Praise for *Cows Can't Jump*

"**Innovative, punchy** and **tender**... maintains a balance of tone, a trueness of voice, laugh-out-loud humour and **stiletto-sharp wit**. Bowne's debut is a performance of real originality and extraordinary promise. I can't wait to see what he does next."

Ray Robinson, author of Electricity

"*Cows Can't Jump* leapt out for its **boldness, confidence** and **humour**. Philip is a gifted and perceptive writer with a fine eye for detail, dialogue and characterisation...a fresh take on the classic rite-of-passage.

Marion Urch, Spotlight First Novel Prize

"*Cows Can't Jump* announces a major talent. Bowne's touch is light, but his themes resonate: faith, family, race, and (whisper it) Brexit. The **prose sparkles like sunshine hitting the English Channel**. Philip Bowne is going to be a superstar."

D.D. Johnston, author of Peace, Love & Petrol Bombs

"Part coming-of-age story, part European travel adventure, Phil Bowne's debut novel **deftly mixes laugh-out-loud hijinx with moments of true poignancy**, and is filled with memorable scenes and a caste of eclectic, authentic characters. **Billy is a brilliant narrator-pilgrim for the next generation**.

Tyler Keevil, author of No Good Brother

About the Author

Phil always wanted to write a book. He started early: at age 6 he penned a short story about an alien befriending a human and attempting to make a cup of tea in the oven. While this story didn't receive critical acclaim, Phil enjoyed the writing process and carried this passion forward through his formative years.

He studied English Literature and Creative Writing at university. While studying, Phil published short stories in literary magazines and anthologies in the UK, US, Canada and Germany. After graduating, Phil spent time in Europe and the US, working and volunteering in various roles and settings: repairing boats at Lake Como, housekeeping at a mountain lodge in California and working with charity Care4Calais in the former Calais 'jungle' refugee camp.

Cows Can't Jump is Phil's debut novel, which he worked on while managing a bar in London. Phil now works as a writer for The Wombles, a children's entertainment brand. He also works on a number of independent writing projects, including a musical set in 1970's Soho and a sitcom set in a failing leisure centre.

Cows Can't Jump

By Philip Bowne

NEEM TREE
PRESS

Published by Neem Tree Press Limited 2020
info@neemtreepress.com

Neem Tree Press Limited,
95A Ridgmount Gardens, London, WC1E 7AZ

A catalogue record for this book is available from the British Library

ISBN 978-1-911107-35-4 Paperback
ISBN 978-1-911107-36-1 Ebook

Printed and bound in Great Britain
by CPI Group (UK) Ltd, Croydon, CR0 4YY

Table of Contents

1

In 2016, I punched my Dad in the face. There's lots of things I did that year that I'll never be able to forgive myself for. A lot more than I'd like. Punching my Dad in the face wasn't one of them. That was one of the few good things I did.

At the start of the year, I was living at home with my Mum and Dad. I was fresh out of school, working the ultimate dead-end job: I was employed as a gravedigger. Mum and Dad had hoped I'd take A-levels, but I wasn't good at anything and I didn't know what I wanted to do. I don't think anyone ever knows what they want to do. People pretend.

I'd quit school as the government announced a referendum on Britain's membership of the EU. Everybody was talking about it. Across the country, it caused a lot of arguments. Relatives, friends, colleagues, strangers in pubs: everyone was fighting. I don't think I had an opinion on the referendum. I don't think I had an opinion on much. I only knew that I disagreed with my parents on everything.

Take religion, for instance. Mum attended church every Sunday, and a crucifix hung in every room of our house. Even the toilet.

There had been one on my bedroom wall until I was fourteen, when I decided that girls might not like it, if I ever got to know any. I took it down and stuffed it to the back of my wardrobe. Mum cried a lot after I did that. She said Jesus would never turn his back on me and that I would come to realise what I'd done was wrong. I didn't think it was wrong. It wasn't like I'd grabbed Jesus by the ear, shoved him in the back of my wardrobe and buried him in a heap of old jumpers. It was just a piece of wood.

It was through the church that Mum found me the gravedigging job. Looking back, I think that maybe her intention was to shock me into developing a career plan. Late in 2015, she sent me to our local church, where I met three men in their fifties. Mum hadn't told me what the job was. It was a surprise, she'd said. I guessed the church was just a meeting point – I figured I wasn't qualified to be a vicar. I thought we would be moving on to somewhere else – a shop, bar or restaurant. But when I arrived in the churchyard, the men were wearing grey overalls splattered with mud. They rested their feet on shovel blades that were planted in the soft wet earth, watching me approach in my ironed trousers.

"Billy?" the fattest of the men said. His name was Wayne. They were all fat, but at different stages of obesity.

They were lined up from the smallest to the biggest, like Russian dolls. The slimmest man was Davey, and the medium man was Frank. His overalls were covered in flecks of white paint.

"Yes," I said. "I'm here to work." I tried to stick my chest out and say the words in an unusually deep voice.

"Grab a shovel," Wayne said. "You can change into your overalls in the church." He had a gold hoop through his left ear and a purple scar on his right cheek.

The overalls were far too big for me and they stank of mud and rot. I imagined that was what death smelled like. I convinced myself that they were the overalls of a man who had died digging his own grave.

The Russian dolls talked and laughed and chewed tobacco. They walked around the churchyard whistling as they clipped back hedges and emptied the bins. Meanwhile, I had to dig until my hands bled.

I got to three feet deep before I collapsed onto my arse and stretched out in the hole. The sky seemed so much further away from down in that muddy pit. I lay like that for several minutes, imagining the dead bodies in the cold earth around me, watching the rooks gather in the afternoon sky. I closed my eyes and relaxed. I liked it in the grave. I didn't like digging it, but it was a peaceful place to be.

Then the dirt hit me. Cold, wet dirt. The Russian dolls chucked mud down at me, shovelfuls of earth on my face and chest. Soil filled my mouth when I tried to shout. The dirt got everywhere. It went down the back of my overalls, in my shoes and eyes and hair. The dolls were laughing at me, howling with laughter as they buried me alive. When they stopped, and I managed to climb out from under the weight of all that earth, I scrambled out of the hole and ripped off my overalls, kicking the mud away and scratching my skin. The dolls were still laughing, patting each other on the back, picking their shovels up and spearing them into the ground.

That first week of gravedigging, Mum made me sandwiches every morning. It never occurred to me to check the logos on the plastic bags she'd wrapped them in. On my third day, I unfolded my sandwiches from a bag embossed with the Virgin logo. The dolls thought this was hilarious and immediately started giving off about my lack of sexual experience. From then on, they referred to me as Virgin Boy.

I wouldn't have minded much except that of course I *was* a virgin. It had been over a year since I'd even kissed a girl, and she'd tasted of pickled onion Monster Munch. As a kid I'd been kind of plump and spotty and girls just weren't into me. But now, having turned seventeen, I'd lost a bit of weight and was maybe emerging as someone you might almost call handsome. "Strapping," was how my Mum put it. The problem now was that I just didn't meet any girls. The only women at work were in coffins.

Dad had tried to give me The Talk soon after I finished school. It was the day of Mum's birthday party and he was a bit drunk. "Listen," he said. "You're coming to that age." He was holding a cardboard plate crammed with the remains of the buffet.

I already knew what he was going to say. He was going to tell me about condoms and chlamydia and water-based lube. Apart from the Monster Munch girl, the only girl I'd ever been close with was Sally Fountain. She would sit next to me in science classes and run her hand along the inside of my leg. I never knew what to do. She'd lean across me to copy my work and I could smell the liquorice on her breath. Sally was always eating liquorice.

After a few weeks of sitting through science classes while my balls fizzed in my pants, we kissed in the cricket nets on the back field, listening to the pick-pock of tennis balls on the clay courts.

The kissing didn't go that well. Apparently normal people don't kiss like they do in the movies. I'd watched DiCaprio kissing women with his tongue on the big screen and assumed that was how you were supposed to do it. Once, I practised kissing like that on the mirror in my room.

Still, Sally and I skipped the last lesson of the day and went back to my house. My parents were at work. She had me on my back, with her top off and her baby-blue bra hanging on the door handle. We nearly had sex, but I was too nervous. No girl had ever seen me naked before. I was so scared. I didn't know what to do. Sally seemed to know exactly what to do, but nothing helped.

Eventually, she slipped back into her school clothes and left. Sally moved seats in our next science lesson, and we never spoke again.

"You don't need to do this, Dad," I said, at the birthday party. "They tell us about it in school." I spotted the banoffee pie on the buffet table and had a flashback to a condom unravelling on a banana.

"No, no, listen here," Dad said. "I don't know how to talk to you about this." Dad and I never talked about anything. Not the weather, or sport, or anything. "What do you want to know?"

"About what?"

"You know, Billy. Girls, dating. That kind of thing."

"Sex?"

Dad was swaying a little, looking down at his cardboard plate. "Ask me anything," he said.

I thought about it. "What do girls want, Dad?"

"What do girls *want*?" he said.

I stabbed a chunk of coronation chicken with a cocktail stick.

11

"In bed?" Dad said.

"In general."

"I couldn't tell you. All I've learnt is what women don't want."

"What don't they want?"

Dad crossed his arms across his pot belly. "They don't want mortgages, or premium bonds or any of that shit." He glugged his beer.

"So, what do they want, Dad?" I asked.

"Isn't it obvious, Billy?"

"No."

Dad bit into a bourbon. "They want a bit of excitement, for god's sake," he said, brown crumbs catching on his sticky lips. "They don't want strait-laces. They don't want tax returns or spreadsheets or photocopiers."

"What do you mean?" I asked.

"They want it dirty, you know? On the floor, in the shower—"

"Oh god, Dad, stop!" I said, cutting him off. He nodded at me and continued to pick at the buffet food. I walked off and locked myself in the toilet, trying to erase what Dad had said from my mind. I swiped through a couple of dozen girls on Tinder as a distraction, but it didn't help. I kept picturing Mum and Dad writhing on the buffet table. It was horrible. Then Mum's friend Mandy started banging on the toilet door.

"Come out, Billy willy," she was shouting and yanking the door handle. I could hear the Macarena blasting in the background. "I wanna dance with you!"

I kept the door locked and waited for Mandy to leave. Once the Macarena had finished, I crept out into the hallway and ran upstairs to my room. I got into bed and hid there until everyone had left.

Being buried alive and repeatedly called Virgin Boy would normally be reason enough to quit a job. But I had to stick at the gravedigging through a long and cold winter. Dad said he'd kick me out if I couldn't hold the job down. So I dug graves until my hands were hardened with callouses, and my forearms were twice as thick as when I started.

Some days the ground was frozen so solid that the shovel would barely break the grass blades. Other days the ground was softer, and it was easy to crunch my shovel through the dirt. It's funny how some graves come easier than others. I always imagined the graves that took longer to dig were for people who took longer to die, like veterans who'd been shot sixteen times in the back but managed to crawl to safety and live for another thirty years.

On the good days, I didn't mind the work. There were days we didn't need to dig any graves, and all we would need to do was clean up the headstones, empty the bins, clip back hedges and water people's flowers. Plus, I enjoyed the precision that the digging required.

First, I had to measure the border of the grave on the grass and mark it by spraying white line marker from an aerosol can. Then I'd take up the turf. We didn't have an excavator, so it was all done by hand, the old-fashioned way. Once I got down a couple of feet, I'd often have to haul out bucketloads of clay and flint. When I got five feet deep, I could stop digging. They don't dig graves as deep anymore. That's the first thing I learnt on the job. Modern graves are five, sometimes only four feet deep. Apparently, it's because of the way we bury people nowadays, in fancy sealed coffins made of steel or heavy wood, which are less likely to be pushed to the surface when water gets into the earth and freezes. It seemed strange to me that people didn't get buried the full six feet underground. It felt as though we'd stopped the tradition out of laziness. We'd rather project manage animated farms on our iPhones or take photographs of lattes and Caesar salads. We don't make time to respect the dead. You can't tell me otherwise. I've seen it. You bury your friends and children and wives and parents in shallow graves.

Wayne told me that we were supposed to dig the graves deeper because animals can smell the bodies and will dig up the earth to eat them. Davey said that we should dig eight to ten feet deep because it'll stop the people digging their way up to the surface when the zombie apocalypse comes. I wasn't sure whether they were serious or not. Either way, I often dug the grave a little extra if I had the time. Six feet deep was always the target – it got tough to shovel the dirt out and lift it onto the turf over my head. My shoulders would ache for hours afterwards.

After you've finished digging, whether it be to four, five, or six feet, the next task is levelling out the bottom. Then you have to climb up and out of the grave, stand on the rim and smooth out the walls with a heavy spade. In Cheltenham, it was custom to line the bottom of a child's grave with sawdust, but I extended that to every grave I ever dug. Nobody wants to see the cold, hard earth as they watch their loved one disappear into the ground.

After levelling out the walls and bottom, you lay planks along the edge of the hole to ensure a firm footing for the pallbearers. Four rolls of artificial turf are lowered over the sides of the grave – the Russian dolls called it butcher's grass, but I never found out why.

On the carpet in front of the hole I would have to place two wooden beams, or putlogs, on which the coffin would rest. Like a waiter setting a table at an expensive restaurant, I'd then lay out the webbing straps used to lower the coffin into the ground. In all, it takes a few hours. I knew the mourners would never see me, but that never mattered.

I grew to like being in the graveyard. The headstones were interesting to read. I started to imagine what the people would have been like. There were some people I liked to visit more than others. They became a posthumous family.

I still remember Annie. She died when she was 26, in 1954. Her epitaph read: 'Mother, dancer, singer and wife. Taken too soon.' I liked to imagine Annie tap dancing on stage, back in the 1950's. I pictured her with red hair and eyes like bluebells. She was short, too. Five foot and a fag butt. In my mind she wore stockings and cream high heels and sang Ella Fitzgerald songs. Men would watch her carefully, but Annie was only interested in returning home to her husband. I had a lot of time for Annie.

After two months in the graveyard, I'd managed to save only £84. Part of the problem was that my Dad had put my rent up to £275 per month because I had a full-time job. Another issue was that every Saturday night, the Russian Dolls made me go out with them to the Six Bells. The first time they invited me, I told them I couldn't go because I wasn't eighteen yet. At that, Wayne insisted I had no choice but to join them, telling me that I wouldn't have a problem getting served because they knew Mickey Two-Shakes, the landlord, and they could introduce me to all the best crumpet. At first I thought they were talking about food, but I later learned it means women. Frank claimed to have dated a girl from Venezuela once, but both Wayne and Davey dismissed that as bullshit.

My Saturdays were spent sitting in the pub, drinking bitter and paying for more than my fair share of rounds. Davey said there was a service charge because I couldn't go up and order the drinks.

"Mickey Two-Shakes says so," Wayne said, when I protested.

"That's right, Virgin Boy," said Davey, licking the peanut salt from his fingertips. Soil was stuck under his nails, and it made me feel sick to watch him.

I fell into a routine. I walked the same paths every day, saw the same faces, dug the same graves. The Russian dolls seemed to revel in that existence – every Friday they talked with hope and expectation of the bets they'd place, and every Monday they'd bemoan the teams that had scuppered their accumulators. All of it was a pointless cycle – they would never win a bet, and their hands would dig the earth until their bodies were buried in it.

After a while I started to hate the work. I hated the Russian dolls even more. They still picked on me – they would throw the dirt I had dug out back in over my head when I was in the grave, just like they did on my first day. I could take that sort of treatment. I was used to being on the receiving end of a joke.

I worked through from October 2015, when the grass was carpeted with brown and orange leaves, into the frosty months of November and December, when the grass crunched beneath the soles of my boots. I worked through the snowfall in January, waking up on dark mornings and drinking bitter coffee and working until it was dark again.

That was how I started 2016 – digging graves. In some ways, it seemed appropriate. In 2016, loads of celebrities died. I didn't know who a lot of them were, but my Mum said it was a pandemic. Before January was finished Mum had cried about losing Bowie, Rickman and Wogan. Ordinary people kept dying too. They died, and we buried them.

I was hoping we might get to dig a celebrity grave one day, but it never happened.

Things changed one morning in February when I couldn't find the Russian Dolls anywhere. Normally they would be gathered outside the front of the church, having a cigarette or laughing about the football results or something that had happened in the pub. But they weren't around. I walked through the graveyard to find them. Grey birds perched in the bare tree branches. Above them, an aeroplane trailed white lines through the early morning sky.

Eventually I saw they were crowded around one grave. It was a grave we'd dug only a few days earlier. I ran over to see what was going on. The grave had been unearthed. I looked down and saw the coffin lid dislodged – the casket empty.

"What's going on?" I said.

The Russian dolls looked at me. None of them spoke.

"What's going on? What's happened?"

"Isn't it obvious, Virgin Boy?" Davey kicked a rock down into the hole. It thumped on the wooden coffin.

"We've had a visit from Tomb Raider," Wayne said.

"What do you mean?"

The men laughed.

"The body snatchers," Frank said, scratching at his paint-stained overalls. I wondered if he'd ever buy new ones.

"Body snatchers?" I asked.

"Somebody's been in and dug her up."

I felt sick.

"Why would somebody do that?" I asked.

"Maybe they lost a bet." Wayne laughed.

"What would they want with a dead body?"

"You tell me, Virgin Boy," Wayne said. "I reckon they wanted a hand or something, you know, like they do when they have a hostage. They send a hand to the authorities, to make 'em pay."

"It's the shock factor," Davey said. "That's why they do it. Shit people up."

"I don't think Cheltenham's the place for a hostage situation," Wayne said.

"You never know. GCHQ's only up the road," Davey barked back.

"What's that got to do with it?" Frank asked.

"I dunno." Davey spat into the ground. A fleck of saliva remained on his chin.

"Have you called the police?" I asked.

"Not worth it," Davey said. "Too much paperwork."

The men laughed again. I felt tears welling up.

"But we need to tell her family," I said.

"Why? It'll only upset 'em."

"It happens more than you might think, Virgin Boy."

"We just fill it up again and carry on. Nothing we can do about it now."

The men started shovelling mud back into the hole. I looked down into the grave as earth began to fill up the empty coffin. The waxed wood reflected the winter sunlight for a moment, and then it was gone, hidden by dirt. I climbed out of my overalls right there and speared my shovel into the frozen ground. I walked away and I didn't go back.

That was in February, on the day Harper Lee died. I remembered reading her book at school.

Every day I looked for work, but I never even got an interview. There's always jobs before Christmas, but as soon as people have shat out their turkey, all the jobs are gone. I realised that I'd quit gravedigging at the wrong time and that I would never earn enough to escape.

One afternoon, when I returned home from another futile job search, I found my Mum in the hallway, filling a hole in the wall.

She had three tubes of Polyfilla on the bookcase and was wearing yellow rubber gloves.

"What happened?" I asked her as she scraped the mixture into the hole with a putty knife.

"Your father—" Mum said. She didn't look at me.

"What about him?" I dropped my rucksack and looked closer. The hole was as big as my head. There was nothing behind it but chipboard. Dad was in the living room with his legs crossed, reading *The Daily Mail*. He let out a loud, purposeful sigh.

"He thought it would help to put a frying pan through the wall."

Dad turned over the page of his newspaper.

"Help what?" I asked.

"If we could afford a house with real walls it wouldn't have happened!" Dad shouted from the other room.

"Well your Father wasn't going to do anything," Mum said to me. "He said I shouldn't bother."

"Your Mother's bought enough Polyfilla to rebuild the Berlin Wall."

I could tell Dad had been thinking about that one for a while.

"Why did Dad throw a frying pan at the wall?" I worried that my parents were losing their minds. Mum walked into the doorway of the living room. I stood behind her, looking in at Dad over her shoulder.

"Tell him, Martin. Tell your son why you threw a frying pan at our wall."

The dimmer switch buzzed like a dentist's drill. I noticed the headline on the front page of Dad's paper: 1 MILLION MORE MIGRANTS FLOCK TO EUROPE. He grunted and kept his eyes glued to the paper.

Mum finally came out with it. "It's GG." GG was my Grandad – my Dad's Father. I never called him Grandad, though. He'd always insisted on GG: Grandad George. "He's dating a woman." She looked at Dad.

"He's a bit beyond dating," Dad said. "He's getting married at the end of the year."

Gran had only been dead ten months.

"Who to?" I asked. It was a shock for me as much as for my parents, but I didn't feel compelled to throw a wok through the kitchen window. If anything, I was happy that GG had found someone.

"Her name's Benny. She's West Indian." Dad was still scanning his paper. At first, I thought he was reading aloud from an article. He looked disgusted with himself at having said the words. "That's why we need to get out of the EU, son. Stop all these foreigners coming and running this country into the gutter. It's like it's illegal to be English, nowadays."

I wanted to point out that the West Indies wasn't part of Europe, but I wasn't brave enough at the time.

"She's thirty-eight," Mum added, shaking her head. I could tell she was hurt that GG was marrying a woman younger than her. "And she's getting all of your Dad's inheritance."

So that explained the frying pan. Dad always was obsessed with money, probably because we never had much. We lived in an old three-bedroom, semi-detached house on the outskirts of Cheltenham. Dad called it a doll's house. We had to squeeze past one another if there were two of us in the kitchen at the same time. If all three of us were in the kitchen, we squeezed around each other – a claustrophobic choreography we had learned from years of treading on each other's toes.

21

The walls were thin – as Dad had proved – and damp. Growing up, I could often hear Mum and Dad arguing when I was in my bedroom at night, trying to sleep. I always wished that I had a brother or sister to be with when the shouting started. But that never happened.

"Should've known not to trust him," Dad said. "It's all dirty money anyway, son. GG has never owned a catering company. He was running a scam at a car park in central London. Twenty years he had it going."

"That's right," Mum said. "We're better off without the burden of spending stolen money."

"I suppose that's why Dad threw a frying pan at the wall," I said. "Because he's so glad to be without the worry of having all that money."

Dad looked like he was considering throwing me through the wall.

"How did GG scam people?" I asked.

Dad took off his glasses. "There's this car park between a hotel and a pub," he said. "Your Grandad tricked the owners of both places into thinking that they didn't own it, and that the other place did. I've no idea how." Dad folded the newspaper in half and slapped it down on the armrest. "He went and collected the money from the machines every Friday for twenty years."

"How much did he make?" I asked.

"Only a couple of million," Dad said, putting his feet up on the coffee table. Mum would normally shout at him when he did that, but this time she let it slide. She had flecks of dried Polyfilla on her forearms.

"So you don't get any inheritance?" I asked.

"Not a penny," said Dad. I thought he might throw something again.

I was struggling to get my head around it too. GG was a millionaire, and he was marrying a West Indian woman half his age. It was a year when anything was possible.

After that, Dad stopped playing badminton on Wednesdays and bought a punch-bag which he hung up in the garage. He lashed out at it every night. Mum didn't like it but reasoned that it was better than having all her kitchenware go through the drywall.

Dad left his red gloves strung over the banister at the bottom of the stairs, which Mum said made us look like a family of brawlers. Dad didn't care. I listened to him punching the leather bag from my bedroom window.

He came out from the garage one evening without his shirt on, gloves dangling around his shoulders. I noticed his chest was barbed with grey hairs and sticky with sweat. Mum called him into the kitchen.

"GG rang," she said. We hadn't seen him since the news about Benny. Normally we saw him a few times a week. Mum was emptying the drying rack of all the saucepans before Dad could get his hands on them.

"What's he say? He's got a boyfriend now?"

I pictured GG on a yacht with his boyfriend. They were feeding each other grapes.

"No," Mum said. "He was talking about coming around with his girlfriend."

"I hope you told him where to stick his African girlfriend."

I wondered whether Dad had forgotten that she was West Indian, or whether he was being a dick on purpose. I could never tell.

"Well," Mum said, wiping down the surfaces with a jay cloth. "It was a bit awkward really. I didn't know what to say for the best."

"Should have told him we don't want anything to do with criminal scum like him." Dad laughed and looked over at me. I wasn't laughing.

"I couldn't say that to your father," Mum said. "He's eighty years old."

"What's that got to do with anything?"

"He's got high blood pressure." Mum started to put plates away. She didn't want to make him angry. She didn't want to have to fill another hole in the wall.

"That doesn't stop him going out shagging, does it?"

I could see Dad getting angrier. His eyes were bright white golf balls and his face was turning the colour of his boxing gloves. I tried to erase the image of GG having a shag from my mind. It wasn't easy. I pictured him rolling around in a bed of money with three women who all had plastic boobs. Everyone was covered in melted chocolate.

"Don't say such horrible things, Martin. Your father's only trying to be civil."

"So what did you tell him?" Dad knotted his arms across his chest. The blue veins in his biceps glowed through his skin. Mum had her back to him, dropping forks into the cutlery drawer. The rattling sound of metal on metal rang around the room.

"What did you tell him?" Dad repeated. Mum started putting away the teaspoons into the drawer and the rattling sound acquired a higher pitch. It was giving me a headache.

Finally, Mum said, "I told him they're welcome any time."

Twenty minutes later, GG's car pulled into the driveway. A tall woman wearing large sunglasses stepped out from the passenger seat. She had on a pink blazer and pressed white trousers with open toe wedges. She wore dark purple lipstick, and her hair was clipped into a neat fade on the back and sides, with short curls on the top. It was Benny. She looked like a celebrity arriving at a film premiere. I thought she looked younger than thirty-eight. I wouldn't have ever imagined GG going out with a young black woman. But then, I'd never imagined GG being with anyone other than Gran, and she was gone, so he needed someone to keep him company. I didn't hate GG for what he'd done. I envied him. GG could still get laid on his death-bed.

Benny and GG walked along our garden path with linked arms. GG was smiling. He had great teeth for a man of his age. I'd never thought about GG's teeth until I found out he was a millionaire. Watching him walk up to the house, I noticed how sprightly he looked. This was the first time I'd seen him walk without his cane since Gran died. When the doorbell rang, Dad took a long drink of water and walked out the back door, boxing gloves still draped around his shoulders.

To start with, things were awkward. Even GG didn't know what to say. The first few minutes were just a frantic exchange of compliments between Mum and Benny about the other's outfit, hair and nails. Benny's compliments were a little farfetched: Mum was wearing a brown cardigan and her blond hair was tied up into what she called a Croydon Facelift. Apparently if you tie your hair up very tightly it lifts your skin and you look younger. I thought it made Mum look even more highly strung than she already was, like her face might split.

I still couldn't believe GG was a millionaire. He didn't look or act differently. But I suppose he had been rich all along. I wanted to forget everything that was going on and go with GG to the cinema or make paper aeroplanes to throw at cats, like we did when I was a kid.

Benny said she had forgotten something and ran back out to the car. She probably knew it was going to be awkward and wanted to let GG do most of the talking. By the time she returned, we were all sitting in the living room. She handed a pot plant to my Mum. It had a tall, spindly stalk with a purple-pink flower blossoming out of the top, like it was on stilts. I was impressed.

"It's for you," she said. "It's an orchid."

It was in a large white ceramic pot. Mum never bought plants. Dad said they were a waste of money because they rot and die. The most exotic plant life in our house was potpourri, which Dad only allowed because it was already dead. Most of the rooms in the house had at least one bowl of potpourri left out on the side. When I first saw one, I thought it was mouldy cereal that had been abandoned on the coffee table. I chucked it all out and washed the bowl. Mum and Dad argued about it because Mum thought Dad had chucked it out in protest. I decided not to own up and left them to it.

"Oh, thank you, Benny. It's lovely," Mum said, carrying the orchid over to the mantelpiece and setting it down next to the gas fire. I could tell Mum was worried that Benny was going to piss away Dad's inheritance on potted plants and garish lipstick. GG could tell, too. He winked at me, like we were both in on some secret. He knew everything was going to turn out OK. I believed in GG.

I could tell that Mum wasn't so sure. She quizzed Benny about the West Indies, but it turned out she had lived in Birmingham for most of her life. GG must have overplayed how exotic she was. He was probably chuffed to have bagged himself a woman as young as Benny.

"I did go to the Caribbean last year, actually," Benny said. "I took my nan to one of the islands. Oh, what is it? I've gone blank. The island beginning with J?" Benny clicked her fingers trying to recall. I couldn't stop staring at her purple lips. They made me think of £20 notes.

"Jamaica?" Mum said.

Benny closed her eyes, her mouth spreading into a smirk. She raised her hands in the air.

"Jamaica?" Mum said again.

"No, she wanted to go," Benny said, finally, and started cracking up. "Get it? Ja-make-her?"

I'll admit that I didn't get it for a few seconds, but Mum clearly didn't get it at all. She hesitated before laughing a little too loudly. Then she jumped up to go and make tea. I was left alone with Benny and GG.

"Where's Martin?" GG asked, settling back into the armchair.

"He's in the garage," I said. "He's taken up boxing."

"Boxing? You're joking. He quit karate when he was a kid because he couldn't hack it."

"He's got a punch-bag and everything," I said.

When Mum returned with the tea, Benny spilled some down her pink blazer.

"Oh dear," GG said, dabbing at Benny's jacket with his napkin. "I'll have to take it to the dry cleaners."

Benny laughed. "He insists on doing my laundry," she said. "I am quite capable of looking after myself, darling."

GG smiled and kissed Benny on the cheek. Benny squeezed GG's hand lightly. It was weird because Benny was so much younger than him, but it seemed like they really did love each other. GG was a new man. I don't ever remember him swooning over Gran like that.

"I love you, honey," GG said. Mum gulped on her tea. It was still so hot that I could tell it was burning the roof of her mouth. Benny kissed GG on the lips. I didn't know where to look.

"I hear Martin has started boxing," GG said. Mum looked at me as if to say, What did you tell them that for?

"My brother was a boxer," Benny said. "He broke his nose three times, but he never lost a fight. You should tell Martin to be careful – it's a game for brutes."

"I'm not too worried," Mum said. "He's only punching a bag. I think it's good for his blood pressure." Mum had the ability to discern the effect of anything on Dad's cholesterol and blood pressure.

"That's where they start – punching the bags, then the speedball, but they get bored and soon they want to fight each other. That's how my brother went. It's a man thing."

Benny sipped her tea. A purple splodge of lipstick had been kissed onto the rim of the white cup. Benny smeared it away with her thumb.

"He's too old for all that," Mum said. But she knew that wouldn't stop him if he wanted to fight. I could see that she hadn't thought about him getting in the ring. Her face turned pale and serious.

"Let him do as he wishes," GG said. "Worst comes to worst he breaks his nose."

"He's not a thug," Mum said. "He wouldn't want to fight anyway. He's against all that."

"So how did you meet Benny?" I asked GG, hoping to get the talk away from boxing. Secretly, I wanted Dad to get into fighting. I'd have loved to see him get punched in the face.

"I met George at the casino," Benny answered for him.

GG placed his teacup on the coffee table. He seemed different – his movements were more assured and confident now that he had Benny. There was something about having a woman that really thickened up his broth. "Benny was winning every hand at the blackjack table. I had to ask what her secret was."

I wondered whether Benny was after GG's money at all. Maybe she was just as rich. Maybe she was wealthier.

"I wish," she said. "I was serving his drinks at the blackjack table."

She *was* after his money.

"How sweet," Mum said. Benny smiled. She hadn't taken her shoes off, which Mum hated. I noticed Mum staring at Benny's purple toenails. "I bet you can't wait for the wedding."

The back door slammed and the whole house seemed to shake.

"Is that Rocky?" GG shouted. He laughed and starting humming "Eye of the Tiger".

Dad appeared at the doorway to the living room. He was topless again, and his bald head and bloated belly dripped with sweat. He had his gloves on. I think he was trying to make some sort of stand.

"What are we doing for dinner?" Dad ignored GG and Benny.

"I was thinking we could get a takeaway. Fish and chips?"

"Sounds good to me," GG said.

Dad looked at GG. His gloved hands hung down by his sides, and he tapped them against his legs. There was no way he wanted to sit and have dinner with GG and Benny, but there wasn't much he could do about it.

"Martin, this is Benny, my fiancée." GG gestured across to Benny, who jumped up and stretched out her hand to shake. Dad didn't know what to do. He hated her – she was stealing all his inheritance, conning his Dad, and disgracing his family name. The neighbours would be talking about it for the next decade. Mum stared at Dad. She was sitting forward in her armchair, urging him to acknowledge her. Benny's hand seemed to be outstretched for hours.

Dad thrust out his red boxing glove for Benny to shake. She didn't seem to know how to react at first. Dad was looking down at the floor, waiting for it to be done with. Benny took the glove in both hands and held it.

"How lovely to meet you, Martin," Benny said.

Dad turned around and trudged upstairs to shower.

GG and Benny went to get fish and chips for everyone, and Mum and I set the table for five. I had to get an extra chair from the garage to make room for Benny. It was much lower than the other dining room chairs, and it looked weird squeezed in at the table.

When GG and Benny returned with the food, Dad was waiting at the head of the table. GG sat facing him at the other end. I was left with the extra chair. My head barely reached the table. I felt like a baby.

Benny placed a bag of fish and chips on every plate. The oil had seeped through the paper and each bag was marked with a large damp patch. Mum poured everyone a glass of Bucks Fizz.

"Here's to GG," she said, raising her glass. "And Benny." It came across as an afterthought. Their names didn't attach. They weren't a real couple, in Mum's eyes. I gulped down the bubbles.

"Thank you, Suzie," GG said.

Mum normally made us say grace before we ate, but that day she didn't bother. Dad ripped open his bag without saying anything. He picked up the greasy chips with his fingers and pushed them into his mouth. Benny was the only one of us without fish and chips. She prodded her fork into a single fishcake which she finished in under a minute.

"Won't you be hungry?" Mum asked her.

"I've got a suit to fit into," she said.

"A suit?" Mum said. "Do you mean a dress?"

"Oh, no. I'm wearing a white suit. I want something I can wear more than once." Benny said. "Plus, it makes going for a pee *so* much easier." Benny chuckled but Mum and Dad didn't find it funny.

"It's the modern way," GG said. Mum looked horrified. Dad was shaking his head.

"And I can't stand chips, anyway. All that grease." Benny was talking and talking. I could tell she was nervous, and I felt sorry for her. She opened her mouth and stuck out her pink tongue to indicate that she found chips disgusting. GG picked up a chip and reached over to put it into her mouth.

"George, stop it," she said. "You're embarrassing me. Stop showing off."

GG stopped. He chewed on the chip with a grin on his face. The awkwardness spurred him on.

"I was meaning to ask you something, Martin," GG said. He wiped his fork clean on his napkin and placed the prongs on the edge of the table. "Something I couldn't ask you over the phone."

Dad didn't look up from his plate. He stuffed a piece of battered fish into his mouth as GG talked. GG held the prongs in place on the edge of the table and pinged the fork handle down. It made a loud twanging noise as it vibrated. Mum looked up from her plate. She would have given me a bollocking for that, I thought.

"Oh, you are funny," Mum said, willing him not to do it again.

GG twanged his fork on the table edge again. It made the sort of noise you'd hear in cartoons, when something bad has happened.

I cleaned my fork off on my t-shirt and started doing the same. Me and GG twanged our forks at each other, in orchestra.

"Billy, stop that."

I didn't know whether Mum was more worried about her best cutlery getting bent or the dining table getting chipped. It reminded me of how she scolded me as a child for bending all the spoons. I'd been watching Uri Geller on TV – the guy that claimed to bend spoons with his psychic powers. Mum was horrified when she came home to a cutlery drawer filled with disfigured spoons. They were all bent to at least a right angle. Even when I bent them all back to normal, she still wouldn't accept that they were usable. Mum threw them out and dragged me to the shop with her. She spent two hours choosing the new ones.

Her face was filled with a similar rage when I twanged my fork. GG and I didn't stop, though. The fork handles shuddered over and over. Dad was acting like nothing was happening at all. He had his face down, filling his mouth with chips – probably to ensure he didn't mouth off at GG. Benny was laughing. Her mouth was wide open; her tonsils jiggled at the back of her throat.

"It's about the wedding," GG continued, twanging the fork in the pause. "I was hoping you could be my best man."

Dad chewed on his food. Benny was clutching her stomach. I didn't think it was that funny. I stopped twanging my fork when she started fanning herself with her hands, breathing as though she was hyperventilating. Dad and GG couldn't look at each other.

"Please, George. Stop now." Mum had had enough. She rose to her feet and held out her hands to GG. "Now, what do you say, Martin?"

GG stopped twanging his fork. It fell onto the floor and Mum glanced to see whether it had left a grease stain on the cream carpet.

"I think your Dad would really love it if you said yes," Benny said. She just couldn't let a moment take its course.

Dad didn't appear to have heard. He hadn't even raised his head. All of the chips on his plate were gone, so he reached over and grabbed a handful of mine. He stuffed them into his mouth and chewed – his jaw moved at a slow, pulsating rate.

"Well, Martin?" Mum was still on her feet. She knew this was the only way to get an answer from him.

Dad swallowed the mouthful of chips. He looked at Mum and said, "I'd love to."

I didn't know how Dad was going to be a best man for someone he refused to talk to.

A week later, Benny asked Mum whether she would like to be a bridesmaid. Benny wanted Mum to wear a suit, like her. Mum was livid. In the evenings, Mum would call Mandy and they would bitch and laugh about how the wedding party would look like a congregation of estate agents.

I wondered why Benny had asked Mum to be a bridesmaid. After all, they had only met once. Apparently, Benny didn't have much in the way of friends or family because she moved around a lot. Both of her parents were dead. Only her brother would be there from her side of the family.

And so, that spring, Mum and Benny played their roles as best they could. Dad pounded the bag alone in the garage, Britain prepared for the EU Referendum, and celebrities kept dying. Dad was upset about some guy called Paul Daniels, who apparently used to be a TV magician.

A few days later, Johan Cruyff died. "Looks like Cruyff took a turn for the worse," Dad said, which I didn't think was funny.

Mum lamented Ronnie Corbett. While the death toll mounted, I applied for hundreds of jobs on the internet. That's all I did, for weeks. I applied for every position, from bin-man to beekeeper – nobody wanted anything to do with me. Until, late in April, on the day that Prince died, I received an email offering me a position at the Eastbourne Summer School for International Students. They must have been the most desperate summer school in the world.

I wrote back immediately to accept. I was seventeen and had spent the last ten weeks scrolling through my phone while picking cotton fluff from my belly button. The school didn't pay a proper wage, but that didn't matter: they offered full board and travel costs, and it was my first chance to get away from Cheltenham and my parents. I saw the job as a free holiday, a break from my normal life. What I didn't know, as I wrote out my e-mail response, was that I was about to meet Eva, and normal would never be normal again.

2

At first, I didn't like Eva. She would crack her knuckles and fingers and make a clicking sound with her tongue when she was thinking. She was always Instagramming weird pictures of cats that didn't belong to her. Little things like that irritated me. And she was hard to talk to. I felt like I was interviewing her whenever we had a conversation, because I asked questions and she answered them and said nothing more. It sounds stupid now. Now that I'm writing all this about her.

The school was designed for foreign children to learn English in the morning and play sports in the afternoon. There were twelve activity leaders, including myself and Eva. The activity leaders stuck together most of the time, because the proper teachers tended to gather in the staff room with their big files and stacks of books, and the catering team were normally out the back of the main building, smoking cigarettes and bitching about the kids with specific dietary requirements. Although I spent a lot of time with Eva as part of the group, I didn't start talking to her properly until I had to look after Mohammed. He was the first thing that brought us together.

Mohammed was a ten-year-old boy from Sirte. His father had sent him to the summer school to keep him away from the warzone in Libya. Bombs were exploding near his home; he told me he'd heard them rattling his windows during the night. While most children would stay at the school for three or four weeks, Mohammed had been sent for the whole summer. Eleven weeks away from home.

Mohammed was usually alone. He spent most of his time on Facebook, watching funny animal videos or reading stuff in Arabic. He was the only child from Libya staying at the school, and the German, Portuguese, Italian, Japanese, Chinese, and Russian children tended to stick to their national groups. I used to sit with him when the other children received parcels from home – lots of the parents sent real paper letters along with sweets or some other homely treat. Mohammed never had a letter from his family.

I told him he'd get a parcel soon, and that it was probably just because Libya was a long way away.

He said, "I don't think so."

I squeezed his hand. It was half the size of my own and his knuckles were lined with white scars that stood out against his dark olive skin. As I comforted him, a door slammed. Mohammed jolted upright and moved closer to me. His eyes became two black marbles and a trail of goose bumps prickled up along his hairless forearm. Eva had briefly walked into the main hall. She was new, and, like me, was an activity leader. We woke the kids up in the mornings, turned their lights out at night and supervised them when they weren't in their lessons. Children that had been playing tag and running around shrieking went quiet when they saw her.

"Time for class," I said, gesturing to the door. Mo looked ill. The tips of his brown fringe had been bleached blond by the hot July sun.

"I will not go today," he said, folding his arms across his chest. His t-shirt was sitting looser on his shoulders and back. He'd been observing Ramadan for ten days and had only eaten before sunrise twice. I told Mohammed to wait in the main hall until I got back. Then I went into an unused classroom. Eva was in there, standing by the tall windows, looking out over the seafront. She looked lost. The school was high up on a hill. From up there in that classroom, you could look out to where the blue sky met the Channel, and struggle to recognise the horizon.

"What do you want?" she asked. She turned around to face me, with her arms knotted across her chest.

"I'm looking for something," I said, surprised to have seen her. We hadn't spoken alone before. She made me feel nervous.

"Can I help?" She turned around and smiled. "What do you need?"

"A gift," I said. "For Mohammed. He's homesick."

"How sweet," she said. "Do I get a gift? I'm homesick too."

I didn't know how to flirt, so I looked at the floor and said, "Maybe."

She pointed at a miniature globe on top of the filing cabinet at the back of the room. It wasn't much. It wobbled on its stand when I picked it up. I pulled it free from its axis, leaving two small holes at each pole.

"I hope he likes it," Eva said.

She helped me wrap the globe in some brown paper and found a box to put it inside. We taped it up, and I wrote Mohammed's name on the top, along with the address of the school.

"Why are you writing the address on there?" she asked.

"So he thinks it's from home," I said. She looked at me like it was a bad idea. I didn't care. I just wanted to make him happy. He needed to know that people cared about him.

I left the parcel outside his dorm, for him to find and open that evening.

Later, when the other kids were settled in their classes, I grabbed a rugby ball and walked with Mohammed up the hill at the back of the school. Granite slabs formed a pathway to the top. Each rock was bordered by delicate blue flowers. The grass on the way up was yellow from two rainless weeks, and only a small patch of green remained at the top, protected by shade from the tree line that ran along its perimeter. The others said that in early June, the hill was gold with buttercups. By the time I arrived at the school, they were gone.

We took a seat on the old wooden bench and looked over the Downs and the distant water. Mohammed ripped a sprig from the bush next to us. He placed the flower in the palm of his hand and picked at its pink spire.

"How does it live, in the darkness?" Mohammed asked, pointing down at the shaded floor.

"Some plants prefer the shade." I picked a pink flower of my own and twirled it between my thumb and index finger. "They become stronger there. Not everything grows in the sunlight."

"What is shade?"

"The cover from the sun."

"This darkness?" Mohammed stretched out his arms, his open palms facing skyward.

"Yes. Where it's cooler."

He repeated the new word under his breath.

"Why don't you want to be in class, Mo?" I said, standing up and passing the rugby ball into his arms. He caught it with one hand, his other tucked the flower into his pocket.

"I am only here so I am not in Sirte." He got up and examined the ball, then began trying to do kick-ups with it. It shot off his foot and bounced down the hill and across the playground.

"Do you miss being at home?" I asked.

"I do not have any home." He sat back down and crossed his legs.

"Your home is in Libya, isn't it?"

"My Dad sent me here for all of summer just so I will not be there. After I am here, I will go probably to Tunis, or to somewhere else, but not to home."

"Is that why you don't want to be in class today?"

Mohammed rubbed his eyelids with his palms and hummed to himself. "What does it matter?" he said, rising to his feet and moving towards the back fence. He looked into the glade behind the school, through the mesh fence.

Dozens of toys were strewn among the overgrown plants. There were footballs, rugby balls and tennis balls, all scattered across the clearing like a minefield. A skipping rope was draped over a high branch.

"Can we go in there?" Mohammed poked his finger through the mesh and looked up at me.

"There's no way in. But we will get them back at the end of the summer." I was sure some of the equipment had been there for years. "What games do you usually play at home?"

"I am very thirsty," he said.

The day was growing hotter. With the sun higher, the area of shade had shrunk. It crept up towards us, a few yards below the bench. I handed a bottle of water to Mohammed. The sweat on his forehead mirrored the droplets which ran along the length of the plastic bottle.

"I can't. I am not allowed this." Mohammed crumpled the bottle in his hand. The plastic crackled. He squeezed either side of the dent he had made to pop it back into place.

"It's going to get even hotter today. I know you aren't allowed to, but—"

"I can't." He looked white.

"You can drink some."

"Not today." He ruffled the sweat away from the back of his head, then dug the flower out from his pocket and, just as I had, ran it between his thumb and index finger. He held it up to his eye, closing the other, and faced towards the sun.

At the foot of the hill the other children poured out from the school buildings. They moved in an excited, colourful wave. Eva was supervising them. She was wearing a white vest top with some denim shorts. Her hair was tied up into a ponytail, revealing her neck and collarbone.

Some of the kids were kicking footballs, others rested down in the reed grass. A group of girls skipped over a long rope and Mohammed saw the boys chase each other, playing war with clasped hands for guns. The wind wandered over from the seafront and stuck to my skin.

As more children came outside, we could hear the rise of voices in a muddle of languages. The hum of the playground floated up to us on the hilltop. Eva was standing with a group of the French girls. They had started singing a song as they hop-scotched on the tarmac. Mohammed got up and looked at them.

From above we could hear the voices merging into the chorus. "*Aux Champs-Élysées! Da-da da-da-da! Aux Champs-Élysées...*"

"Do you know the song?" I asked. Mohammed had told me his mother was Tunisian and that she had taught him French. A crowd was gathering around the girls. There must have been fifteen of them singing.

"It's called '*Les Champs-Élysées*'," Mohammed said. "I sing this song with my mother, before the bombing." On the playground, the children continued their chorus, and the girls with the skipping rope stopped and joined in. Eva had been teaching the kids how to sing the song. I figured she was French at the time. It was before I really knew her.

"*Au soleil, sous la pluie; À midi ou à minuit; Il y a tout ce que vous voulez; Aux Champs-Élysées.*" I imagined the waterfront wind would carry their voices for miles inland.

"What is it about?" I asked.

"Paris," Mohammed said. The girls finished their song and Mohammed clapped his hands and cheered for more.

"What does it mean?" I asked.

"The Champs-Élysées is the most famous street in Paris," Mohammed said.

"But what are the words?"

"At the Champs-Élysées; in the sun, under the rain; at the middle of the day; or the middle of the night; there is everything you want; at the Champs-Élysées." Mohammed smiled. I had been taught the song in GCSE French, but I hadn't remembered any of the words. I'd failed French completely.

"Aux Champs-Élysées!" he giggled.

"Maybe you could teach me the words," I said.

"I will." Mohammed continued humming the tune. "I would love to go," he said. At the shore, the white capped waves crashed into the rocks on the waterfront. "I have never been to Paris."

Neither had I.

Halfway through the lunch hour, we came down from the yellow hilltop. I left Mohammed sitting in the shade, holding on to my bottle. I walked inside for water. I felt empty, covered in a second skin of sweat. I drank as much as I could.

When I went back outside to check on him, he wasn't there. I checked the school buildings. Nothing.

I asked Eva whether she'd seen him.

"I haven't seen him since this morning," she said. "Is he OK?"

I didn't answer. I'd already made for the hill, nearly trampling over a few of the girls lying in the long grass.

The clouds had etched a black spot in the sky away to the East. But he wasn't there.

I yelled his name between lungfuls of hot air. Still nothing. Propping myself up against the bench with my back to the school,

I looked through the mesh. It frustrated me to see how close the footballs and the other toys were.

As I rattled the fence, "Champs-Élysées" started up again.

Looking down over the playground, I saw Mohammed standing beside Eva and the French girls, clapping his hands. Eva was waving at me to come back down, smiling and laughing. She handed Mohammed a bottle of water and he unscrewed the lid, taking a long drink.

When the bell rang, calling the kids to dinner, I didn't speak to Eva. She had tricked me, making me run around in a panic when she must've known where he was all along.

Instead, I went to collect the parcel I'd left for Mohammed that morning. I was going to give it to him myself – I wanted to see his face when he saw it. But when I got to his dorm room, it wasn't there. There was no sign of the box anywhere. I checked all the rooms, just to see if one of the other kids had been around and hidden it. But that was impossible. The building was locked during lunchtime, and they had all been in lessons before. I went looking for Eva, checking the playing fields, the staff room, the classrooms; she'd disappeared.

I went back into the unused classroom where we found the globe. She was standing there in the same spot, looking out over the water and the rolling hillside. A tugboat whistled out at sea. Its engines left a pathway of foamy water in its trail, all the way across the Channel.

"You moved the parcel," I said. She had her back to me and didn't turn around straight away.

"Yes, I did." She was still looking out over the Downs. "It's cruel to lie to him."

45

I looked up at the filing cabinet where Eva found the globe.
It was back on its axis, like it had never been touched. Not only
had she taken the parcel away, she had put the globe back in its
place. At the time that felt like she was rubbing my face in it
somehow. It pissed me off. I grabbed the globe from its axis and
part of the plastic cracked.

Eva didn't say anything.

I ran up to the hilltop, to the fence and the glade. The skipping
rope still dangled on its branch. I stepped back and squeezed the
globe in the palm of my hand. Running my thumb over the smooth
plastic, I traced my fingertip from Sirte, past Tunis and Malta,
across the Mediterranean, between Sardinia and the Balearic
Islands, up through France to Paris, and then across the Channel.

I raised my head and threw the globe up and over the fence.
It carried in the wind and cracked against a tree stump, resting
somewhere out of sight, hidden in the long grass.

I didn't want anything to do with Eva after that. She didn't
seem interested in talking to me, either. We ignored each other.
I felt useless. She made Mohammed feel happy and loved, and
she had disregarded everything I'd tried to do. It pissed me off.
I'd never done anything worthwhile. All I'd done was fail my
GCSE's and dig holes in the ground for dead people. I thought
that helping Mohammed would make me feel like I'd done
something good for a change.

A few days passed. We continued to ignore each other. But
I struggled to make friends with any of the other activity leaders.

They were all so different to me and talked about things I didn't like or understand. Things like K-Pop and Rugby League. I was close to packing my bags and leaving the school.

A few more days passed. At mealtimes in the canteen, Eva tried several times to catch my eye. I kept my head down and ignored her. This was well over a week after the Mohammed incident. Looking back, I was too immature to look her in the eye and smile back. It didn't stay that way for long, though. The school was so small that we would have to start talking again at some point. I knew that, and I dreaded it. I was useless at conflict, and worse at resolution. I didn't know how to say sorry or thank you. Symptoms of an only child.

We'd never have got together if Eva hadn't caught Paulo smoking. Paulo was this fifteen-year-old Italian boy who didn't say much. He looked older than I did, and as a result I had avoided him stubbornly, but he never caused us any problems. I was walking across the school to my dorm when Eva came running over. I was the only other person around. The other staff were putting the kids to bed. It was almost 11pm.

Eva said she could see someone out on the playing field but didn't want to go over to them on her own. She led me to the edge of the field and pointed into the darkness. Paulo was standing on the playing field, below the hill where I threw the globe. I noticed a glow of orange in the darkness, and I could smell smoke in the warm air. When we walked over, Paulo didn't run away or put the cigarette out. He just watched us, sucking on the filter tip and blowing out clouds of smoke.

"How's your day been, Paulo?" Eva asked him. I expected her to grab the cigarette from him and stamp it into the ground. I thought she would be angry and shout at him for breaking the rules. But she was calm. She spoke to him like it was the most normal thing.

Paulo didn't say anything. The rizla crackled as it burned.

"Tell us why you're out here, Paulo," Eva said.

The boy finished his cigarette and picked up a bottle of Teacher's. He unscrewed the cap and slugged it without a flinch. Eva didn't stop him drinking either. I wondered how he'd managed to get tobacco and whisky. His chin was furry with the beginnings of a beard and he was probably six feet tall, but I couldn't get served in those days, and I was supposed to be his guardian.

The lights in the schoolhouse were off, but the bright moon shone over the seafront like a lighthouse. I could hear the distant waves crashing along the shoreline with an uneasy rhythm. The boy took another long swig of the whisky and then screwed the cap back on. He plucked a filter tip out from the packet in his pocket and pursed it between his lips. Then he pulled out his pouch of tobacco and filled a paper, stuffing the tip at one end and rolling it into a neat stick. He was sitting down on the grass by this point. When he sparked the lighter, I saw his eyes were bloodshot and his cheeks were wet and shiny.

"What are you doing out here?" Eva asked again.

Paulo was smoking his cigarette and pulling clumps of grass up from the field. He held the grass between his index finger and thumb and singed it with his lighter flame. Eva went to sit down next to him.

"My father died today," he said. "His heart stopped." His English was excellent – he didn't need to be at a summer school to improve. Most of the kids didn't need teaching – their parents were just rich enough to get rid of them for a few weeks.

48

Eva moved in close to him and picked up the Teacher's. She took a long swig and passed the bottle over to me.

I gulped down a mouthful.

"I'm sorry," Eva said. "Don't worry. You won't be in trouble."

I don't think he cared about being in trouble. Eva put her arms around him and he started crying. She squeezed him and stroked the back of his head. Then Eva was crying, too. Paulo had his eyes closed so tight that they looked like clenched fists. I wondered how I'd react if Dad had a heart attack while thumping the punch-bag. I couldn't imagine myself crying about it, but then I couldn't imagine him dying either. I still didn't know what to say so I had another go on the Teacher's.

Paulo pulled away from Eva after a few moments and wiped his face with the palm of his hand.

"I didn't know him very well. He lives in Spain," he said.

"I didn't know my father," Eva said. "I grew up with my mother in Switzerland, but I was born in Paris, where my father is from."

I didn't know my father either, even though he'd been around all my life. I don't think anyone can really know their father. Not properly. Standing there in the dark, I had an urge to pretend to them that my Dad was also dead.

A couple of the other activity leaders walked out from the schoolhouse towards their bedrooms on the other side of the school. We didn't say anything. They were close by, talking and laughing loudly about one of the teachers who owned a banana lunchbox. They didn't notice us.

Eva pinched his tobacco and rolled two cigarettes. She passed one to me and put the other in her mouth. Paulo lit our cigarettes: Eva's first, and then mine. We smoked in silence, passing around the Teacher's until my belly felt full of fire. I tried smoking the cigarette but it made me cough a lot and it tasted of ash so I stopped. Eva smoked her cigarette down to the stingers. That's the only time I ever saw her smoke. She wasn't a smoker.

We stayed with Paulo a while. I didn't say too much. After an hour, Eva led him back to the schoolhouse and found him a private room for the night. I waited for her, and when she returned I hugged her for the first time. She had taken the Teacher's from Paulo. As I took another gulp, she cried into my chest. Her breath smelled of mouthwash, but cigarette smoke still lingered in her hair.

She sang the song into my ear, slower than usual, each sound a delicate song of its own. Her mouth was close to my ear, and, even though I was holding her, she rocked me in lullaby. "*Au soleil, sous la pluie; À midi ou à minuit; Il y a tout ce que vous voulez; Aux Champs-Élysées.*"

We stayed out there well into the night, sitting on a couple of meadow stones, throwing pebbles into the blackness. After another hour of sipping the Teacher's, Eva said she should get to bed. I could have stayed out all night.

Paulo went home to Italy the next day. I didn't see him again. I woke up late with a heavy head from all the whisky, the smoke-smell stuck to my hair and clothes.

Thursday June 23rd 2016 was the night of the referendum. The British public were given the chance to vote on whether Britain should remain in the EU. I was done hearing about it. It was all people talked about. My parents had been going on about how leaving would be the best thing Britain could do, about how things would go back to the good old days, about how we would look after our own first.

It was a bigger deal to Eva than it was to most of the others at the school. She'd baked a cake – vegan banana bread iced with 12 golden stars on a blue background – the EU flag.

I wasn't old enough to vote. I was to turn 18 only a matter of weeks after the referendum. Eva was annoyed with me, but I couldn't help when I was born. She made me watch the news with her all night as the results came in. A few of the other staff tried the banana bread but it tasted like soil and it had sultanas in which make me feel sick. I had to eat it because it meant a lot to Eva and I was dying to have sex with her. Sometimes I'd lie awake at night and the voices of the Russian dolls would come back to me, yelling, "Virgin Boy! Still got your L-plates on?"

I had to do something with Eva. I was waking up every morning with a rock-on. It didn't help my sexual frustration watching Eva running around in little denim shorts and crop-tops that showed the small of her back and the curve at her hips.

The news reporters were confident that Britain would remain. Most people were. The polls were indicating that more were in favour of remaining. A few of the other staff watched the TV with us in the common room once the kids were all in bed, but they dropped off one by one, losing interest. Before long it was just me and Eva, and the TV.

At 4:40am, it was clear that Britain would leave. Normally I'd be fast asleep by then, but Eva kept yelling at the TV and saying how stupid British people were and how the stock market was going to crash and how Europe's back was broken.

"Billy, I can't believe it's true. Is it really true?"

I put my arm around her. She picked up the half-eaten banana bread and threw it at the TV. David Cameron's face was smeared with vegan marzipan.

"Fuck you, Britain," she said. "Do you realise what this means?"

I didn't really realise what it meant. I don't think anybody did.

Eva didn't talk for a little while. She watched the discussions and dissections closely. She lay across my lap, and curled her body into a ball, head rested on my thigh. Her smooth, brown neck was staring up at me, waiting to be kissed, but her eyes were fixed on the news.

After another hour of staring in disbelief, Eva grabbed me by the hand and we left the main house. The TV was left on, and the EU cake smeared on the TV and the carpet. She led me to my room, and when I unlocked it and went inside, she stripped off her t-shirt and lay down in my bed, on her front. I felt like my balls were swelling and turning bluer and bluer with every moment.

I was lucky to have a room to myself. It was in an old Portakabin, with one other room in. They normally used mine for piano lessons, but when the summer school needed to use it, they shoved a single bed in there. There was a guy called TA staying in the room next to mine. He was also an activity leader, but never really spoke to anyone. We'd barely said a word to each other all summer.

There was an upright piano at the end of the bed. Sometimes my toes caught the keys on the upper octaves in the night, and I'd wake up at the sound of an out-of-tune note. But I wasn't fussed. It was better to have my own room rather than share with another guy, like the others did. It meant I had some privacy.

I got into bed next to Eva and moved my face next to hers. She giggled as I tried to kiss her. Our teeth kept banging together and I didn't know where to put my hands. They were on her hips for a bit, but then I thought I should mix it up and started rubbing the top of her back. On reflection, it was similar to how you'd wind a baby.

Thankfully, Eva didn't burp. Her breathing grew heavier. It was like she was blowing up a balloon in my boxer shorts. I felt awkward that it was pressing against her stomach while we kissed.

She pulled my t-shirt up and over my head and unbuttoned my cargo shorts. I should've been enjoying the moment, kissing her and making that my only thought. But images were racing through my mind: diagrams of vaginas in GCSE Biology textbooks, bikini-clad models in Mum's clothing catalogues, David Cameron's red face, Union Jacks and vote/remain pie-charts. It was supposed to be the best night of my life, but all I could think about was Brexit.

I started thinking about whether Eva was only jumping into bed with me because of Brexit. It felt reactionary. It felt like maybe she was just teasing me, that she'd let me get so close to having her and then take it all away, put her clothes back on and disappear like Sally Fountain had before.

My room proved a difficult space to be intimate. I was nervous about having sex with Eva, of course. She was older than me by two years, and I felt sure she must have been with a handful of guys. My imagination convinced me that she had dated international businessmen and millionaire poker players – people that were better than me in infinite ways. I never found out how many men she had been with. I don't think knowing would have helped. I was already worrying about chlamydia and herpes and warts and gonorrhoea because I didn't have a condom and I didn't know what any of those infections were, but people always seemed to get the piss taken out of them if they happened to contract them.

The springs in my mattress were broken and reverberated like a gong chime whenever I moved. Eva said it hurt her back. There was no room on the floor either. After nearly an hour of kissing, my lips were sore. We were naked, and I was panicking about how to touch her. I still didn't have a clue what to do. Thankfully, Eva took control. I'll never forget when she grabbed my hand and guided it across her chest, brushing my fingertips over her breasts, down, down, tracing the curve of her flank all the way to her hip, and across the flat plane of her stomach.

"Are you OK?" Eva said. The moment felt heavy in the air. It was how I imagined the seconds unfolded in agonizing slow motion before a natural disaster. I opened my mouth to speak, but desire had thickened in my throat. For a moment I couldn't talk.

Eva didn't seem to mind. She giggled and smacked me on the chest, then jumped on top of me. The mattress gonged.

I woke up and Eva had gone to work – she was supervising breakfast. I rolled over to check my phone and Mum had texted me saying "Great result!! Xxx" with a couple of Union Jack emojis at the end. I felt like replying and telling her that I'd managed to lose my virginity so we both had reason to celebrate. Instead I just replied with the thumbs up emoji.

I didn't care about Brexit. I didn't really know what it was, or why people were so angry about it. I didn't follow the news. Eva talked about Brexit less and less. She even said we wouldn't speak about "The B Word" anymore. She seemed to have accepted that things would be different. I wasn't sure how it even affected her. Over the next few weeks, I spent most nights in bed with Eva. On one occasion, I lasted over ten minutes.

But it wasn't just sex. Eva and I went for long walks over the Downs when we had time away from work, and she talked to me about everything she loved. These things included, but were not limited to, Russian literature, running across the tops of cars when drunk, chai tea, steam trains, wind farms, hydroelectric research projects, composting, sewing, pottery, bird baths, mosaics, nutmeg, World War II, Gary Numan, oxbow lakes, mushroom stew, and Freudian psychoanalysis. I accepted that she had a wide and eclectic taste, and I loved the way she loved things. She always talked about Freud and how we all want to shag our dads and kill our mums. It might have been the other way around. I didn't tend to listen too closely when she talked about that stuff.

One day we went to Brighton, and Eva led me along the seafront. We walked past the pier, where people were eating and drinking and looking out towards the hope of the horizon. The air smelled of seaweed, lager, sun cream and chips. Two Union Jacks fell flat in the still air. The colours had faded from the flags and the paint had chipped away on the poles. We walked underneath the pier and saw the rotten pillars, coated in algae, lichen and moss.

Eva walked a couple of miles inland, following a river until the sounds of the seafront disappeared. I didn't know whether she knew where she was going. But I didn't care – I followed. We came to a nature reserve. It was either that or an abandoned area of countryside. We weren't following a track, just walking into nowhere. Grasshoppers rustled in the weeds. I didn't like it. The pollen made my nose itch.

"Do you know where we're going?" I remember asking her that a lot. It didn't seem like she did.

"Keep walking," she said. "We're almost there."

The grass brushed against my bare knees. Further along the river, I saw a bridge. It took another twenty minutes of walking upriver to reach it, and that's where we stopped.

It looked like a disused railway bridge. Eva ran up to the concrete pilings and started climbing into the framework.

"Are you sure that's a good idea?" I asked. People had obviously been there before because there were boulders in place at the bottom to allow you to climb up. Eva hoisted herself up onto one and grabbed onto the iron bars. "I don't think it's safe."

She ignored me and pulled herself up, disappearing into the metal. Desperate not to be shown up, I followed her. I was worried about plummeting into the water. Swimming had always been difficult for me, and I was never any good at adventurous stuff. I'm scared of heights.

Even so, I scrambled onto the boulder and grabbed the bars as Eva had. I had no choice. It wasn't easy to pull myself up – not as easy as she had made it seem. Once inside the framework, though, it was simple enough to climb up onto the bridge itself. Blue and red graffiti had been sprayed all over the metal. Along the ledge, someone had written in huge letters: If at first you don't succeed, call an airstrike.

The rails were rusty and chipped. They ran halfway along the bridge, and then stopped. A large section of the floor had been removed. It was hard to tell whether it had fallen away with time or been destroyed. It was a thirty-foot clean drop straight into the river. White-capped rushes moved below – the noise of the current hissed up through the hole in the bridge. Eva was standing at it, looking down. She had taken her shoes off, and her toes curled over the edge. Her toenails were little red shells.

I walked along the bridge, as close as I could get. In the distance, the candy-cane swirls of a helter-skelter climbed into the skating clouds. A Ferris wheel turned behind flapping flags, and the skyline was punctuated with tent tops.

"Don't get too close," I said. The water was bursting along so loud below us that I'm not sure she heard me. She didn't say anything. She just looked down at the water. Eva was drawn to things like that. I stepped closer to her, slowly, careful not to catch her by surprise. I didn't want her to fall. The water didn't look too deep.

"Go easy," I shouted. A carousel was going around at the fairground. The plastic horses galloped around in circles.

"What are you worried about?" she said. "It's just water."

I relaxed as she turned and stepped away from the edge.

"It's dangerous."

Eva smiled. Her eyes were burning gas – bright and blue.

She stepped in close to me. The sunlight glowed around her jaw, and a shadow settled on her cheek. She took off her sandals, stepped out of her shorts, and peeled off her vest top. She was wearing a blue bikini. There were tiny gems in the pattern of a diamond on her hip. Her hip bones jutted out like two small knuckles.

Honky-tonk piano noises at the fairground wandered over from across the river. Screaming and shouting voices muddled in with the melody. I used to be one of those voices – eating candy floss from a stick, throwing balls at hoops for prizes that nobody ever won.

Eva pressed her cheek into my shoulder, then, with a slight twist of her head, touched her lips to my neck. They were salt-and-pepper kisses, barely pressing the skin. I felt a little thrill as my hands settled on her hips, and I could feel the goose bumps prickle up on her sides. That was the only true thing in the universe at that moment. It didn't last for more than a few seconds. She slipped away and smiled at me. I was floating off, somewhere above the bridge, into the candy-floss clouds.

But then Eva stepped back towards the hole in the floor. She turned around and jumped up into the air. She had her hands crossed over her chest. As she dropped, her hair whisked upwards above her head like a parachute, and then she shot down through the hole in the floor. Down, down, down, into the river. I heard a splash, fainter than a bar of soap dropping in dishwater. I rushed forwards and looked down. It was an unbearable drop.

I waited for her to reappear on the surface, for her to burst up for air like a mermaid, look up and laugh at me, diamond-eyed, and then pull her hair away from her face and swim along the river. I waited a few seconds, but she didn't appear. That was the moment I should have jumped. Nothing was said about it – she didn't tell me to jump. But that was what I was supposed to do. Instead, I stood up there and took a picture of her swimming.

There're only two types of people in this world – those who lead and those who follow, those who jump and those who don't, those who stay and those who go, those who take photos and those who are in photos. I didn't jump. That was my biggest mistake.

Moving to the side of the bridge, I climbed onto the iron ledge. There were rivets hammered into the metal – small bumps that pressed into the soles of my feet. I looked for her. The water ran away to sea downriver. All the way along the riverbanks, the leaves and branches of willow trees hung over into the water like girls on their hands and knees with their hair thrown out over their heads. Logs and branches were dragged along in the current, and further on, the small whitecaps formed plaits in the surges. Way off in the distance, I saw Eva floating along on her back. Her feet kicked in the water, but she wasn't struggling. The river carried her.

Eva's arms performed slow, rhythmic strokes: up, back, and behind her head. An arm would raise up every few seconds, then swish back into the water behind her. Her stroke seemed to hold still in mid-air, hands and fingers relaxed. Her hands made a tiny splash as they broke through the surface water. They were skimming stones, racing out towards the horizon.

Eva was from Lucerne, Switzerland, and it was only a matter of time before she had to leave.

The day Eva left, I walked her to the train station, down the long winding paths from the summer school where we had spent the last few weeks together, right down to the bottom of the hill, back to the real world where people have to run for trains and stuff cardboard sandwiches into their mouths between changes, where suited men haul their briefcases around, shackled to their wrists. I wheeled Eva's suitcase down the road and it kept clipping my heels and toppling over. Eva walked on ahead, several metres in front of me. She always hated being late.

By the time we got to the station, Eva's train had already left. Pissed off, she went to buy an espresso shot and a punnet of cherry tomatoes. She refused to talk to me for ten minutes. We waited in silence for the next train, her suitcase wedged between us on the bench.

"I'm going to be late now," Eva said. "I told you we would be late."

I reached for a cherry tomato, but she slapped my hand away.

"Don't leave," I said. "Stay."

"You know I can't."

"You can."

"I don't want to be in this country any longer. I'm not welcome."

"That's not true."

"Britain doesn't want all of us foreigners here. Taking your jobs."

"Not everybody."

"Whatever you say."

"You could stay in England. You can do anything you want to."

"I have a new job, Billy. In Zurich."

"You'll get a better job here."

"Billy, I must go."

"Don't."

"You can come to see me when the school is finished."

"Yeah?"

"Of course."

In the twenty minutes we spent waiting for the next train, I dreamed about going to live with Eva in Switzerland. Everyone was shitting their pants about Brexit. While the country was trying to get rid of foreigners and keep more from coming, I was going to up and leave, live with Eva and enjoy a simple life in the Swiss mountains.

I looked across to her. The black handle on her suitcase was extended upwards, like two prison bars between our faces. She was always hard to be close to. Intimacy was foreign to her. Eva could never cuddle to sleep, and she hated holding hands. I mean, she jumped off a bridge moments after I kissed her, so I should've seen that coming.

The train hummed in and the doors swished open. Eva got up, kissed me twice on the mouth and held my cheeks with her sticky palms. I said goodbye, and then she was gone.

3

A few days later, my time at the summer school came to an end, and I returned to my parents and GG and Benny. Before the train arrived at Cheltenham Station, I'd already decided that I would not be home for long. The way I saw it, I needed to save only a few hundred pounds with which to pay for my escape. Then, I could move to be with Eva.

We were texting each other every day, but Eva had told me she didn't like spending too much time on her phone, and she would sometimes not reply for a few hours. She would occasionally call me before she went to sleep, but these would often be cut short. If Dad heard me talking through the wall he would bang on my door and tell me to shut up if it was late. The infrequent communication served as extra motivation for me to move out to Switzerland and be with her. I refused to be forgotten.

How long would it take me to get a few hundred pounds? I figured I could do it in under a month, and I figured I wouldn't even need a job. One afternoon in the spring, before Eva, I'd wandered around town on half-hearted job hunts, and found myself in WH Smith, in the section with all the notebooks. I wanted to start writing a diary. Something to keep my mind occupied while I sorted everything out. I liked the look of the

Moleskine notebooks. They had a touch of class. I picked up a bright red one and decided I wanted it. The leather felt like a Bond villain's driving gloves. But then I'd looked at the price ticket – £22 – and had put it back on the shelf.

But travelling home from the summer school, I'd had an idea. On my first day back in Cheltenham, I returned to WH Smith and found the Moleskines. I chose a red one and carried it to the jiffy bag section, with all the brown paper bags for posting parcels and letters. I found one that fitted the notebook and slipped the Moleskine inside. Then I walked upstairs. WH Smith in Cheltenham has a post office on the first floor. They have post offices in quite a few of their stores. I just wrote out my name and address on the jiffy bag and sent it to myself first class. It cost me 69p. I walked out and nobody thought anything of it.

I started sending notebooks to myself every day for a week or so, and then selling them on eBay. It was an earner, and better than working. I calculated that if I could sell a Moleskine for £15 every day, I could fly out to Eva in a matter of weeks. It gave me hope, stealing all those notebooks.

The best thing was, I could re-use the jiffy bags that I was sending to myself, so that made things less sketchy because I didn't have to steal a jiffy bag and the notebook every time. I got a few USB sticks as well, but they weren't worth as much.

Course, that would've been way too easy. Before long, I got caught.

I went into Smith's and did the usual thing: walked around for five minutes, found my notebook, mooched around a bit more, flicked through magazines and skimmed over the tabloid headlines – they were usually accompanied by pictures of Boris Johnson or Kim Kardashian.

I crammed a Moleskine into a jiffy bag and strolled upstairs. Looking back, I got too cocky. I ran the same con every single day. The staff must've caught onto the fact it was a bit weird for a teenage boy to post letters of the same size and weight, addressed to the same place and person, *every single day*. But I didn't think it'd be an issue.

I'd just got to the front of the queue to be served by Jules – the redhead in her mid-thirties that looked like she'd happily burn down the Post Office at any given moment. She'd served me there several times before. I imagined that Jules didn't care – she'd have happily processed the envelope and asked no questions. But before I had the chance to send the letter, I felt a hand grip me by the elbow.

"You'll have to come with me," said the man that'd grabbed me. His name badge read Justin and below it, in block white capitals, it said: MANAGER.

He led me through to their back room and invited me to sit down in front of sixteen CCTV monitors.

"I know what you've been doing," Justin said, as he fiddled with the CCTV controls and the images on the screens started zipping back in time. He stopped rewinding as the monitor showed me walking through the front door. We watched my perfect crime in agonising slow-motion. "And I know it's not a one-off. If it was, I'd have let you off the hook. But you've been stealing every day. I've been through the footage and the police are on their way."

I've never been so close to shitting myself without it happening. "I'm sorry," I pleaded, close to tears. "I'm desperate. I had no choice."

"Nobody is that desperate for Moleskine notebooks and USB sticks." He had an annoying mole above his left eyebrow. "You can't live on them, you know. Try stealing food and water if you're that desperate."

I didn't want to admit to flogging them all on eBay, so I kept quiet and waited for the police.

The police inevitably took ages to arrive as it was a non-emergency. I thought about asking Justin to borrow a magazine or newspaper to help pass the time, but he didn't seem to be in the most obliging mood. He waited with me in his office, filling out spreadsheets and angrily clicking on desktop icons when they took longer than three seconds to load. I thought about running away. But if I'd tried to leg it, he probably would've caught me – he was tall and lean and looked like the sort of twat who had a blog about all the half marathons he ran for charity at weekends. Plus, I reasoned that I was in enough trouble as it was, and I probably wouldn't make for a good fugitive.

When the police finally arrived – a man and a woman – I was quite relieved. I wanted it all over with. Part of my stupid seventeen-year-old head thought it would be OK to get arrested and thrown in prison. I figured that I'd get to move out of home and have my own room and loads of new mates, and girls might think I was cool because I don't think any of the other boys in my year had even been close to prison. I thought about the prison gang I'd fall into and the mysterious codename that I'd be known by. Eva would probably like it, too. I'd got the impression from one of Mum's gossip magazines that women love a bad boy.

Justin explained the situation to the officers. They listened to him with their arms folded and when he was done, the male officer, PC Alan World, asked me to follow them downstairs to the car. They'd have to take me into the station and make a record of the incidents, they said. I was in total shock. Justin thanked the officers and they shook hands. He picked up two grip strengtheners with foam handles and tensed them in his hands as we left.

When we got outside, PC World handcuffed me and bundled me into the back of the car. I tried to keep my head down in case somebody on the high street recognised me. The tears finally came, but I was proud that I'd managed to appear tough in front of Justin. He was a total dickhead.

The officers didn't say anything for a few seconds, and then PC World turned around from the driver's seat and said, "That's some stunt, kiddo."

The female officer giggled from the passenger seat. Her body armour bounced up and down on her shoulders. "It's genius," she said.

"We're gonna let you off with a caution. Only because you're a smart kid and I've not heard anything like this in all my years." PC World was smiling now. I couldn't work out why. "But you must return anything you've taken, and we have to let your folks know. Jesus, I've never seen anything like it. Posting yourself whatever you want. They'd have never caught on if you weren't so obvious about it."

Was PC World giving me advice on how to be a better thief? I hadn't even given any thought to how stupid his name was. It can't have been easy being PC World. He must've been dying for a promotion. But I didn't think about any of that until after.

I got a caution and a slap on the wrist and promised I'd never do it again. I wouldn't. I couldn't. I was barred from WH Smith and all other Post Office branches in Cheltenham. I thought that was harsh, but I was lucky not to be going to court. The officers dropped me home and explained to Mum and Dad that I'd been caught trying to shoplift. They didn't explain that I was trying to steal by manipulating the postal service, or that I'd been stealing every day for the past couple of weeks. They were weirdly nice to me, thinking back.

But even with that version of the truth, my Mum and Dad still went mental.

I turned 18 a few days later. My parents withheld all presents and celebrations as punishment for the shoplifting. GG sent me a card with £20 inside, but that wasn't going to get me to Eva.

I spent the day at home watching films and eating salted popcorn. I liked to chew the kernels that didn't pop in the microwave. When I got bored of that, I scrolled through the birthday wishes on Facebook. Most of them were from people who'd never liked me. I swear that some of them were from people I'd never met. I clicked on a few profiles and saw that everyone seemed to be doing much more interesting things than I was, which wasn't saying much. I did get an uninspiring "Happy Birthday x" from Katie Marshall, who I used to fancy in school. I spent a while looking at her pictures, but I couldn't think of anything besides Eva. I clicked through Eva's social media for the twentieth time that day. She still hadn't posted anything since two days earlier when she'd shared a video about the exploitation of elephants in Thailand.

After that, I sat on my windowsill and tried to sketch the front garden – the perfect trees and hedges, the cars and the rooftops. It looked like a Lego set. It didn't take me long to realise I was useless at drawing. All the lines I drew were laboured and sharp – they didn't look right.

But while I was drawing, my Mum came back from work early. There was a car waiting outside on our drive – a black Mercedes. A man was sitting in the driver's seat, engine idling.

I thought it was just somebody waiting to pick up one of our neighbours, but then Mum ran over to the car and got in the passenger side. They drove off, and I remained on the windowsill.

I didn't move from the windowsill and an hour later the Mercedes reappeared, and Mum climbed out. She ran her fingers through her hair and tucked a few loose strands behind her ear.

Happy fucking birthday, I thought.

At 6pm, my friend Tommy knocked on the door. I was relieved to see him. We'd fallen out a few months before after I wouldn't let him copy my answers during our GCSE Chemistry exam. As a result, we hadn't spoken much since leaving school. I'd sent him a few text messages, but he never replied. I figured he was still pissed off at me, and I regretted not helping him with the answers. That said, I got a D, so he wasn't missing out on much.

I was surprised that he'd come to see me. Tommy's as stubborn as a wet match. He looked taller and thinner, and his face seemed leaner and greyer and sadder than before.

We chatted at the doorstep for a bit, and he explained that he wasn't annoyed at me anymore, and the reason he hadn't responded to my texts was because he'd smashed his phone up after an argument with his mum's boyfriend. He wished me a happy birthday, pushed a lottery ticket into my chest, and punched me hard on the shoulder.

"Put some shoes on, Bill," he said. "Let's go for a beer."

We went out and bounced from pub to pub until midnight, holding conversations that never really met. I got drunk and talked at length about Eva, and he talked in parallel about gambling and football and a show about the zombie apocalypse on Channel 5. When the Two Pigs shut, we walked around town for another hour, stopping at various points where things had happened throughout our school years. We reminisced about throwing snowballs into car windows as they drove past. We laughed about the boy who used to tie his shoelaces to his bicycle pedals. We laughed so much that we came to realise there was nothing to laugh about anymore. We realised that all those memories had long faded, and that we'd grown into different people. People we never expected to be.

After a bit, we started to sober up and it seemed we'd totally run out of things to say. But as the evening began to get awkward, Tommy said, "Listen, if you want to see this girl, I've got a plan for how we can make some serious money."

The next day, I woke up around one in the afternoon. When I went down for a glass of water, I found Mum with a whole group of other women around her age, about ten of them. I walked in and their eyes widened and many of them put their teacups down on their saucers to examine me. Mum hadn't noticed me. She was standing in the middle of the room, reading aloud from a piece of paper that she must have picked out from the bowl full of them on the coffee table.

"When I was fifteen, I got pregnant and my Mum kicked me out of the house. She never found out that the father was her boss, and they're married now. My son doesn't know who his Dad is."

"What?" I said.

Mum looked up and saw me staring at her. "That's not mine!" she said. "We're secret sharing. I'm reading the secrets out. That's not my secret."

All the other women peered at me. None of them said anything.

"She's telling the truth," one of the women said. She was fat and her second chin bounced with the movement of her lips. "But that's not my secret either. I'm just saying, she's telling the truth."

The rest of the women all nodded and looked around, examining each other's faces to see if they could determine who the secret belonged to.

"You can join us, if you want. It's all anonymous." A woman sitting on the sofa budged up to make room for me. She was skinny. Her collarbone jutted out like a coat hanger.

Mum picked another piece of paper and read it aloud, "My husband and I have sex twice a year. When we do have sex, we have the lights off and I imagine he's Tony Blair."

71

A few of the women giggled. Many of them tried to look as stony faced as possible, trying not to give anything away. I imagined that was my Mum's secret – that she imagines Dad is Tony Blair when they have sex. The thought made me feel sick. But I convinced myself that it wasn't my Mum's secret because her and my Dad always voted Conservative.

Nobody spoke after each secret was read. It was just a recital of everybody's deepest fears and woes. I didn't see the point in it.

"I lie to people and tell them I voted for Britain to remain because I'm scared people will think I'm a racist." Five or six of the women started nodding their heads and one muttered, "You're not the only one."

Mum kept flying through the secrets. "I hate dogs. My friend had a dog that always used to jump on me, so one day I fed it chocolate." The women gasped. Mum paused for effect. "It died."

When Mum finally reached the end of the secrets, she invited the women to put down their tea and cake and sit on the floor in a circle to reflect and meditate. The fat woman peeled herself away from the leather sofa and groaned all the way down to the floor. I remained on the sofa, watching as the women held hands in a circle on the floor. The larger women couldn't cross their legs, instead resting on knees that clicked under the strain of their bodies. Mum went and put a CD in the stereo. Simply Red.

"Thank you for sharing today, ladies," Mum said, as Mick Hucknall's voice began to fill the room.

I wondered if Hucknall was alive, and if so, whether it might be worth a £10 bet on him to be the next celebrity to drop dead.

"I think this has been an extremely transformative experience for all of us," Mum continued.

The ladies nodded. Some had their eyes closed.

"We should do it again," the skinny woman said.

"Yes," the other women agreed.

A lady that had said nothing until this point began singing the chorus to "Holding Back the Years." The ladies didn't hesitate to join in.

"I'll keeeeeeeeeeeeep, holding onnnnnnnnn. I'll keeeeeeeeeeeeep, holding onnnnnnnn."

They started to cry after that, clenching hands and biting lips, tears wetting their wrinkly cheeks. I needed to get out. I ran upstairs and showered, dressed and left. On my way out I passed Dad in the front garden. He had the kettle and was pouring boiling water between the slabs of our garden path.

"What are you doing?" I asked him.

"We've got ants under the path. Thousands of them. Trying to kill them off." Dad hunkered down and poured a pint of boiling water onto the slabs. A cloud of steam shot up into the air, and hundreds of ants ran out from below the path. Dad tried stamping on them and poured the remainder of the water over as many ants as he could. A puddle of floating dead ants remained, along with hundreds of other living ones running around, mourning. Dad went to fill up the kettle again. "It's an invasion," he said. "Enough is enough."

I got to Tommy's and banged on his front door. It took a few minutes, but eventually the door opened.

"What's up?" Tommy said, answering the door wearing only football shorts. He had a skinny, hairless chest and I could see the faint outline of his ribs. I was always glad when he answered. His Mum made me nervous, and Simon, his stepdad, would have probably told me to piss off.

"I needed to get out of the house. My Mum's started this weird secret sharing group."

"A what?"

"This group of women all sit around and write down their secrets, then put them in a hat. My Mum reads them all out."

"But it's all anonymous?"

"Yeah. Why does it matter?"

"Was there anything dirty?"

"Well, one of the women confessed that she and her husband only have sex twice a year or something, and when they do, she turns out the lights and pretends he's Tony Blair."

"Blair?"

"I know."

I went inside and waited for Tommy to get dressed. His house was totally different to mine. The wallpaper was peeling away from the walls in places. It stunk of smoke, too. His Mum always chain smoked at the kitchen table. I remember her sitting there smoking when I was a kid. She didn't care that Tommy was asthmatic.

When Tommy came down, he scooped up the day's post from the doormat.

"What are you doing?" I asked him. He picked up a lighter from the kitchen table and went out into the back garden, taking a seat at the rotting wooden table.

"Burning Simon's post."

Tommy didn't even bother reading the letters before setting them on fire.

"Why?"

"Because he's a dickhead."

I couldn't argue with that. "Do you burn it all?"

"When I catch it in time. I'm hoping that he'll go bankrupt soon. He's in a lot of debt. He's only with my Mum cause she pays his way."

"Want a hand?"

"Go ahead."

I went and grabbed a can of Lynx from Tommy's bedroom and a lighter from the kitchen, before returning to the garden. I opened a letter in a white envelope. It was Simon's bank statement.

"Here, hold this up," I said.

Tommy pinched the corner of the paper between his finger and thumb and held it at arm's length away from his body. I sparked the lighter and sprayed the deodorant through the flame. The spray caught fire, and the deodorant spray transformed into a flamethrower. The flames shot nearly a metre out of the can, disintegrating the paper in seconds.

"Let's have a go," Tommy said.

We took turns to use the flamethrower on the rest of the post. I watched the flames consume the papers – bills, warnings, final reminders, all scattered across the patio in ashes.

Once all the post was cremated, we walked to the racecourse so Tommy could explain his money-making plan. He claimed that to understand it properly, I'd have to see the spot where the scheme would unfold. I followed him through a gap in the hedges, about half a mile down the road from the entrance to the racecourse itself.

We walked along a dirt track, past a caravan park. Overarching trees blotted out the grey sky. All I knew was that it was near to Prestbury, a village just outside Cheltenham. The track ended and opened out onto a wide stretch of green turf, where cloud shadows raced over the grass plain. In the next field there were huge cows grazing on the thick grass. The racecourse was so far below that the brush fences looked like matchsticks.

We walked down the hill, onto a trail that bordered the racecourse. All that separated the trail from the racecourse itself was a low metal fence. Tommy's spot was half a mile along the bridleway, where the bushes thinned out. He rushed up to the fence and hooked his fingers through the rusty mesh.

"When the horses shoot past, you can hear the whips crack on their hindquarters," he said. "It's so loud down here, it's like they're slashing you with the whip."

Tommy sounded like he knew what he was talking about. I'd never heard the word 'hindquarters' before. I didn't expect to be able to get so close to the racecourse. But the horses would run past five or six metres away from where we were standing. The brush fences were close enough to see where they'd been clipped.

"So, what's the master plan?" I asked him. He was staring out at Cleeve Hill in the distance. The buildings near the top looked like doll's houses.

"We shoot the favourite of the Gold Cup," he said.

"We shoot a jockey?" I asked.

"No, dickhead. We shoot the horse. Bet on an outsider and shoot the favourite with a BB gun. Then our boy comes through and we win our fortune."

"Seriously?" I couldn't believe we had walked all this way to hear this crazy idea. "I thought it was gonna be better than that."

"Hear me out," he said. "We take out one of those instant money loans, say £10,000, and put it all on a horse with odds at 10/1 – that's £100,000. Five or six races, we'll be laughing. You'll be well out of your overdraft."

"Surely people can find this track? People must come and watch the horses from here."

"Never seen a soul down here. Been coming since I was a kid."

"But they'll know something's up if a horse drops dead while it's running."

"BB guns wouldn't kill it. We'd just slow it down."

"But we'd get caught. They'd find the ball bearings in the horse."

"They won't penetrate the skin. It'll just feel like a shock and then it will bounce off. Come on, think of all that money you could have. You could take your missus to Timbuktu."

I pictured me and Eva on a beach somewhere, and then I pictured me and Tommy huddled up with camouflage draped over our heads, faces smudged with war paint. I imagined myself pulling the trigger, popping a shot into the horse's flank. Tommy was right. Working at some shitty job I would have earned a couple of hundred a month. Without Tommy's plan, it would take months to get the money to go out to see Eva. And all the time I worried she might meet someone else.

Tommy's plan was crazy enough that it just might work.

We went to look at guns that afternoon. There was a shop just out of Cheltenham that sold air rifles, BB guns, shotguns, scopes, silencers – everything. Tommy picked out an automatic BB gun. It had a scope already attached. He said there was no way we could miss with a scope to aim through and not a chance anybody could catch us if the gun made no noise. I got caught up in his enthusiasm. It was easy to get dragged along with Tommy's ideas.

Tommy bought the gun. It cost him £200. He didn't even think about it, he was so set. There was no talking him around once he'd made his mind up. I couldn't wait to shoot it. As soon as we left the gun shop, Tommy bought some beers and we took the gun out into the fields beneath Cleeve Hill, not far from the racecourse. Once the beers were done, I rested the bottles beneath an oak with cracked bark, near the edge of the field. Tommy let me shoot it first.

I pushed the stock into my shoulder and supported the barrel with my left hand. I'd never shot a gun before. With my left eye closed, I looked into the sight and fixed the bottleneck in the cross-hair. I imagined the horses passing through the view of the sight, in a blur of racing colours. Then, right before I pulled it, the image of the black Mercedes came into my mind, and I pictured shooting through the windscreen, ripping the man's head off his shoulders. I saw it all. It felt good to think of it.

With that, I squeezed the trigger and the ball bearings sprayed out and crashed through the green bottle. A thousand glass diamonds scattered across the cold soil.

I thought about how I'd show Dad I could make money and we could do all the things we'd ever wanted. Mum could go off to the Bahamas; Dad could play golf with businessmen on Tuesdays. We could get out of the suburbs. That's what had driven Dad crazy. I was sure it wasn't about GG getting married again, or the arseholes he worked with. It wasn't about Brexit or the new speed cameras on the M5 or even about immigrants. It couldn't have been.

I imagined walking home with millions in cash stuffed into briefcases, opening them up in front of Mum and Dad and throwing it up in the air, watching the money float to the floor. Mum and Dad would jump around in it and dance as the Queen's head flashed all around us in purple and red showers. Mum would stop her affair and Dad would stop boxing. We could forget about GG and the inheritance we weren't getting, and everyone could get on again, like when Gran was around.

Best of all, I would have the money to go and see Eva, and we could travel the world together. I could buy her champagne every night and we could live on a yacht.

Tommy was a genius.

While Tommy and I were preparing to shoot a racehorse, my parents still hadn't noticed that I didn't have a job. I wasn't even sure they cared. Mum was busy with Mercedes Man and Dad was obsessed with his punch-bag. I took to running around the racecourse every morning – sometimes I would go twice in a day. It seemed that the more I learned about the layout of the course, the more likely it was that the plan might succeed.

One afternoon I had to stop to get my breath back by a service gate. It led into the expensive part of the racecourse, where the punters get the best view. The Owners and Trainers restaurant was along from the gate, where the rich horse owners eat and drink on race days. It's a semi-permanent marquee with two floors. There are stables on the left-hand side, on the other side of the chain link fence, next to the restaurant. I'd been studying it all on my runs, trying to see if there was anything that might help me and Tommy. Until that day, I hadn't learned anything useful.

As I was stretching out my hamstrings, an old man was walking towards the service gate where I was standing. He was dressed like a farmer in a green sweatshirt, brown flat cap and black trousers. He stopped every few steps, placed something on the floor, and then picked it back up again and walked a few more steps before setting it back down. It looked heavy. I walked towards him, and when I got to him, he was breathing hard with his hands on his hips. His cheeks sagged with age and were pocked with liver spots. Grey hairs bristled in his ears, and black hairs lingered in his nostrils. He had a white moustache that fell over his lips like two wilting petals. In his time, he must have been well over six feet tall, but now his back was bent in the middle and his posture was hunched. On the floor at his feet was the biggest bottle of whiskey I've ever seen.

"Need a hand?" My breathing was back to normal but my head was covered with sweat. He was still panting.

"Could you?" he said. He had a country accent. The words all seemed to jumble into one. "I'm Sam."

"Billy," I said and shook his hand. "Where do you need to take it?"

"I dunno what's to be done with it, to be honest. We'll take it back to the stables and the rest of 'em can decide whether they want it. I don't even bloody drink the stuff."

"Why do you have it?"

"There was a horse had a fall and broke both its front legs. Snapped like breadsticks. I work in the vets' quarters here, see. I'm retired, though. I just do it for the day out. It's not much pay, but you can't stop at my age."

I was struggling to understand him. He spoke in long sounds. There were no gaps between any of the words. I didn't want to interrupt, though. I liked listening to him talk.

"Alls I do is get the winners to piss in a bucket. They check it all these days, see. Alotta cheatin going on."

"So how did you get the whiskey?"

"That's it." He scratched his cheek and it sounded like sandpaper. "So this horse breaks its leg, comes into the vets straight away. There's alotta blood pumping out everywhere, real messy show it was. Their hearts beat faster when they're racing, see. They break their leg and their heart goes even faster still. The owner of this horse is a little Chinaman. Tiny little fella, barely five feet tall. Anyway, he comes into the vets where they're working on his horse, sees the state of it and bursts into tears. He thinks his horse is gonna die, see. Can't blame him, really. What with the amount of blood all over the place. I tried telling him that it wasn't gonna die, and that the vets should be able

81

to fix her up OK, but he doesn't understand a bloody word of English."

I wondered if the Chinese man did speak English, but just didn't understand a word Sam was saying. It was difficult enough for me.

"He went away and came back the next day. That was yesterday. We had his horse all bandaged up and she was sleeping. He breaks down in tears again, expected her to be dead, see. He was crying and grabbed me and cuddled me like I was his mother. He really loved that bloody horse."

"So he gave you the whiskey to say thanks?"

"He rocked up just now carrying this great big bloody bottle of whiskey. Cradling it like a bloody new-born, he was. A gallon of whiskey. Can you believe it? What's a man my age gonna do with a gallon of whiskey? I can't even lift the bloody thing to pour a drink. He doesn't even know I'm not the bloke that fixed his horse up. I had nothing to do with any of it, and now I've got this thing."

"I'll help you carry it."

"Thank you," Sam said. His cheeks were red from his rant about the Chinese man, and he still hadn't caught his breath back. The blood vessels showed in bright red lines beneath the surface of his cheeks. I picked up the gallon of whiskey and started walking towards the service gate with Sam. He unlocked the gate and led me down to the stables. I set the bottle on a stool.

"I owe you for that," Sam said. "Would've taken me all year to carry that bloody thing back."

"I don't mind. This is an interesting place to work, I bet."

"You could help me out if you want," he said. "I'm gonna clean out these stables then I gotta go and pick up a load of straw and medicine from down Gloucester way."

"I'd like that."

"Really?"

"Yeah. I need a job."

"Well, I struggle to get it all done on my own, see. But I can't tell 'em that 'cos they'll find someone else. Someone younger." Sam looked at me and scratched his cheek again. It made that same sandpaper sound. "I tell ya what. I'll give you what they pay me, and you can just help me out with it. I don't do it for the money. There's no real money in it. I just do it to get out a bit. People die sitting in chairs all day long. It's no good for nobody."

"Are you sure?"

"I'll be glad of the company more than anything. Anyone asks, I'm your Grandad."

I mucked out three stables with Sam. He gave me a pitchfork and showed me how to separate the bits of shit that the horses had left in there from the good straw we could re-use. Sam went around and picked up smaller droppings that we couldn't get with the fork. Once we'd got rid of all the bad straw, we moved all the dry straw against the corners and walls. Then we got all the wet straw (Sam called it 'bedding') and put it in the wheelbarrow. Once all the dirty bedding was out, I swept the floor again, and we let the floor dry. Sam had to pick up the new straw in the afternoon. He said we didn't need to make the new beds in a hurry because there weren't to be any more horses there until the Showcase in October. The Showcase was when Tommy and I planned to shoot the favourite.

After we finished mucking out, Sam closed all the stable doors and locked them, and then we went back out the service gate and into Sam's car. He drove an old Nissan Micra that had rusty wheel arches and missing hubcaps.

He said he'd owned the car since 1987. Before I was even born. Sam started the engine and it choked a little before he got it going.

"She's never let me down. No use replacing something if it's never let you down."

He drove out of the racecourse and went straight over the roundabout at the exit. We were going to a farm just out of Gloucester to fetch the new straw, and then into Gloucester itself to pick up some medicine supplies for the horses.

"How are we going to get the straw back to the racecourse?"

"In here, my boy."

The Micra was true to its name – it was made for picking up the kids from school, not delivering bales of straw.

"Where?"

"We have to make a couple of trips. But we'll get it done. You need to be somewhere?"

"I don't mind. Don't you need a truck for this type of stuff?"

"I shared this car with my wife for twenty-odd years, and it don't feel right to get rid of it. Especially not for some big truck. I'm not a trucker, Billy."

"Fair enough."

"What do you get up to when you're not out running then?"

"Not much."

"Why aren't you at college? You're what, sixteen?"

"Eighteen."

"You look like a youngster."

"I didn't get enough GCSE's. Otherwise I would be at college."

"I doubt you're missing much. Not every lad your age is lucky enough to sweep up horse shit." Sam winked at me and turned the radio on. I laughed, and we both leaned forward to help the Micra crawl uphill.

We drove out to the farm and filled the Micra with six bales of straw – four in the back and two packed into the boot. Sam didn't speak to anyone when we were there; he said we didn't need to. Then we drove into Gloucester where Sam went into a veterinary supply centre and I waited in the car. Ten minutes later he came out with a small box with a handle and we drove the half-hour ride back to the racecourse.

As we drove, I asked the question I'd been building up to.

"Do you bet on the horses?" I'd wanted to ask Sam for tips since the moment I'd met him. Tommy hadn't figured out who to back yet. Neither of us knew much about horses.

"Sometimes."

"I might bet on a horse at the Showcase."

"Wouldn't bother if I were you. Fool's game, betting."

"Can you give me a good tip?"

Sam looked at me but didn't say anything for a while. He went over a roundabout and then looked back at me.

"Now I hope you don't think I'm gonna go shouting about horses."

"I was just wondering if you had a tip."

"I may have."

"Do you win much on the horses?"

"I used to bet a bit, but it's not good to. I'm too old for that. Need to stay honest, once you get to my age. Him up there will keep you honest once you start getting on." Sam pointed up to the sky. I don't think Sam was religious – he was frightened.

"Come on, if you were my age which horse would you fancy?"

"I'm not giving you a tip. Even the bloody experts don't know."

"One horse?"

"One tip?"

"Yes," I said. "Any. I'm not going to put much on it. Maybe a fiver."

"OK. I'll give you one tip. But you ask me for any more tips and we won't work together anymore. I don't like to talk about gambling. Betting ruined my brother's life. He lost everything – house, wife, kids, job, car. Didn't have shoes on his feet by the end of it. It's a sickness, gambling. Can be, anyway. People don't know they're beat."

"I don't have much to lose."

"I'm not sure. I don't want to get you hooked into it, see."

I needed to get a tip out of him. He had been in horse racing his whole life. I imagined all the names of all the winners floating around in that old head of his. I needed one. Sam clenched the leather wheel and his knuckles turned white as his hands flexed. I looked out the window, to try to make it seem like it didn't matter to me. Inside I was panicking. All Tommy and I needed was an indication of which horse to bet on – we could sort the rest out.

Finally, Sam spoke. "OK. I know what it's like to have a flutter. I know what it's like, being your age. It's a thrill."

"I've never bet on a horse before."

"Well then." Sam tapped the steering wheel as he thought. "On the Saturday, in the World Hurdle, there's a very strong runner called Akimbo. Outsider. Not many will look twice at her, but she's a strong little thing. If I'd a fiver to burn, I'd back her."

"Akimbo in the World Hurdle. Thanks, Sam. That means a lot."

"You'll have to let me know how you get on. I'll have some work for you at the Showcase. If you fancy it. I could use the help."

I took Sam's telephone number. He didn't have a mobile, so he wrote down his landline number on a scrap of paper. After we'd finished our last run to pick up straw, he dropped me off at home and waved as I opened my front door. I turned back and looked at him, smiling in his tiny old car. Then I saw that Mum was wandering about on the opposite side of the street. She was holding her mobile outstretched and staggering about like a zombie.

"Mum?" I called across the road. "Mum, are you OK?"

She didn't say anything. Her features were cold and flat, her eyes fixed on her mobile phone.

"Mum?" I yelled.

Mum's eyes snapped into focus. It was like she woke up from a trance.

"Mum. What's happened?"

"Oh, Billy, come here," she said. "Come here! You need to see this!"

I ran over.

"I caught the little bastard," she said.

"Caught who?" For a moment I worried that she knew about the gambling plot.

Mum showed me her phone. The Pokémon GO app was open. Mum had just caught a Weedle. She spent the next hour out on the street trying to catch a Jigglypuff. It turned out that one of the women from the Secret Sharing Club had got her hooked on Pokémon hunting. Things just kept getting weirder.

A couple of days later I went to see Tommy at the Frog. I told him I had news.

When he asked me what it was, I closed my eyes and sipped my pint. I took it as an opportunity to wind him up. He'd always been a show-off. He'd always been the one in the know. This was my turn.

"What is it then?" he persisted. A fat man walked past carrying three pints of lager gripped in a triangle. One of them dropped and smashed on the floor near our spot. I had to wait for the barmaid to fetch the brush and clean it up before I could tell him.

"I met a guy that works in the stables at the racecourse. He's nearly eighty, and he's been in racing his whole life. He's given me a tip."

"No way?"

"Yeah. Akimbo, in the World Hurdle on Saturday."

"I bought you a gun," he said.

"What?" I said. "How the hell did you afford that?"

He always had to trump me.

"Don't mind about that," he said. "And don't worry about paying for it when we win. I'll sell it on once we're done with it."

If I had my own gun there was no backing out. When I thought about it, I wanted to do it as much as when we had been down to the track. I needed the money to see Eva, and that seemed like the only realistic way to go about getting it. We were talking less and less every week. There's only so much you can say when you live thousands of miles apart. I needed to see her in person. I had thought about asking GG for a loan when I found out about his money, but I didn't have the backbone. I didn't want him to feel like he had to throw money at me, just because he was getting married. He had enough going on.

I wasn't planning on putting £10,000 on the horse, as Tommy had suggested. I just wanted enough to go and see Eva. I had nothing keeping me in Cheltenham. No job, no commitments. If I could win enough to start a life out in Switzerland, I'd be chuffed. I calculated that £3,000 would be enough to set me up abroad. With odds of 5/1, I would have to bet a minimum of £600. That didn't seem too bad. I knew that I'd end up betting more, though. Me and Tommy were in this together. If I could take a loan of £3,000, I'd bet it all.

"Baba Ganoush is the favourite, so we might need to shoot her." I'd researched the horses on my phone. I made sure I deleted my internet history afterwards. I was paranoid the police would investigate my activity.

"But whichever one comes round the bend ahead of Akimbo, we take them out. It can't fail."

"What if it does?" I said. "What if we miss, or if we get caught? Could we get arrested?"

"We won't get caught."

"How do you know?"

"Nobody goes down that track. The jockeys won't see us. They won't hear the guns go off. The horses are so loud when they run. It can't go wrong."

"But what if they come round the bend and Akimbo is last. What if Akimbo falls at the first?"

"It'll work, Bill. Stop shitting your pants about it."

"Well, it's a lot of money. I'm already in my overdraft."

"It's not a lot of money. Not compared to what we can win. You should ask your boyfriend for more tips. We could shoot again on the Sunday."

"I can't. He didn't even want to give me Akimbo. And he's not my boyfriend."

"Well we can work it out for ourselves."

"Maybe we should just concentrate on shooting one horse at a time."

"That's a thought."

"What's that?"

"We should try and shoot a horse before the race. See what happens."

"Where are we going to find a horse?"

"There's loads round here. If we go out of town a bit and into the fields, we'll find dozens of them."

"I don't want to make shooting horses a regular thing. We know what would happen."

"But maybe there's a certain spot that you can shoot that just drives them totally mental, and they lose the plot. That's what we need."

"I don't want to make a horse go insane."

"They'll live. We need to do our research."

When I got home from the pub, there was a large parcel in the hallway. I could barely squeeze past it to get through to the kitchen. It was for Dad.

Mum was sitting on the bottom step, talking to Mandy on the phone. I only caught bits of it. "I just don't know what to do," Mum kept saying. Mandy was her friend from Slimming World. Neither Mandy nor my Mum were fat; they were women that felt they were obliged to spend their entire lives 'dieting'. "I told you about the boxing, didn't I? I just don't know what's come over him. He's lost his mind."

I walked past. Mum didn't acknowledge me. She coiled a strand of hair around her index finger as she spoke.

"I don't even know where he is, and this great big parcel has arrived. He was meant to be home four hours ago. I cooked a lasagne – that's gone cold. I'm well within my rights to open the bloody thing."

Mandy must have reassured Mum that she was, because five minutes later I could hear cardboard and Sellotape being ripped open. I was up in my room, watching clips of Baba Ganoush online. She was a beautiful horse – soft brown eyes and strong, rippling muscles. It seemed cruel to shoot her. Every race I watched, she won. Baba Ganoush was way ahead of the rest. She could take a beating, too. The jockeys gave her a lashing to get her over the line quickest. That got me thinking. I paused the video and inspected her muscles closely, deciding it would probably take more than one pop to slow her down. She could really run.

Mandy must have waited on the end of the line while Mum opened the parcel, because shortly after the cardboard tearing noises, she shouted, "I knew it, it's a fucking speedball. What did I tell you?"

So Benny was right: first the punch-bag, then the speedball. Maybe Dad would be getting in the ring soon. It's a man thing. I certainly had no desire to get punched in the face in front of a crowd of people.

Mum carried on ranting to Mandy for a few minutes, before telling her that Dad had just pulled into the driveway and she had to go. As soon as he walked in the door, Mum was onto him.

"What the bloody hell do you think you're doing?" she said. "Where on earth have you been?"

"Why have you opened my parcel?" Dad replied. His leather shoes tapped on the wood flooring in the hallway. "Can't you read?"

"Well I didn't know what you could be buying, the way you've been acting lately. I was entitled to open it."

"Entitled?" Dad laughed.

"You're sending this back first thing. You are not turning this family into *Fight Club*."

Dad ignored her and walked out. I watched him out of my bedroom window as he carried the speedball to the garage. For the next twenty minutes, I heard his drill whizzing screws into wood, and for the next hour after that, the speedball drummed against the framework like impatient fingers tapping on a tabletop.

Meanwhile, GG and Benny were busy preparing for the wedding. Benny had quit her job at the casino, and they were coming around more often to talk about their plans. Their main problem was who to invite. Many couples ruthlessly trim their guest list, but that wasn't a problem for Benny and GG. They were exceptionally short on friends. I didn't think of this as a reflection on GG's personality. Most of his mates were dead. Plus, GG had been a bit of a loner since Gran died. Benny had already declared that her brother would be the only guest from her side. She said she didn't have many friends because she moved around a lot. I wasn't so sure.

Dad started sleeping on the sofa. Mum said he was to sleep down there until he sent the speedball back. He didn't see why it was such a problem. I don't know why Mum was so het up about it, either. Dad's physique was improving by the day. He'd only been boxing for a few weeks, but the fat was melting away from his face, and his gut had shrunk. Despite the fact Dad had been banished to the sofa, I could tell Mum thought he was looking good. She would rub his shoulders if he was cooking in the kitchen, and I noticed her squeeze his bum once, when she thought I wasn't looking. I needed to get out of there.

I'd been messaging Eva every day, but she often took a few hours, or days, to respond. I tried to convince myself that I liked it. I told myself that messaging Eva 24/7 would destroy all the romance, dissolve all the mystery, and it wouldn't give me a chance to miss her. I was kidding myself, of course.

When she eventually responded, she would tell me all about her work and how she felt like she was helping the world and how she wanted to start making jewellery out of recycled metals. I lied and told her that I thought it was a great idea. She would write about how she missed being in bed with me and the things we used to do, and how I used to tickle the small of her back until she drifted off to sleep. But things were still difficult. Eva would ask about when, or if, we would see each other again. It felt like things were coming to an end.

I called her one evening and we talked about everything.

"It's been so long, Billy," she said. "I don't know how much longer I can do this."

"Soon I'll be able to fly out to you," I said.

Of course, I couldn't tell her that I was planning on placing a £3000 bet on an outsider, and shooting the favourite to ensure my bet came in. She would have ended it on the spot.

"What happened to you moving out here? I can't wait forever."

"I will, once I have all the money I need."

We were having fights like that more often. Eva was getting impatient. You worry what your girlfriend is thinking when you share the same bed. Eva lived halfway across Europe. It scared me to think that I'd never know what was in her head.

Dad's boxing obsession didn't stop at the speedball.

One week before the Showcase, I got home in the early evening and heard the usual sounds coming from behind the garage door: Dad grunting, thumping bags, and the monotonous clang of metal dumbbells clanking on the concrete floor. But there was something new – a man was yelling – a man who wasn't my Dad. I stopped by the door and listened.

"That's it, smash, smash, smash! Left, right, duck! Don't piss about, Martin. Are you a woman, or what?"

I couldn't tell if the man was beating my Dad up or encouraging him. I stopped outside the garage door for a few minutes to try to figure out whether I knew the man's voice. Dad didn't have many friends – he hated everyone that he worked with over at the Eagle Tower, for any number of reasons. Some were old and pompous and never offered to make anybody else a cup of tea, others were too young or had stupid haircuts or talked about football too often or didn't hold doors open or say hello in corridors or respond to e-mails quickly enough, even when he could see they were on Facebook. Dad used to rant about it all at the dinner table. Mum would laugh along like it was all a joke, but we both knew it wasn't.

"Alright," the voice said. "Take five. I'm going for a fag."

The garage door opened before I had a chance to move away.

"Who the Konnie Huq are you?" the man said, pulling a cigarette out from his shirt pocket. He was much less imposing than I expected – shorter than me, skinny, baby-blond, around thirty-five. His cheeks were pocked with ice-pick scars and deeper, pitted hollows – the aftermath of teenage acne. I was always too scared to pick my spots, in case they ended up scarring.

"I'm Billy," I said.

"He's my son," Dad shouted from the garage. He was sitting down on a leather bench – the sort you find in gyms.

"Tuna," the man said.

I went to stick out my hand but he didn't notice and I quickly put it back in my pocket.

"I'm your Dad's coach."

"He's not interested," Dad said.

"Is he any good?" I asked.

"Not bad. Do you box?"

"No," I said. "But I like running."

"Running?" Tuna said. "What use is running?"

"I think it's good for my headspace."

"Your headspace? What is that? You got a big space between your ears, have ya?"

I laughed, but it wasn't funny.

"Careful, Tuna," called Dad. "You'll need to give the little snowflake a trigger warning if you want to swear."

"Bollocks!" I said.

Tuna was looking at me as though I'd shown up wearing soiled trousers. I could see Dad shaking his head in the background.

"Why are you called Tuna?" I asked.

"Never you mind," Tuna said, flicking his cigarette down the drain, then pulling the garage door shut.

I went into the house and asked Mum if she'd met Tuna.

"Who's Tuna?" she said.

"Dad's boxing coach."

"Coach?"

"Yeah."

"He has a boxing coach?"

"I just met him. He's in the garage shouting at Dad."

"For goodness' sake," Mum said. "Will there ever be an end to this?"

"I don't think it's a bad thing. At least he's exercising."

"You wouldn't understand. Why's he called Tuna, anyway?"

"He wouldn't say."

"Why not?"

"I don't know."

"Ridiculous. Totally ridiculous. He's probably been in prison so he can't tell us his real name. That's where people get those sorts of nicknames. Prison."

"I doubt it."

"Did he look like he'd been in prison?"

"I don't know. What does somebody that's been in prison look like?"

"You can just tell. Did you think he seemed dodgy?"

"No dodgier than any of the other convicts I've met."

"That's not funny. It's not funny to joke about these things. You can't trust anyone, Billy. He might be planning on burgling us. Perhaps he's part of a gang. A prison gang. They're probably all named after fish – like codenames."

"That explains why Sea Bass was loitering in the back garden."

"What's got into you? It's not funny, Billy. It's serious."

I didn't care what my Mum said. Tuna didn't seem like the type of person I would expect to be a burglar. Besides, it wasn't like we had much to steal. Even if he had been in a prison gang, I didn't think he seemed so bad. Everyone has nicknames. I got called Skips at school because Lauren Edmonton spread a rumour that I smelled of prawn cocktail flavoured crisps. I don't even like prawn cocktail flavoured crisps, so it can't have been true, but I made sure that I sprayed deodorant after every lesson and I changed into a clean shirt after lunchtime every day.

Maybe Tuna just smelled of tuna.

Since I'd said I wasn't prepared to go along with Tommy's research project and wander around the countryside shooting horses, he'd taken to shooting cats.

I was round his house one day and he stuck the BB gun out of his window when a ginger tom cat was taking a poo on his lawn.

"Watch this," he said, squeezing the trigger and hitting the cat on its flank. The cat shrieked and sprinted towards the back of his garden, scrambling up the fence and away. "See, it works." Tommy turned around and grinned.

"What the hell are you doing?" I said. "We're not shooting cats. That is not happening."

"I just wanted to put your mind at ease."

"How is shooting a cat going to put my mind at ease?"

"I just thought you'd like to see that it works."

"What do you mean? Did you think I was under the impression that cats would shoot back if you shot at them?"

"I don't know."

"Please don't ever do that again."

"I shot a cow the other day."

"What?"

"I went out to the fields by Cleeve. Shot a cow."

"Why?"

"Research."

"You can't call it research when we're gonna be shooting a horse."

"They're similar."

"Cows and horses are not similar."

"They are."

"Well what happened?"

"Why should I tell you?"

"Because I want to know."

"You'll shit your pants and run off to the RSPCA."

"Tell me."

"Forget it. Listen, we need to take our loans out today."

"Really?"

"We can't leave it too late, else the money won't come through in time."

Taking the loan made it all seem real. More real than walking down to the racecourse and seeing where it would happen. I was £1,000 in my overdraft – the bank was still charging me £5 a day for being in the red.

"How much are you going to borrow?" I asked him.

"As much as I can. I think I'll be able to get four or five grand."

"Shit."

"It won't go wrong. We know it won't. We're betting each way. That means we win money if she's in the top three. Plus, the bookies are doing a special offer. You get your money back if you bet each way and the horse comes fourth."

That sounded promising to me. 5/1 wasn't the longest odds. There was a chance she could have won the race without any intervention. But Baba Ganoush was quick. She was really quick.

"I don't think I'll risk that much," I said.

Tommy was on his computer, filling out the form for an instant money lender. He requested a loan of £2,000 from one place, and £2,000 from another. The loans would take three days to reach his account.

"Your turn," he said, once he'd finished filling out his details. I had to run back home and grab my passport and provisional driving license. I thought about all the money I'd have when it was all over. When I got back, I went to sit at his computer and processed my details. I requested £3,000. Taking that amount meant that I'd have to pay £3,500 back to the company. I didn't even think about taking the £3,000 and going to Switzerland without gambling it on Tommy's plan. I wanted to go for good, not just a holiday. The interest repayments on top didn't matter. If Akimbo won, I'd have £15,000 to my name. I couldn't resist it. I'd never had an opportunity to make that kind of money. At least if we messed up, I wouldn't be the only one with a huge debt to pay off. Dad would've beaten the shit out of me if he found out.

"I saw this video of a guy that bet his whole life on red," Tommy said. "His house, car, life savings, everything. It's crazy. He's there watching the wheel spinning, and the ball trickles over the wheel. Red, black, red, black, red, black, red, black – zero."

"No way?"

"He lost it all," Tommy said.

I didn't know why he was telling me that after we had taken out thousands of pounds in loans to gamble.

"Serves him right for being so arrogant," Tommy said. "He let his whole life spin away on a roulette wheel. We're in control of our risk. That's why it's perfect."

"We're in control," I said. "Totally."

"When we win, I'll have £20,000, you'll have £15,000. There's racing on Sunday too. We could put another six or seven thousand on a horse then. It wouldn't even matter if we lost. We'd still be loaded."

Tommy was right. We would be loaded.

When I got back from Tommy's, Mandy was at our house. She had a "can I speak to the manager?" haircut – a dyed red bob, spiky at the back, with a sharp fringe. Her and my Mum had been shopping. I walked into the kitchen and they were drinking wine, wearing matching white tuxedos.

"Stop! Freeze! The name's Bond," Mandy said. "Mandy Bond."

Mum started laughing. Mandy stood up and twirled around with her hands clasped to mimic a pistol. Then she started pretending to shoot me.

Mum began singing the 007 theme tune. "Dum, d-d-dum, dum, dum dum, dum, d-d-dum, dum." Mum was clutching her belly. Her laughter caused her whole body to convulse. I hated it when she laughed like that. It looked like she was coughing up a furball.

Mandy was laughing too, and drunk, but not as drunk as my Mum.

"Do you like our suits?" Mum said. "Don't I look *fabulous*?" She got up and twirled like Mandy had. It was only 7pm. "Mandy's a bridesmaid too. Can you believe that? She only met Benny today."

Mandy raised her glass of red wine and closed her eyes, "Me and Benny go way back."

Mum squeezed the cork out of another bottle of red. She took a glass down from the cabinet and filled it to the brim. I spotted her mobile phone on the counter. The Pokémon GO app was open on the screen. I wondered if she'd started using Tinder, too.

"Have a drink, baby boy." Mum handed me the glass. "We've been out Pokémon hunting. I nearly caught a Bulbasaur."

"How's GG?" I said.

"Oh, he's fine. Still marrying a slut," Mum said. She gulped down her wine and grabbed the glass I was holding.

"Don't speak about them like that," I said.

"Don't be so precious, Billy boy," Mandy said. "Your Mum's only playing."

"No she isn't," I said. "She's jealous because Dad's not getting any of GG's money."

Mum got up and came up close to me. Too close. She was right in my face. Her cheeks were flushed red and her mascara had been smudged into black blotches. "That's a very horrible thing you just said."

"It's true. You're bitching because you can't go to the Bahamas."

"Do not talk to your mother like that," Mandy said. "It's disgusting."

"I don't want to go to the Bahamas, you stupid boy. We just don't like to see GG be taken for a ride."

I could see where Mum's lipstick had cracked and flaked away around the corners of her mouth.

"Have any of you actually asked her why she wants to marry him? Maybe she loves him."

They both laughed. "She's already married, Billy. She's a con-artist."

"What?" I said.

"It's a scam, you silly boy. She marries GG, divorces him, embezzles the money, and lives happily ever after with her real husband, who's probably some drug dealer from Croydon. She's worse than a whore." Mum ruffled my hair and laughed in my face.

I hated her right then. If this was all true, then I didn't see what was funny about it. "Wait – how do you know?"

"I know, Billy. I have my sources. Like Mandy said, we are MI6 now." Mum laughed and made the gun with her hands just as Mandy had.

"Why did you think she was interested in GG?" Mandy said.

Mum laughed again. "What thirty-eight-year-old woman wouldn't want to marry a man twice their age? Apparently the sex is something else."

I walked out. Dad wasn't in to hear any of it. That's probably why Mum had got bladdered so early. I'd never seen her like that before. She was so angry about it all, when she'd been so calm about it when we first found out. And where had she got this notion that Benny was already married? Maybe it was because the situation was ruining her marriage. Her husband spent half his time lashing out on leather bags, the other half out of the house. We didn't know where he went. He was never around. That's why Mum hated Benny so much. She blamed Benny for all her difficulties. Maybe it was Benny's fault. But Mum had her Mercedes Man. She made her own problems.

I went out to the garage and pulled the metal door open. I flicked on the light and the bare economy bulb came to life a few seconds later. Dad's gloves were hanging on a bracket attached to the bricked wall. His punch-bag dangled from the beam in the middle of the room, and the speedball was attached to the wall down at the back. I picked up the red gloves and slipped them on. They were too big for my hands, and they wobbled when I tried to tighten the straps. I thumped the bag. I lashed at it with upper cuts, jabs and hooks. Shadows dashed across the brickwork as the bag swung in the lamplight. I kicked it and butted it with my head. Shoving it away, pumping my knees into it, the metal chains that attached the bag to the hook squeaking with every blow.

I was making so much noise shouting and grunting and working away at the bag that I didn't hear Dad's car pull in. He must have seen the light breaking out from the edges of the garage door, because he pulled it open and looked in at me. His car's engine purred in the background. When he lifted open the door, all I saw was his black silhouette set against the headlights.

I didn't stop. I carried on hitting out at the bag, each blow harder and faster than the last. Dad watched me for a few moments, and then turned around, pulled the door shut, cut the engine and went into the house.

On the first morning of the Showcase, the day before we were due to shoot the horse, a wedding invitation dropped through the front door. Dad opened it while we were eating breakfast. He read it aloud to me and Mum. "Dear Martin, Suzie and Billy. You are cordially invited to the wedding of George and Benny on Saturday 17th December, at Burbridge House. We have no friends and would be really grateful if somebody could witness this sham marriage. Love, George and Benny." Dad put the card down on the table.

"What does it really say?" Mum said. "Burbridge House isn't cheap."

"'We have only a small guest list and we encourage you to share this invitation with friends and family.'"

"As if!" said Mum.

I was sick of them. It didn't matter if Benny was after his money. I didn't see why it mattered. GG was enjoying the last few years of his life. It was his money anyway. If he wanted to marry her, then why the hell shouldn't he?

"Your Grandad's marrying a blackie." Dad started laughing. "And he expects our friends to witness it!"

I got up from the table and walked out. Once I won my money, I thought, I was out of there for good.

On my way to the racecourse, I passed middle-aged men in tartan jackets, many drinking beers already. By the roundabout outside, there were two boys around my age selling flapjack from a little table.

"Lucky Flapjacks!" they yelled as the crowds walked in past them. I could hear them before I saw them. By the time I walked past the boys, there was hardly any flapjack left. I thought they must have made loads of money, and I regretted not thinking of a similar idea myself. But it soon became clear that people had been grabbing the flapjack and walking away without paying. The boys were pummelling flapjacks into the heads of those who were stealing, so there wasn't much stock left.

It was only 10:30am but there were dozens of parking attendants in bright orange hi-vis jackets pointing people in different directions. I met Sam in the car park and we went through the gates together, to avoid any problems with security. He looked pale and said he didn't sleep much. His movements were laboured and he said there was a terrible pain in his side.

I made sure to fill up all the water and clean up around the stables so Sam didn't need to do anything. When I'd finished, I made him a cup of tea and then went to explore the grounds. I posted a selfie of me at the Owners and Trainers Tent, because rumour had it Michael Owen was in there eating smoked salmon and poached eggs with Jeremy Kyle and I hoped my being there might impress Eva. But she didn't like it and shortly later Tommy messaged me and told me to take it down. He said it could be used as evidence.

At the Owners and Trainers Tent, there were three guys staring at one of the windows, pointing and shouting. I walked up to them, to see if I could get any information about the horses.

"That one," the man in the middle of the three said, pointing at a spot on the window. "I'll have a hundred quid on that one."

"He's mine," another one said, pointing to a different spot on the glass.

"Hundred on him," said the third man, at which point they all shook hands.

"Three, two, one, go!"

All three men started yelling.

"Come on, my son!"

"You've got it!"

I couldn't work out what was going on. The ground floor of the Owners and Trainers Tent was empty, except for the waiting staff laying up the tables. I wondered if they might've spotted Michael Owen and if they were betting on how fast he could eat his brunch. There were no races on either. It was still early in the morning. I moved closer to the three men as they yelled and watched the window closely. They were betting on the droplets of water sliding down the windowpanes.

Sam couldn't do much all morning. He had to keep stopping and sitting down. I thought it was just because he was old, but just before the third race, Sam asked me to call him an ambulance.

"I can't move for it, now," he said. "Thought it'd pass but I can't move at all now. It's like there's a knife in my side."

I pulled out my phone and dialled 999. I'd never made an emergency call before. It made me nervous. "What's your emergency?" The voice on the end of the phone was female. She spoke like I could tell her the most tragic thing in the world had happened and she wouldn't be moved in the slightest.

"It's my friend, he's got a pain in his side. He can't move."

"How old is he?"

"He's in his late seventies."

"Where is he?"

"We're at Cheltenham racecourse. By the service gate."

"OK. An ambulance is coming. I need you to stay on the phone until it arrives, is that OK?"

"Yes," I said. The crowd in the grandstand roared as another race came to an end.

"Has your friend had symptoms like this before?" the woman asked.

"Have you felt like this before?" I asked Sam.

"There's been a pain there for a while," he said. "It's on and off. You start to ignore pains as you get older. They become part of the furniture."

"He's had pain there for a while," I relayed to the woman on the phone. "It's on and off. But he thought it would pass."

"OK," she said.

"I'm sure it's nothing," I said to Sam.

"Must be a big old bit of nothing to hurt this bloody bad."

"When will the ambulance be here?" I asked.

"Soon," she said. "Just make sure you stay on the line."

It took forty minutes for the ambulance to come. I stayed on the phone to the woman the whole time. She asked me loads of questions about Sam and told me to make sure he was comfortable, and I gave him some water and tried to keep him relaxed. While we waited, Sam told me stories about when he used to go blackberry picking over Cleeve Hill. He told me about climbing trees near Southam, and about how his mother raised him and his four brothers alone, while his father was away at war during the 1940's. He told me about when he collected frogs in a milk bottle and released them in the middle of his school assembly. His long, flat mouth split into an open red wound, bleeding laughter. He told me lots of stories. Most of them were about him as a teenager, or a kid. I didn't know much about his adult life. It was clear that Sam thought he was going to die, and I guess it's your youth that comes back to you when you're at the end.

It was difficult not to cry. I thought if I cried, that would only upset him. I promised him I'd look after the stables while he was gone. I knew that I wouldn't be able to, though. The next day, I had to shoot Baba Ganoush. I'd planned on telling Sam I was sick. I hated the fact that I was going to let him down – part of me thought about abandoning the whole idea – letting the horse run its race and if it won, it won. But I knew that was never an option. There was too much at stake.

The blue lights appeared and the men in their green shirts and trousers jumped out of the van. I dread those blue lights. It means something bad has happened, whenever you see them. I walked away and let them talk with Sam. They loaded him onto the ambulance. Sam was clutching his side the whole time. Before he went, I squeezed his hand. It felt cold. We didn't say anything to each other. After that, they closed the doors and drove off.

When I got home, Mum and Dad were having an argument about the fact Dad had burnt three pieces of chicken cordon bleu. The smoke alarm was screeching.

"This is why you can't fend for yourself," Mum shouted from the kitchen. "You're useless. Totally useless." She was standing over the three offending pieces of chicken cordon bleu. The breadcrumbs on each piece were black. Dad was in the hallway, slapping the smoke alarm with a tea towel. A pan of peas was boiling over on the hob.

"They're not burnt," Dad yelled, still whipping his tea towel at the smoke alarm. "They're well-done."

"They're charred," Mum said. "We can't eat that. It's carcinogenic."

"What?" Dad screamed back from the hallway.

"Carcinogenic!"

"How do you get this thing to shut up?"

"It'll give us all cancer. You can't eat burnt food, Martin. Didn't you see it in the paper? It'll give us all cancer."

"How the hell do I turn this thing off?"

"I don't suppose you care about cancer, anyway. Do you?"

"How do I turn this shit off? What are the neighbours going to think?"

"They'll think that you're a useless fuckwit for burning a chicken-cordon-fucking-bleu."

"Shut up!"

"You're useless, Martin. Press the button for fuck's sake!"

At that, Dad punched the smoke alarm and it flew across the hallway and slammed down onto the wooden floor. Parts of the plastic casing broke away, but the alarm was still ringing. Dad kicked the alarm and it smashed into the door, sending the batteries skidding across the laminate wood. But even that didn't stop it.

"How do you kill this thing?" Dad yelled. He picked up the indestructible smoke alarm and walked onto the front lawn with it. Mum grabbed the baking tray and slammed it onto the bin. The three pieces of carcinogenic cordon bleu dropped into the black bag. Then she turned the gas off and the pan of boiling water reduced, although most of its contents were bubbling away between the black metal grids on the hobs, having spilled out. The sound of the smoke alarm faded away, and Mum went to sit down at the kitchen table, peeled a satsuma, and began tearing apart the segments, piece by piece.

That's when the noise started up. I looked out of the kitchen window and Dad was looming over the smoke alarm with the garden strimmer, hovering the blade just above the cracked white box.

"What on earth is he doing now?" Mum said, peeling a white strand of flesh from her satsuma segment.

"He's about to start strimming the smoke detector," I said.

"What?"

Dad pressed the strimmer blade down onto the smoke alarm, and white shards went flying out in all directions. The case split open and scattered across the front lawn. The wire fragments shot against the kitchen windows like they were being spat out from the eye of a hurricane. Graham from next door came past as Dad switched off the strimmer, the lawn dotted with pieces of white plastic. Some of the pieces had even skipped over our front hedge and landed in the road. Dad rested his hands on his hips and smiled.

"Hi Graham," Dad said, smiling and waving as Graham power-walked past our house and down the road.

I went up to my bedroom with a bowl of Bran Flakes and a banana. I didn't want to be around anyone, especially when my parents were close to killing each other over a piece of chicken cordon bleu. I wanted to be alone. I ate the bowl of cereal and drank the milk that was left at the bottom of the bowl. Dad had picked up all the fragments of the smoke alarm and the lawn looked the same as it always did. I ate the banana and threw the skin out of my window, into the front hedge. After I was done eating, I started drawing horses in one of my leftover Moleskine notebooks. I was supposed to return them all, but I figured I could get away with keeping one or two. I sketched out a few horses, imagining their muscles powering across the finish line and winning me thousands. It was a long night. The nerves filled up my belly and shot around my whole body with each heartbeat. But more than anything I was excited. I had waited so long to be rich. I had waited so long to see Eva. I was confident that the race would bring me everything I wanted and get me out of that house.

I didn't get to sleep until the early hours that night. Mum and Dad had been arguing all night, but finally suspended their dispute around midnight. I wasn't sure exactly what the fight was about. I thought I heard Mum shout something about IBS which is something to do with having the shits. But then Dad started yelling about Iain Duncan Smith so I didn't know what was going on. They were fighting about anything and everything around that time.

I got into bed, closed my eyes and covered my head with a pillow. But I couldn't sleep. I thought about the race. The guns. The pressure. What would happen if it went wrong? I thought about Sam. I was worried that he might have died. Was there anything I could have done to prevent it? Selfishly, I wondered if him being taken ill was a bad omen for mine and Tommy's race fixing plan. I allowed myself to imagine all the worst-case scenarios in my head and convinced myself that they would all come true. After a while I had to sit up and switch on the lamp to calm down. I checked my phone. Eva had sent me a link to an article about overfishing in the Pacific. It came as a great relief. I read it without any real interest but replied saying that I thought it was terrible what these people were doing to the fish and that I hoped things would improve. I also said that I missed her, and that I couldn't wait to see her again soon.

Then I turned the light off, closed my eyes and fell asleep.

Saturday – race day. Me and Tommy weren't talking much. My stomach was chewing itself inside out. I went into town in the morning to buy green blankets and face paint. We needed camouflage for the BB guns. The face paint felt right – we were going to war, we needed war paint.

I met Tommy at 10am. Akimbo would have been having her breakfast. She had no idea what she was going to do to the lives of a couple of boys. We walked down to the racecourse the same way he had shown me before – along an old bridleway, through a gap in the hedges near the village of Prestbury. Everything felt good. The town was full of people wearing tartan, sipping coffees, smoking cigarettes and filling buses to the racecourse. They were all idiots betting big on horses that they didn't know were going to win them anything. We knew we were going to win it all. It was just a case of waiting for it. Our race started at 12:30pm.

Tommy had been down in the middle of the night and had hidden the guns in bramble bushes next to our spot. He had thought things out. He wasn't stupid. When we got halfway down the track, he tied tape across it, blocking it off for pedestrians. The tape was blue and white and had Police Line Do Not Cross written on it. It looked genuine.

"Are you sure about that?" I said. "Might get people interested."

"Nobody comes down here anyway, Billy. I'm just giving people a good reason not to come any further."

I couldn't argue with that. He seemed ten years older than he normally acted. Everything was considered. We walked further down the track and Tommy taped across the path at the other end. We were cordoned off. We had nothing to worry about.

It was a long wait until the race started. We could hear people talking over a tannoy in the distance, and I could see the crowds stirring as the grounds started to fill with racegoers. Tommy pulled the guns out from the brambles. We got them in position. I covered the gun barrels with the green blankets and we painted brown and green onto each other's cheeks and foreheads.

113

The horses would race past my position first. I was expecting the green and yellow of Baba Ganoush, but we were prepared to shoot whichever horse looked like winning. The front horse was going to get a shot in its back leg from me, and then 50 yards further along, Tommy would shoot it again. With the main competitor out of the picture, Akimbo would surely come in for a top three finish. She was the second favourite. Tommy had done his reading.

At midday we got into our positions. We both knew what to do. Tommy said it was a good idea to minimize the amount of movement we made, just to make sure we didn't catch anyone's eye. I didn't see how we would. The grounds were way off in the distance, probably at least half a mile. The racecourse itself sits in a basin below the Cotswold Hills. We were positioned way out below the hills, looking back at the stadium and the grounds. The track must have been forgotten about, or never discovered. There weren't any footprints in the mud, except our own. I felt good about it all. I just had to shoot the damn thing.

The race started with the pop of a starting gun and the horses broke out. I put my headphones in to listen to the racing commentary on the radio.

"Baba Ganoush is off to a flyer and first to show, Hoof Hearted is slowly away. As they settle, it's Baba Ganoush leading the pack, with Rolling Maul and Auntie Freeze tucked in behind. Akimbo is looking sharp in fourth." The commentary buzzed in my ear.

I looked over to Tommy. His eye was fixed in the sight of the gun. Lying down in the bushes, it was hard to see him at all.

The commentary picked up. Tommy said it would be around a minute and a half before the horses reached our spot. They'd been running for thirty seconds or so.

"It's close here. Rolling Maul is still running strong, and there's nothing between Auntie Freeze and Akimbo. Baba Ganoush leads by a hair."

I pulled the earphones out. The horses were coming close to us. I could hear the tread thumping into the ground. It reminded me of Dad out in the garage, pounding his punch-bag. As they came closer, I drew my eye into the sight. They were coming around to the final furlong. It was easy to spot Baba Ganoush. I recognised her from the videos I'd seen. Those four white socks. I wasn't going to let her win. She was just ahead of the pack, but the others looked like they were still in it. Akimbo was sitting in fourth, but I didn't think about it. She would come through with a place. She had to.

I fixed the green and yellow chequers of the jockey in my sight. Baba Ganoush was flying. Her tail whipped out behind her in a blur. Her hooves ripped up huge chunks of grass and turf. The sound of the running horses was growing louder with every moment. Tommy was right about the noise. The cracking of whips on the horse's hindquarters was hair-raising. It made me feel uncomfortable.

My finger felt for the trigger. I had Baba Ganoush fixed in my sights. My hands were shaking as I stalked her movements down the barrel of the gun. I could see the muscles in her legs tensing and relaxing between each step. I pictured the ball bearing ripping through the skin and bringing her down. But it was too late to think about it, I had to do it.

Baba Ganoush was only a few feet away when I squeezed the trigger. The shot zipped out and hit her on the flank. It worked. She fell out of step. She lost her balance, but she was still running.

I was relieved that it hadn't killed her. They carried on around the last bend. Baba Ganoush was still out in front, Akimbo was in fifth, maybe sixth.

Tommy shot at her again, twice. It must have sent her crazy. She reacted the same – falling out of step, appearing to lose her way – exactly what we wanted. But after a moment, she was running faster than before. It had spurred her on. She was winning.

I plugged my headphones into my ears again and got to my feet.

"And Baba Ganoush is well away here, followed by Rolling Maul, Auntie Freeze and The Good Stuff in fourth. Akimbo trails in fifth place."

"Shit," Tommy yelled. "How did that happen?"

I fell to my knees and pressed my forehead against the grass. It was cold against my skin. None of it was real. Baba Ganoush ran stronger when we shot at her.

"Wouldn't you run quicker if someone was shooting at you?" I said. "Why didn't we see that?"

"We're screwed. It's all gone." Tommy had got up and come to sit by me.

I thought about what Eva had said to me a few days before. If I don't see you soon. I had nothing. I was up to my balls in debt and my girlfriend had gotten sick of me letting her down. Dad was going crazy, Mum had started drinking. Everything was ruined.

Tommy ditched the rifles back in the brambles. We didn't move from our spot for a while. There was nothing to move for.

I watched another race go past, the horses rushing by us, winning other men money they didn't need.

Tommy left after that. He said he needed to think things through.

I thought about ringing Eva and telling her everything. She might have sympathised and hopped on a flight to the UK, to come and stay with me. I knew how unlikely that was, though. She was waiting for a reason to call it off. That would have been it.

I stayed by the track for a while, thinking it over. Adding the £3,000 I'd borrowed from the loans company to my pre-existing overdraft, I was down £4,000 plus interest. It would have taken me a year to earn that. If I told Mum and Dad they would have disowned me. I didn't dare take out another loan – that would have ended up with more costs and I'd never clear the debt. Besides, my credit rating would've been too low for a bank to even look at me. GG was the only option.

The race kept replaying through my mind. The way Baba Ganoush ran crazy after we shot at her was like watching a bull kicking out at the rodeo. Wouldn't you run faster if someone was shooting at you? The words ran through my head again and again.

On the walk home, traffic lined up in every direction – people were running to their cars to try to get out faster. All the footpaths were crammed with men walking towards the town centre. Buskers played guitars and sang Irish songs on the street side. There were only a few pennies in their open guitar cases.

I didn't want to be among the crowds of drunks, so I dipped off the path into town and cut through Pittville Park. The whole place was deserted. I walked up to the lake in the middle of the woodland. The swans were sitting out on the grass verges. I went to sit on a log. It was too much to take in. I could still hear the noise of all the racegoers walking down into town. They were yelling and chanting and singing, drunk and carefree.

Late on in the afternoon, I ran to GG's. I had no choice.

I banged on the front door. A few moments later, the door opened. It was Benny. She was wearing a grey tracksuit with reading glasses balanced on the bridge of her nose.

"Oh, hi honey. How are you?" Benny said. "Come in, please."

"I need to talk to GG," I said.

"Of course, he's in the kitchen. Is everything OK?"

"Not really," I said.

Benny opened her arms and gave me a hug. "Whatever it is," she said. "Just remember: all things pass."

I wanted to cry as Benny squeezed me tightly into her, but I bit my lip to hold back the tears. After a few moments, Benny let go. "I'll leave you boys to it," she said. I walked through to the kitchen.

"Hello, my boy. What can I do for you?" GG said. He was sitting down at the kitchen table.

I hadn't planned what I was going to say. I just had to ask him. He grabbed two bottled beers from the fridge, popped off the caps and set them down on the table.

"I'm in trouble, GG," I said. "I lost a bet."

"Betting's a fool's game," GG said. He sipped on his beer. He already knew what I was going to ask him. "How much did you lose?"

"Four grand. You can't say anything." I drank the bottle of beer. It was some Californian pale ale. GG didn't drink pisswater beers like Dad did. GG placed my empty bottle in the sink and picked out a new one from the fridge.

"Four thousand pounds?" GG said. "How on earth did you get that kind of money together?"

"Promise me you won't tell Dad?" I said.

"Why would I?" he said. "Your Dad already hates me enough. Have you been selling drugs?"

"No. It was a loan," I said. "It was stupid. I thought it was guaranteed to win me money, but it turned out I was wrong."

"Always the way," GG said. "I had a friend that would talk just like that. He pissed away his whole life on the horses."

"Can you lend me four thousand pounds? I can pay you back in full. I promise."

"Billy, you can't chase it and chase it. You chase your money for too long you end up in the gutter."

"I know," I said. "But it wasn't just a bet. I was convinced that the horse I backed would win."

"What are you, the rocking-horse winner?"

"What are you talking about?"

"You never heard the story?" GG said. "The young lad, Paul. His mother doesn't love him. She's always fretting because there's never enough money. The kids even hear the house whispering, 'there must be more money'." GG got up and paced around the kitchen.

I didn't say anything.

"So this Paul kid gets a rocking horse for Christmas. He spends hours on it, working himself up into this state where he

119

can predict the winner of any race. He tells his uncle and they start betting, winning more and more. They end up winning a fortune. A hundred thousand pounds. Something like that. Only, the kid dies after they win it. Dies in the night. Now, what's the use in that?"

"I'm not talking about some stupid ghost story, GG. I just need you to help me get out of trouble."

"Billy, I can't do that."

"You're a millionaire. I never ask you for anything."

"It's a lot of money. How do I know you won't bet on another horse? Didn't you hear me? Betting's a fool's game."

I got up and walked for the door. GG pulled me back.

"I can help you out, Billy. I just can't let you gamble it away. It's criminal."

"Criminal? You're the con man."

GG didn't say anything.

I wanted to tell him that Mum was shagging some guy with a Mercedes, and that Dad had abandoned us for a boxing coach called Tuna. I wanted to tell him that my whole life was ruined, that I was going to lose Eva – the only thing in the world that was worth getting up for. I just needed a second chance. He could have made everything OK.

"Wait here," GG said, and he walked out of the room. When he returned, he dropped something into my hand.

"That was your grandmother's engagement ring," he said. "It's fifty years old."

I looked at the stone. It reminded me of the gems on Eva's bikini. I remembered seeing it on Gran's wrinkly finger. She used to wear it every day. I'd tried it on, as a kid. It looked expensive.

"I'm not saying go out and give it to your girlfriend and marry her as soon as you get the chance. I'm not saying sell it, although you can if you really need to. It's up to you. You can keep hold of it. It would be nice for you to give it to the girl you love. There's a lot of love in that ring. Your Gran wouldn't like to see it go to waste."

I looked at the diamonds next to the yellowed callouses at the bottom of my fingers. GG walked through to the front room. Benny was sitting on the sofa reading a book. She smiled at me. GG asked her if she would like a cup of tea, or something to eat.

"You must stop your Grandfather," Benny said. "He dotes on me like a new-born puppy!"

I smiled, but I couldn't stay there any longer. My hands were shaking.

The front door rattled as I slammed it shut – the brass knocker clapped on the door frame. I went back home and ran up to my bedroom. Gran's engagement ring was the only thing in the world I had that could get me to Eva. The ring was a bit dusty, but I blew it all off. The dust floated away like dandelion seeds – the particles flickered in the beams of sunlight that broke through my blinds. I didn't want to sell it. It felt wrong – it still does. It's still one of the worst things I've ever done. Worse than shooting any horse. But I had to do it. I ran to town and into the first jewellers I could find.

They bought the ring for £350 – cash. Not nearly enough to clear my debts, but enough to get me to Eva.

After getting the money, I went into the travel agent on the high street and booked the first flight to Zurich.

4

I didn't tell Mum and Dad I was leaving. Not directly. I left a note saying I'd gone to visit Eva and I might be away some time. And then I was gone, on a bus with my rucksack. Soon I was at Gatwick Airport.

It was the first time I'd flown on my own. Normally Mum and Dad took care of everything. I was scared. I didn't know where to go. Eventually I found the departures and saw my flight listed on the board. I queued to check in, panicking that I'd forgotten my passport even though I checked it was in my bag every two minutes.

My nerves settled slightly after check in. I didn't like going through the security checks. I felt like they were going to pull me aside and stop me from flying – maybe my parents had phoned them and told them to stop me leaving the country. My bag, belt, phone and keys went on the conveyor belt and through the electronic box, and a bald-headed man frisked me. His hands came uncomfortably close to my balls, but he gave me the all clear, and I was through.

In the departure lounge, I bought a continental adaptor for my phone charger. Then I changed my money into Swiss Francs. After paying for the flight, transport to the airport and the adaptor, I was left with £184. I changed the lot and received only CHF212.

After that, I finally phoned Eva with the good news.

She was at work in the recycling plant in Zurich, but she picked up after a couple of tries. I was surprised that she answered. She took her job too seriously. Every day she commuted from Lucerne in order to pick out plastic, metal and paper, separating it all – saving the world.

"What's up?" she said.

"I'm coming to Switzerland," I said. "I'm at the airport."

She didn't say anything.

"Can you believe that?" I said.

"How can you afford to, all of a sudden?"

I could hear tin cans crumpling beneath the weight of an industrial crusher. "I can't," I said. "I bought a one-way ticket."

"How much money do you have?"

"Nothing," I said. "Less than nothing. I lost it all. But what does it matter? I'm coming to be with you."

"So, you're going to come and live off my money?"

"No, I–"

"That's not happening. I can't believe you would expect that of me."

I didn't know what to say. I'd expected her to be wildly happy. "But I'm about to board the plane."

"Are you kidding me?"

A conveyor belt rumbled. I could picture her still leafing through the rubbish as she jammed the phone between her ear and shoulder.

"How do you have no money? You have a job, don't you?"

"I'm sorry. I lost all my money. I placed it all on a bet. A stupid bet, on a stupid horse that Tommy thought would win. I thought it would win me enough money to take you away somewhere."

"What?" she said. "You lost all your money on a bet?"

"We thought it was going to win."

"Are you stupid?"

"No, we shot the favourite."

"You shot a horse?"

"Yes. I hate that it happened but now I'm coming to see you and I'll fix it."

"What is wrong with you?"

Tin cans crushed and baled.

"I risked everything to get the money to come and see you. I had to do something."

"I won't be here."

"What?"

"I'm going away."

"With who?" I said.

"I don't want to see you, Billy."

"I'll fix this," I said.

"Cancel your flight. I won't see you."

"Can't you wait for me?"

"I've waited long enough."

I started to explain that I couldn't cancel it, but she had already hung up.

But what was I to do? Where else could I go? I boarded the plane. All I thought of was Eva. I tried not to think about the debt. Whenever I did, I pictured myself in thirty years, worn down and weather beaten, bald and fat and lonely, drinking Doombar at a Wetherspoon's at ten-thirty on a Wednesday morning – still paying off the interest from the loan.

On the plane, I looked out of the window for much of the journey. A power plant puffed trails of smoke into the clear sky. Then we crossed the channel. Ferries appeared as tiny dots. France passed below us, a patchwork of green and yellow fields. As we travelled over the Alps, the cabin rattled through pockets of turbulence. I always imagined turbulence wasn't a real thing – that the pilots got bored in the cockpit and decided to shake the joysticks around for fun. As the plane started its descent, I looked for a building that might have been the recycling plant where Eva worked. I saw cars and lorries moving down the motorways, like ants. I imagined a giant version of Dad with an enormous kettle, pouring boiling water down over the ant-like cars and people.

From Zurich, I caught the train to Lucerne. When I arrived, I was crying. There was nothing I could do to stop it. I'd tried to contact Eva but she wasn't answering her phone or responding on snapchat – even though I could see she'd opened my messages. 80,000 people live in Lucerne, and I didn't know Eva's address. I walked along the lakeside and watched the water slop against the concrete shore of Lake Lucerne. Eva had told me all about Lucerne, and I recognised the mountains from pictures she had shown me on her phone when we were at the summer school together. Mount Pilatus towered over the city from the distance, collecting the only clouds in the clear sky around its summit. A sailboat bobbed out in the open water, its mainsail reaching up from the boom. From a distance, it looked like the fin of a giant shark lurking below the surface. There were other boats too, some tied in at the lakeside, and one rowing boat, Julia, letters fading from the wet wood. She was rotten through to her hull.

I found an Irish pub on the waterfront, just along from the rowing boats. Inside, the walls were covered with four-leaf clovers and Guinness adverts and Irish tricolours.

The locals stared at me and I felt self-conscious that I'd recently been crying. A fat man lifted his coat off an empty stool for me. His shirt sleeves were rolled up, revealing forearms splattered with mud. I threw my rucksack down next to him and ordered a Guinness, because that's what all the other men were drinking. The few women in the bar were swirling red wine around bowl-sized glasses. For a minute or two I sat with my pint, pretending to be busy. I was trying to calculate what percentage of my total budget I'd just spent. The Guinness cost seven francs, so I made out that I'd already blown over three percent of my money. I think I might have started crying again because the fat man on the adjacent stool spoke to me in a concerned tone in German. "English?" he asked, when I didn't respond.

I couldn't deny it.

"Christoph," he said, stretching out a large, worn hand. As he spoke I watched his chin move. It was dotted with prickly hairs, like a raspberry.

"Billy."

He had the sort of handshake that made everything seem OK.

"What brings you to Lucerne, Billy?" A half-crescent of froth lined his top lip. The foam gushed to the bottom of my pint in an avalanche, settled, turned black.

I glugged down half of it and placed the glass back down on the bar.

"My girlfriend. I came here to take her away somewhere, maybe America or Australia. Somewhere far away."

"Oh, super! And she is coming?" Christoph swiped the cream from his upper lip.

"She doesn't want to see me." I could feel the foam bubbling up at the back of my throat.

"So you don't travel?"

"She changed her mind. I'll go back to England tomorrow."

"You can go alone, no?" Christoph patted me hard on the back with his big hand.

"It's a bad start, getting dumped on day one."

Christoph said, "Then it can only be better," laughing from his belly. His gut was pregnant; swollen into a perfect globe. I could imagine peeling up his shirt and finding it decorated with a map of the world. "Why go home now?"

"How come you speak such good English?" I asked.

"Ah, you are kind. My wife and I, we met in London. It is an amazing city. We go back at least once a year. Something amazing happened to Diana there, before we met. Something spiritual. A miracle, perhaps."

The conversation was getting a bit weird, so I just nodded and complimented his English again.

"Listen," said Christoph. "Here is a question. If somebody who speaks two languages is called bilingual, what do you call somebody who speaks many languages?"

I didn't know.

"Polylingual," said Christoph. "So what do you call somebody who speaks only one language?"

"Monolingual?" I guessed.

"No, English!" Christoph laughed hard and clapped me on the back. He had a point. There are four languages in Switzerland and I couldn't speak a word in any of them.

I spent the evening at the pub with Christoph and his wife, Diana. They told me about their farm, high on the hillside on the way out to Pilatus, about how their children had all left Lucerne, about their cows and sheep. We played darts and Christoph spoke about his passion for Guinness.

"I could have it with my breakfast cereal," he said. "If she would let me." He nudged Diana. She was markedly slim in comparison to her husband. Blond hair fell over her shoulder, fading grey, but she was still young in the face. In her day, she'd probably been the most beautiful girl in the town.

The bell rang for last orders.

"Come and stay," Christoph said, placing his hand on my arm. "Help me on the farm tomorrow. Stay as long as you like. Share our bread."

"I would," I said, "But I've booked the night at a hotel." I hadn't booked a night at a hotel.

"Tomorrow?" Diana said.

Christoph cheered. "Yes! I'll meet you here, at eight thirty."

"In the morning?" I asked.

"Of course in the morning," Christoph said.

I left The Shamrock and walked out along the docks. I don't know why I didn't go with Christoph that evening. I stood by the lakeside, looking at the view. The moon was a silver medal suspended above the mountains, and streetlights cast long flames across the lake.

The rowing boat Julia was still tied up to a bollard. It could have been there for years. Parts of the rib had cracked away, and rust had grown thick over the rowlocks. Chucking my bag in first, I made camp for the night on the bottom boards.

Silhouetted against the evening glow of the city, the high-rise buildings hung in the night air. I lay down on my back. I could hear fish making knife-breaks in the cool water, in lullaby. If Eva had been there she would have pressed her fingertips into my armpit for warmth. I wasn't cold – the beer was warming me. But the night was getting colder, and I was sobering up.

I lay in the boat for a while, thinking of Eva. The cold wooden planks pressed into the bottom of my back. I thought about when we were at the summer school, and the day we went to Brighton – the day I failed to jump from the bridge. Afterwards, once she'd emerged from the water and the sun had dried her, she was in a strange mood. The only thing she'd talk about was Brutalist architecture.

I hadn't known what Brutalism was when she'd first mentioned it. Brutalism: the word had rolled around my mouth like a Werther's Original. I'd assumed it was something to do with sadomasochistic sex. Luckily, I'd looked it up on Wikipedia and learned it wasn't anything to do with whips and chains or erotic asphyxiation. Apparently Brutalism was an architectural movement that flourished from the 1950's until the mid-1970's. Concrete was often used for its raw and unpretentious honesty, contrasting dramatically with the highly refined and ornamented buildings constructed in the elite Beaux-Arts style. I didn't know what that meant, but that's what the Internet said. To me it just looked like a bunch of ugly concrete tower blocks and multi-storey car parks. They looked like inner-city sea defences. Built to last a thousand years or survive the next A-bomb.

But that day, after the bridge and the jump, it was all she would talk about. We were eating veggie burgers down by the seafront. I'm not a veggie – it was Eva's choice. I wanted to find a quiet place where we could kiss and I might be able to get my hand up her shirt. But she would only talk about Brutalism, and how beautiful the buildings were.

I could never see beauty in a concrete building. Maybe that was why she wouldn't see me. It's hard to be in love with someone that can't see beauty in the things you do. That night in the boat, I started thinking of her as a concrete tower with no windows or doors, as something I would only ever know from the outside.

At some point I fell asleep, but I soon woke up shaking with cold. My feet were wet because I hadn't realised there was a long, thin crack in one of the bottom boards, which allowed water to dribble into the hull. I climbed out and sat down at the waterside, slapping my sides to get my circulation going. I put on several layers of clothes and jogged on the spot. But although I warmed up, there was no way I could get back to sleep.

I wandered the deserted streets of Lucerne, imagining that Eva was asleep behind every shuttered window. Maybe I passed within metres of her. Eventually, I returned to watch the sun climb to the summit of Mount Pilatus.

I'd turned my phone off to save battery, and when I turned it back on and saw a stack of notifications, I got all excited thinking that Eva was trying to reach me. But they were all messages from Mum on the family WhatsApp group. She called it the family WhatsApp even though only me and her used it. Dad hadn't even mastered texting. It had taken her a while, but she'd obviously realised that I'd really gone. The messages went from angry to panicked to sad. I felt awful about that. But I also felt frustrated that even in Lucerne I couldn't escape. Nobody can escape these days. The world has shrunk.

I wrote back that I was fine and was staying with Eva and that she shouldn't worry. I sent a picture of me with the mountains in the background because Mum liked that sort of thing. I tried my best to smile and look like things were OK and I hadn't slept in a wrecked rowing boat. Then I added that I didn't have any roaming data so I wouldn't be able to stay in touch anymore, so she shouldn't worry if she didn't hear from me.

After that I sent half-a-dozen pleading messages to Eva. Reading them back, I sounded pathetic and stalkerish. In any case, the only replies I got were from Mum. She sent a line of crying faces. Then she sent a long and weird warning about terrorists – "like that jeehadee in Nice" – who she said were everywhere in Europe. Then she sent a croissant emoji, which I guess was because she thought Lucerne was in France. Mum had become very enthusiastic about emojis.

When I was done, I turned my phone off and went to meet Christoph. I wasn't expecting him to show up. It seemed like the sort of thing someone would suggest after a few beers and then realise was stupid in the morning. But Christoph came early. I was thankful. I needed a meal and a hot shower. He drove us up to his farm, half an hour south from the city, near to Alpnach, at the foot of Pilatus. The car rumbled through the hillside. Pine trees lined the roadside in regiment, upright, like soldiers.

"You look tired, Billy," Christoph said. "Did you party all night?"

"Hotel wasn't much good," I said. "Damp."

"You can sleep for an hour. But my cow, she will give birth this afternoon. I want you to be there."

I'd never seen anything give birth before.

Their chalet looked out over the lake. While Christoph ran out to check on his heifer, Diana showed me to their spare bedroom. She was wearing a cream jumper with chocolate icing smeared on her breast. As I showered I could smell cakes baking. When I went back into the bedroom, Diana was cranking the Venetian blinds, locking out all light. I lay down on the bed and fell asleep within minutes.

An hour later, I woke up with Christoph shaking me.

"It's time," he said. "She's almost ready."

I had no idea what he was talking about.

"Come on. You can't miss it." He handed me a small plate with a thick slice of double-layered chocolate cake and a glass of milk. "I'll be in the barn."

I stuffed the cake into my mouth, swilling the chocolate pieces around with the creamy milk. I walked through a corridor lined with old family photos. Christoph hadn't always been so fat. One picture showed him and Diana with their two boys out by the lake. Christoph's shoulders were twice as broad as his hips, his stomach flat, legs thick, brown and barbed with hair. He stood proud in swim briefs. Diana was covered up: hat, sunglasses, skirt and blouse.

I went out to the barn. The smell of shit reminded me of working with Sam. I thought about him briefly and hoped that he had recovered. I regretted not going with him to the hospital. I should have gone to visit him. Maybe, I thought, if I had done the right thing then, I wouldn't have ended up in such a mess with Eva and the money.

Christoph showed me inside the barn, where the cow was sectioned off in a pen. She was standing up, covered in mud and dust and straw. Two hooves were emerging from her vagina, and a thick string of mucus dangled from her vulva.

I'd never seen a cow's vagina. It bagged up, crinkled; ready to spit out a new life. It was one of the most hideous things I'd ever seen.

"Isn't it beautiful?" Christoph whispered.

I smiled.

"You might have to help me ease her out," Christoph said, examining her backside. "If she struggles, we pull the calf from the hooves."

"I can't do that," I said. I didn't think I was scared of animals. But there's something alien about livestock – you only ever see them on TV or in children's books or in your dinner.

"Sure you can," he said. "You can't be so negative, Billy. She will know."

The cow mooed.

"What do we do now?" I asked.

"We wait for her. She won't be long." Christoph moved to the corner of the barn and showed me a large black tub full of what looked like rotten grass. "This is silage. A cow's dinner. How does it smell, to you?"

"Rural," I said, and took a seat on a small wooden stool, behind the cow. Christoph laughed, and joined me.

"A few years ago, we had a terrible time with the cows," he said. "Everything was normal, the calves were coming strong, and we were doing so well. I was even going to build a second barn. But one day they just started disappearing. One here, one there. We didn't know what was going on."

I picked up some straw and started ripping it up into tiny pieces as he spoke.

"I searched for hours, Diana too. We lost ten in one week. We thought someone was stealing them."

"Who was it?"

The cow shuffled her hind legs, grunting.

"It wasn't anyone," he said. "They were committing suicide."

I laughed. The cow's ears flopped down over her head. There was something deliberate about her posture. Her front legs were slightly cocked, like the coy hands of a magazine model posing nude.

"I'm not joking," he continued. "They were jumping off the cliff, just down from here. I didn't understand. I found them finally, as I walked along the cliff's edge. I looked down and they were all piled up in the valley. They'd all jumped off at the same spot."

"Cows can't jump," I said. "It must have been an accident. They must have strayed too far."

"Once is an accident," he said. "There were twelve cows down there." He looked troubled by the memory.

I said, "Animals aren't capable of suicide." I thought how common a sight it is to see cows out grazing on the green plateaus in the Alps. They don't just fall off cliff edges. Not that many.

"It must have been something I had done. They felt like slaves or prisoners or something, having me lock them up in a cowshed. They hated me. They would rather throw themselves off a cliff than be around me any longer."

"I'm sure that's not the case," I said. "Cows can't hate."

"You don't know much about cows, Billy."

I shrugged. "Did you fence in the suicide spot?"

"No, no. I thought about it," he said. "But then I thought if they want to die, they'll find a way."

I couldn't think of any other way a cow could kill itself.

Christoph continued, "So I started sleeping out here with them, and eating my dinner with them, to show them I was a friend. One of them."

"What did Diana think?"

"She wasn't happy. I thought we might be divorced. She said I had lost my mind, I was paranoid, obsessed."

"What happened?"

Christoph spread his palm in front of him and thumbed the golden callouses at the bottom of each finger. They were worn, useful hands, spotted with patches of vitiligo. The white patches looked as if they were spreading, like marbling meat.

"They stopped jumping. I still sleep out here once a week."

"That must be difficult," I said. "Even in winter?"

Cracks of daylight shot through the wooden panels of the barn. It would be hell in winter.

"Of course," he said. "That's why I drink so much Guinness."

I thought about how cold I had been the previous night, in the autumn after several pints. He must have had to get through a whole keg.

"I think it's time to get her out, Billy. Are you ready?" Christoph rubbed his palms together. I felt queasy. The silage had a smell that reached down my throat and hooked at my stomach.

"What do I have to do?"

Christoph talked me through everything. He described what he was doing as he attached a set of calving chains to the protruding hooves – making loops above and below the knee. I felt like a trainee vet.

"Pull when I say. Easy! We pull out and down when she is straining, and try to ease her out when she isn't."

"Right." I still had no idea what to do.

Christoph double checked the chains and we took one each. The heifer groaned. It resonated around the barn. We tugged at the chains.

"More!" Christoph urged.

I braced my knees and squatted, putting all my weight through the chain. I imagined the calf curled up in the foetal position, rolled into a ball with its head jutting out, hooves tucked beneath its chin, preparing to emerge into the mountain air. It wouldn't budge. It was a tug of war: two men losing against an unborn calf.

"It's not moving," I said. The chains were cold and breaking the skin on my palms.

"Shut up, and pull," he said, grunting as his top lip curled onto his gums.

We heaved harder, urging the calf out. For the amount of force we were putting through the thing, I would have expected it to catapult out and splat on the wall.

"Here she comes," Christoph said.

The calf's head appeared. The head stretched the heifer's vagina to the point that it might split. The amniotic sac covered its face – it reminded me of when my cat got a Tesco bag stuck over its head, and my Mum grounded me for a week because she thought I'd tried to suffocate it.

From there, it didn't take much to get her out. The chains jangled and fell slack as the calf slipped out from its mother and onto the floor. Its black skin was shiny, leathery, covered in gunk. Christoph quickly punctured the sac and ripped it away. A rush of afterbirth spilled out, landing in a steaming pile. I dropped the chain, inspecting the blisters on my palms. The mother soon shuffled to her feet, licked the new-born, cleaning the fluid away with her pink tongue. Christoph hugged me.

The calf strained, trying to stand. I watched as it tried to prop itself up and take its first feed. It was soon on its hind legs, but not quite strong enough to be completely free standing. It was doubled over, resting its weight on its knees.

"You can name her, if you like," Christoph said.

Flies fizzed around the afterbirth. The calf wobbled over to its mother, nuzzling into its teat. I remembered a fact Eva had told me once, about cows emitting enough methane to damage the ozone layer. I wasn't even sure whether that was true.

"Call her Eva."

We washed up in the house. I had another shower and scrubbed the slime and hay and stink from my skin. Then I called Eva. The human Eva, not the new-born calf. I didn't know what I wanted to say to her. I just wanted her to hear my voice and to hear hers, and to feel like everything was going to be OK.

I pressed the phone to my ear. Diana was chopping vegetables in the kitchen. The knife thudded against the wooden board between each ring in the receiver. Eva didn't answer.

I got dressed and joined Diana in the kitchen.

"Hungry?" she said.

I was starving. But having only recently pulled a calf out of a cow's vagina, I didn't have much of an appetite.

"We can have chicken and potatoes, later." She wore a blue and white apron tied closely around her neat little waist. "For now, I can poach some eggs?"

"That sounds amazing, Diana. Thank you."

Diana clinked a pan full of water onto the hob and flicked the gas on. Christoph returned from cleaning up, but in the same clothes.

"Chicken?" he said.

Diana smiled. "Yes, chicken. Always chicken for you."

"Thank God for chicken!" Christoph said, holding the raw bird aloft in two hands. He was like a kid after eating a bag of sweets. "Do you believe in God, Billy?"

His serious tone jarred with the uncooked chicken in his hands.

"Put it down, Christoph," Diana said. He dropped the chicken down on the counter, kissing his wife on the forehead.

"I'd like to," I said, wondering if it was a trick question.

"Well we have to baptise Eva tonight." Christoph lifted his bum onto the kitchen counter, letting his legs dangle on the cupboards.

"You baptise the calves?"

"Yes, all of them. I began baptising them when they started jumping." A ginger tomcat pattered into the kitchen, collar bell tinkling. Christoph jumped down off the counter and scooped it up in his arms, scratching its chin. It purred. "Are you not baptised, Billy?"

"Yes, I was, as a baby." Of course, when I was a baby my Mum had me baptised. You're stuck with faith the same as cancer or dementia. It's all out of your control.

"And what about now? If you could be without religion, you would be?"

"That's a decision I don't need to make," I said, dodging the question in case they tried to convert me.

"Diana, tell Billy your story." Christoph kissed the cat on the nose.

"What's this?" I said.

"My wife has proof of God," he said. "Something that happened to her, years ago."

"Christoph," she said. "You know I don't like to tell this story."

"Please." Christoph dropped the cat and pulled a chair out for Diana. She picked a plate from the drying rack and put it away in a cupboard. "Diana," Christoph urged.

Diana picked a broom from the corner and swept crumbs into a neat pile by the door. She ignored him. "I don't want to speak of it," she said. "I hate remembering."

"It's a troubling story," Christoph whispered to me. "It's a special story, Diana. I promise I won't ask you to tell it ever again, just tell Billy what happened. I've made him curious now."

I was curious. Once there's something to be known it's unbearable to go on without knowing it. Diana stopped sweeping. She had her back to us, facing the door. After a moment, she untied her apron, hung it on the back of the door, then joined us at the table.

"This is not an easy story for me to tell," Diana said. "But it is true, every word. So please, don't question it. I cannot explain it, but it happened."

"Of course," I said. Christoph nodded.

Diana licked her finger and dabbed at tiny crumbs on the tabletop. "I visited London," she began. "Years ago. When I was young, a little while before Christoph and I met. I stayed with my cousin, in Clapham. One evening it was late, and very dark, I was lost. I was alone, completely alone. Just me."

"Sure," I said. She looked confused at why I had spoken.

"The only way I knew to get home was through a dark alleyway, a tunnel. There was a man there. A big man, alone, right in the middle. He was waiting there. I thought about it a while, about whether I should do this or not. I thought I could pretend to be on the telephone, but he would know. I thought something bad would happen."

"Tell him what you did, Diana!" Christoph clapped his hands in anticipation. It didn't seem to matter that he had probably heard the story a dozen times before.

"I said a prayer. A few words, for protection, safe passage. And I walked through the tunnel."

The water bubbled up to the brim of the saucepan.

"It was fine, I walked through past the man and nothing happened."

The tomcat jumped up onto the counter, sniffing around for something to eat.

"But that's not it," Christoph said. "Tell him."

"Give me a chance," said Diana. "I was called to give evidence, soon after that night, as it turned out that man did attack a woman. He raped her." She paused. Christoph squeezed her hand. "Right there, he did it. The place where I passed through just fine." She locked her fingers together.

I was silent. Hairs on my back prickled up like pine needles. "Do you believe the prayer protected you?"

Diana ignored me. She didn't look at me or Christoph. She just stared into the table.

"In court, I saw him, the same man, on trial, I knew his face. He was charged with rape and sentenced to five years in prison."

"That's all he got?" I said. I wasn't sure whether either of them heard me.

"When I gave my evidence, my statement, about when I was there, and was it him I recognised, the judge asked him why he didn't attack me, why I wasn't the victim – something I had been thinking about ever since I heard the news." Tears lingered on her cheeks. The water spilled over the saucepan, bubbling and evaporating over the edge into hot air. Christoph jumped up and reduced the gas, bridging a wooden spoon across the saucepan.

"You'll never guess what he said."

Diana paused a moment before saying it.

"He said, 'Why would I attack her, when she was walking with two big men?'"

Christoph was grinning. I felt a cold rush travel down my spine.

Then Diana said, "I was alone that night, completely."

That evening, Christoph, Diana and myself went out to the barn and baptised the calf. Christoph lit candles in jam jars and hung multi-coloured bunting along the wooden beams. Diana and I watched as Christoph patted the calf on its head.

"We are gathered here today to baptise this child," Christoph began. "And to recognise that she is the child of God."

"Is it always like this?" I whispered to Diana.

"What do you think?"

Christoph held the calf's face between his hands and kissed its head.

"Water is used in this ceremony to symbolize the water of life," he continued. "Let us remember that the water used in this baptism is the symbol of immersion in the life of God. The life of God surrounds us, fills us, and flows through us, as us." He signalled to Diana.

She handed me her candle and picked up the red bucket, then poured some water over the calf's head. The calf jolted and tried to squirm out of Christoph's grasp, but he held on to the animal tight, dipped his index finger in the remaining water, and marked out a cross on the calf's head.

"Baptism marks the beginning of a journey with God which continues for the rest of our lives," he said. "Let this be the beginning of our journey with Eva."

The candles flickered around the barn. I walked outside with Diana while Christoph tended to the calf. The hillside was in darkness, the distant lights of Lucerne fizzled out one by one, like fingers pinching out the flames of matches.

"Has he always been so religious?" I asked her. We were standing a little way out from the barn. Below us, telegraph poles punctuated the shoreline, connecting a wire all the way around the hillside and down into the basin, to Lucerne. Down on the lake, all of the sailboats were tied up at shore. The empty tongue of water stretched between the dark mountains, and along through the valley.

"That was nothing," she said. "He used to drive the calves to the lake and baptise them in the water." A few more lights flicked off in the town. "It was all after I told him about what happened in London. He was never a believer in anything before that."

"He's a dedicated man," I said.

"Yes," she said. "A calf was born on Christmas day a few years ago. He called her Jesus."

I laughed and thought of my Mum. She would've given all the cows Biblical names.

"Do you think you will sort things, with your girlfriend?" she said.

"I hope so," I said.

"I think you would do better to travel alone. Women are nothing but trouble." She laughed. In the darkness I couldn't see the creases around her eyes and mouth.

"I don't know. I want to see Eva," I said. "Even though it would be good to just forget about her."

Christoph wandered out from the barn. "Billy," he called. "I'm going to have one beer before I go to bed, if you would like to?"

"Sure."

He walked back into the house. Diana and I stayed outside.

After a minute, Diana said, "So what happened with Eva? Why did you break up?"

"She said it's because we are so far from each other."

"But you are here now," Diana said.

"I know," I said.

"Some things just can't be explained." Diana stroked the hair on the back of my head. I felt like a six-year-old boy again. "Will you go to see her?"

"I might do, tomorrow. To say goodbye."

"Maybe," she said, her hand moving away from my hair and resting on my shoulder. "Of course, she won't want you if you chase her."

"No?"

"If you want her to want you, you have to make it clear that you don't want her. So, you should probably get as far away from her as possible."

We both laughed. The ginger cat rubbed its head against my leg, pacing a figure eight between my legs.

"I want you to know something, Billy."

The pine trees along the hillside shivered in the breeze. The picket fence away to the left of the farm rattled as loose barbed wire clinked on the metal gate. The cat ran away.

"What is it?" I asked.

"You can't tell Christoph," she began. "I mean that. Never."

"Of course, Diana."

"I just have to tell someone."

"What is it?" I asked.

"What I told you about the alleyway in London, about how I prayed to God to protect me–" She paused. Her eyes weren't looking at me anymore; she was staring out at the lake, into the starless sky. "I made it up, Billy," she said.

"Why?"

"To protect Christoph."

"From what?" I asked. She moved closer to me, wrapping her fingers around my forearm. Her wedding ring pressed cold against my skin.

"It was me," she said. "I was attacked." She buried her head into my chest.

As I held her, I watched more and more lights go out in the distance. One light glowed brighter than any other. I looked at it for too long, wondering what it could be illuminating. I drew my eyes away from it, burying my nose and face into Diana's hair. It smelled of vanilla and almonds. The glare had made an impression on my sight. It fogged my vision. I rubbed my eyelids with my fingertips, trying to make it go away. I could still see it behind my eyelids when I closed my eyes.

The next morning I woke up early and Christoph gave me a lift to Zurich. Diana wasn't around when we left.

"You will have to visit again," he said as we pulled into the train station. "On your way home, perhaps. Or maybe we will see you when next we are in London." He stretched out an open palm to shake my hand.

"That would be lovely, Christoph." I jumped out of his car and grabbed my rucksack from the boot. He got out and shook my hand again. That same reassuring handshake.

"You know you are welcome any time. And good luck with the lady."

"I'll need it," I said. I couldn't look him in the eye.

"You know, I wouldn't be who I am without Diana." He put his big hands on my shoulders. "I'd like you to have something," he said, running back to the front of the car and fumbling around the glovebox. As he did, a pack of tourists emerged from the train station. I wondered how many of them were about to be dumped by their eco-girlfriends.

Christoph returned and placed a silver crucifix necklace in my hand. I lifted it between my index finger and thumb. It was as delicate as a daisy chain. Christoph smiled as I raised it close to my eye and watched the sunlight flash from the twirling cross.

"I want you to take this with you," he said. "And just remember, it's not all bad."

Inside the station I stared up at the departures board. Names of faraway places flashed at me in yellow pixels. Berlin, Frankfurt, Milan, Rome, Munich. I wondered how far my money would take me.

I went to sit down on a bench outside. In a way, I wished I'd stayed with Christoph. I could have helped him with the calves for a month and been fed for free. I'd have been comfortable. I could have even done a few baptisms. I could have been ordained.

But I couldn't stay knowing what Diana had told me. I couldn't bear having to look at her and know what happened – knowing what Christoph didn't. I played with the cross on the necklace he had given to me. I wondered how he would react if he knew the truth.

Eva would have been in her first hour or two of work, picking trash off the conveyor belt, watching the endless stream of junk flow past her. Maybe she was thinking of me. She had to be.

I got up and admitted what I'd known all morning: I was going to visit Eva at her place of work.

It took me an hour on Google to work out I needed to get on the 78 – the bus that runs out to the north of Zurich, to Hagenholz, where Eva worked. Then it took me another hour to find the stop.

When I was finally aboard, the bus moved out of Zurich and through huge green spaces. It would be hard to know you were anywhere near a city at all. I jumped off near Hagenholz. The recycling centre was a short walk along the main road. I had no idea what I was going to say to her, if she was even there. But I had to try.

The sign at the main gate read Hagenholz Recycling Centre. I walked inside and crossed a small wooden bridge that led over a man-made pond. The reception was a small cabin with magazines scattered across coffee tables and a spectacled man sitting behind the desk. I was the only visitor.

"Good morning," the receptionist said. He was in his mid-fifties and he had more hair in his nostrils than on his head.

"Hello," I said. "I'm looking for Eva Stamm. She's a recycling operative in the centre."

"Of course," he said. "May I ask what business you have with her?"

"She's an old colleague," I said. "I'm visiting Zurich and she promised to show me around."

He tapped on the computer keyboard and clicked the mouse a few times.

"Oh dear," he said. "She's gone away for a while." He clicked the mouse once more and jerked back into his chair, with his hands clasped around the back of his head.

"Could you help?" I said. "I have no way of contacting her."

He moved forward in his seat. "Would you like me to give her a call?"

"If you could."

He walked over to the filing cabinet behind his desk and opened one of the drawers. His fingers tapped over the metal partitions.

"Got it," he said. He didn't seem used to having visitors. Dialling Eva's mobile number into the land line, he smiled and coiled the wire around his finger. It looked like a phone from the 1960s, with its receiver attached by a white cord to the dialler.

She answered after two rings.

The receptionist spoke to her in German for a couple of minutes. Then he looked up at me.

"What is your name?" He put his hand over the mouthpiece.

"Christoph," I said.

They spoke in German again, then he handed me the phone. The cord didn't stretch far, so I had to lean over the desk.

"Eva," I said.

"Billy?"

"I'm sorry, I'm at the centre. I need to see you."

The receptionist was shaking his head, doodling on a scrap piece of paper.

"I'm out of the country."

"Where are you?"

She was silent. As I waited for her response, the receptionist plucked a walkie-talkie out from his drawer and garbled something into it in German.

I persisted. "Tell me. I have to see you."

"I told you not to come."

"Where are you?"

"I'd rather not say."

"Just ten minutes," I said. "Give me a chance to talk to you. Then I'll leave you alone. Just tell me where you are."

She was silent for a few more seconds. The receptionist stretched out his hand to take the telephone from me. He was rising from his seat, coming closer, trying to paw the phone from my ear. I scooped up the telephone dialler from the desk and managed to move away from his grasp. The wire was taut – stretched to its maximum length. It would either snap or the plug would shoot out of the socket if I moved any further. The receptionist got to his feet and lumbered around the desk.

"I'm in Slovenia," she said.

"Where?" I said. The telephone wire was tight as a banjo string.

"In Bled," she said. "Meet me here at the start of my birthday. I'll be at the church at midnight."

The receptionist grabbed the telephone from my hand and the cable shot out from the dialler. The line went dead.

After I'd been escorted off the premises, I waited for the 78 back to Zurich. I didn't mind. I knew where I had to go, and I was set on getting there as soon as I could. With not enough money to get a train, I worried whether I'd get there at all. I'd never hitchhiked, and the idea of it scared me. It was too far to walk the whole way – I'd never make it in time. I didn't know exactly where Slovenia was, but I thought it was somewhere near Russia. I knew nothing about it and that scared me.

I thought about it on the bus. Eva's birthday was on the 5th of November. I remembered explaining to her that she shared the date with Guy Fawkes. She'd said to meet her at midnight on the start of her birthday, which meant I had to get there on the night of the fourth. I had eight days, including that one.

The problems were all financial. In addition to the beer, I'd spent CFH4.80 on the bus fares. The train to Lucerne had cost me CFH30, leaving me with CFH137.80. By the time I'd converted that to Euros, I'd have even less. I knew that it was never going to be enough, but I had to try.

I Googled the town, just to make sure she hadn't made it up. She hadn't – it was there. A small town in Slovenia, 600 kilometres from Zurich.

I started walking.

At the time, walking to Bled didn't seem to me that stupid. I found a route on Google Maps that said it would take 130 hours; I could make it in eight days so long as every day I slept for eight hours and walked for sixteen.

On my first day of walking, it took me two hours to get out of Zurich and its suburbs. Then I walked for five hours, crunching the soles of my trainers through dirt and gravel and mud, trudging along roadsides, past the mounds of harvested plants heaped up in adjacent fields. I walked until the blood swelled in my feet.

By the time it was nearing dusk, the road signs said I was 22km from Zurich. I started to run, shouting at myself to go faster. But my backpack bounced on my back and it soon started to hurt, so I rolled down the grass verge and sat in the dirt until I felt better.

I had the last of my water and continued onto Grüningen, a small town south east of Zurich. I walked until the sun melted below the horizon. Then the moon appeared, transposed onto the black sky. I walked through the night, thinking only of Eva.

Few cars passed. I followed the empty roads until I could walk no longer. I didn't want to sleep outside in the cold but I didn't have much choice. Eventually I found a spot to lie down in a bush on the outskirts of Niederurnen. I placed my backpack under my head and waited for the sun. Even though there was nobody around, I was terrified. I could hear animals making noises I'd never heard before. Growling, screeching and screaming through the black night.

I was still ten miles or so from Glarus, the next town. I was nowhere. I've never been so alone. My feet ached and now that I had stopped walking, I was quickly getting cold. I tucked my knees into my stomach and curled into a ball. I couldn't settle my thoughts – I expected to be mugged or beaten or abducted at any moment. I tried to calm my breathing, holding my breath for seven seconds and then slowly exhaling, but that didn't work either. I decided I had to focus on something to take my mind away from how scared and lonely and cold I was. There was only one thing I could think about. I thought about Eva.

I remembered one night in July at the summer school, when my suitcase went missing. I got back to my Portakabin at about 11pm and all my things had gone. The bed was neatly made, and the piano lid was closed. The room looked like it had been cleaned out and prepared for someone new. I worried that the school had discovered that Eva and I were sleeping together in my room and had decided to sack me.

There was a note on my pillow. It said, "Marine Parade Beach." I recognised it as Eva's handwriting – the neat curls and joins of the letters made my stomach go all weak.

I ran down to the beach. It wasn't far from the school. Eva was sitting on top of my suitcase, facing out to the water.

"I needed a deckchair," Eva said. "Hope you don't mind."

I dropped down into the sand and flicked off my trainers. Eva was barefoot, her hair down and blowing in the wind. I stroked the top of her foot.

"How did you get that down here?" I asked.

"My private helicopter."

We spent an hour sitting out, looking at the water, watching the flashing buoys bobble in the distance.

"The sea is so ugly," she said.

"How?"

"There is a whole new place across it. With new people, and languages, and cities and mountains and desert."

"Why is that ugly?"

"Because the sea is stopping me."

"You can fly right across it."

"But I shouldn't have to. I should be able to walk the earth as freely as I wish."

"But that doesn't make sense. There's always other places."

"Yes," she said, toying with the pink and blue anklet above her right foot. "But the sea is stopping me from reaching them."

"And?"

"It teaches us something, doesn't it?"

"About what?"

"Barriers. Borders. The restrictions put upon us."

"But we're free to travel wherever we want."

"Are we?"

I thought about the times I'd spent in the south of France as a kid. I'd never really been anywhere besides that.

"I think so."

"It's blocking us from new experiences. A whole sea that could drown every person on this planet. It's ugly."

I didn't know how to talk like she did – I couldn't grasp what she meant. Part of me thought that was her way of telling me that she didn't like me. We held each other to keep warm, and after another hour the tide had moved out, revealing a new stretch of rippled sand. There were ridges formed by the waves, like the fingerprint of the sea. Eva got up and walked to the shore. I imagined the water retreating as she approached, forming a path for her to walk the world as freely as she wished. But at the water's edge, she stopped. The sea water tickled over her toenails. I was left with the cold hollow in the sand, where she had been.

I slept for two hours that night on the side of the road in Switzerland. Before the night was out, I'd started walking again. As I walked, I decided I would have to try to hitchhike large portions of my journey. After one day my body was broken and I was already way behind schedule. Plus, my phone was dead and without it I had no idea of the route. I now had only seven days to get to Bled. My feet were blistered and cracked around the heels. I needed to wash, but I didn't even have drinking water.

So instead of walking into Glarus, I waited at Niederurnen in the morning light with my thumb stuck out, hoping to hitch a ride east towards Innsbruck. I didn't know anything about hitching.

I watched the faces as they drove past me and into the city. Many kept their eyes dead ahead, fixed to the road, unblinking. Many made a signal with their index finger in a circular motion, which I later learned meant that they were only driving around the local area. One man stopped in the first twenty minutes of me offering my thumb to the road, but he was heading west towards Geneva, and that was no use.

I waited three hours before a truck stopped. The brakes squealed, and the truck let out a long horsey sigh. Out jumped a woman in her mid-forties.

"Wohin gehst du?" she said. Her hair was bright purple and she was wearing a pair of frayed denim shorts, despite it being late October.

I didn't understand the question, so I pointed and said, "Innsbruck."

"Innsbruck? Kein Deutsch?" She had good legs and her calves were incredible. She was not how I expected a trucker to be. "English?"

"Yes," I said. "I'm going to Innsbruck."

"Sorry," she said. "I go Ancona."

I couldn't think where that was. I recognised the name – it sounded vaguely like a football team.

"Italy," she continued. "There, I must get ferry for Croatia. Innsbruck is far, I think." She shrugged and climbed back into her cab. "Good luck." She smiled and slammed the door shut.

"That could work for me," I said, but she didn't hear. I said it again but she'd started the engine and it roared over my voice. I ran up to the cab and opened the passenger door.

The woman looked horrified. "What are you doing?" She cut the engine and the silence made me even more nervous.

"If it's OK, could I come? I've never done this before. I don't have any money."

"But I do not go to Innsbruck."

Her little hands gripped the steering wheel tight. Something about her reminded me of my Mum's friend Mandy, which made me hate myself for fancying her.

"I'm trying to get to Slovenia. But it doesn't matter how I get there."

"Slovenia? Is a long way," she said.

"Croatia is a lot closer than here."

"OK, come."

"Are you sure it's OK?"

"Yes, yes, come!"

I chucked my bag onto the middle seat and climbed into the spare seat, by the window.

"My name is Klara," she said.

"I'm Billy. Thanks for stopping."

"You look like, how do you say... you need a nice ride." The way she said it, with her accent and everything, it sounded like a line from a porn film. It felt like all the blood dropped out of my stomach and down into my crotch. It was like how I felt when I used to be paired with Sally Fountain in science class.

I think it took me a long time to say anything. "I was walking all night," I said. "I thought I'd have to walk all the way to Slovenia."

"Please, sleep. It is a long drive."

"How long?"

"I think, eight hours to Ancona. The ferry is through the night. In the morning, we are in Dubrovnik."

"What are you taking to Croatia?" I asked.

"Everything." She threw her head back and laughed. The bracelets on her wrists jangled as she manoeuvred the truck around winding country roads. "Where are you from?"

"England. A town called Cheltenham."

"I do not know this," she said. "I am from Czech Republic. Near Prague. But today I come from Munich."

"Isn't this the long way round to Croatia?"

She laughed her girlish laugh and I leant forward to ensure she wouldn't notice the bulge in my crotch.

"Longer, yes. But I get very tired when I must drive so far. I must stop and sleep, so... This way is good, I think. I like the water. Sometimes long is good," she said, and she laughed again.

She was so small that she had to sit on a heavy winter coat to lift her to a comfortable driving position.

"I like the water, too," I said, before putting my head back and falling asleep.

Klara woke me up two hours later. She placed a Coke on the dashboard and dropped a paper bag containing three warm hamburgers on my lap. A trail of drool had escaped from the corner of my mouth and run across my chin. I swiped it away as fast as I could, but I was certain she'd seen.

"You didn't need to buy me food," I said.

"Yes," Klara said, biting into a double cheeseburger. "It's OK."

"Thanks." I unwrapped the first burger and finished it within a minute.

"You are hungry," Klara said.

I nodded, chomping through a mouthful of mashed up bread and burger.

"Where are we?" I asked, once I'd swallowed.

"Como. North Italy. Is beautiful here, no?"

I looked around. We were in a service station car park. A fat man was filling up his 4x4 with diesel opposite us. Klara laughed. She was always laughing. I wished I could be as happy as she was.

We finished our food and Klara started driving again. We went around Milan and continued down through the north of Italy, racing towards the coast. I watched her calves flexing and relaxing on the clutch and accelerator pedals as we moved.

"Whooeee, here we go!" yelled Klara. I jumped with shock and laughed. "I do this," she said, bouncing in her chair, "to be awake." She reached over to me and pulled open the glovebox. "You can be the DJ," she said.

The glovebox was stuffed full of CDs. I pulled out a bunch of them. The only one I recognised was Stevie Wonder. I pushed the disc into the stereo and the first three tracks skipped and couldn't play. The disc must have been scratched. Then track four came on and Klara smiled and turned the volume up. It was "Sir Duke". She wound the windows down and bounced along to the horns. The wind lifted her hair above her head and she started laughing and singing.

"You do not know these bands?" Klara said. "You are like baby. You make me feel old."

"You're not old," I said.

"Your mother is how old?" Klara asked.

"She's fifty next September."

"Fifty?" Klara tipped her head back and laughed again.

"What's so funny?" I said.

"I am sixty."

"No way," I said.

"Yes. I am old as the mother of your mother."

That made me feel a little sick. It didn't make me stop fancying her. I just couldn't believe how young she looked. I thought she was twenty years younger.

"How do you look so young?" I asked.

She laughed again. She laughed all the way to Bologna.

A few hours into the drive, I could tell Klara was starting to tire. She started talking lots, adding in words of Czech and German when the English escaped her. From what I could pick up she was telling me about Catholic parents who had disowned her for abandoning the faith. And a man, possibly her ex-husband, who now lived somewhere in the French Riviera. I learned that she was not married and didn't plan on marrying again. She played the trumpet and double bass and used to play in a jazz quartet in Kraków.

As we passed Cesena, Klara told me that she was moving to Dubrovnik, a city right at the southern tip of Croatia, out on the coast.

"I want to make a restaurant," she said. "A pizzeria on a boat. What do you think? Is good idea?"

I couldn't tell if she was taking the piss or not, so I said it sounded like a great idea.

"I want to have a small kitchen, some customers, and a handsome Croatian man who will drive the boat. Do you know boats?"

"No."

"Shit."

"Are you really setting up that business?" I asked.

"I don't have any plans. It's nice to dream. Why are you here and with no money, Billy?"

"I have a little."

"A little?"

"Yeah. It's in Swiss Francs. Maybe €90?"

"Shit," Klara said. "Why only this?"

"I lost the rest."

"How?"

"I gambled it on a horse. It was supposed to win. Now I'm trying to get to my girlfriend. She's in Slovenia."

"She is from there?"

"No. She's from Lucerne."

"Why then Slovenia?"

"I don't know."

"Why not?"

"She broke up with me. I'm trying to find her."

"That is nice."

I didn't know what Klara meant by that so I kept quiet, peeling my shoes away from my heels with my toes.

"You still have a long journey from Dubrovnik," Klara said.

"I'll get there," I said, still not entirely convinced I would.

We got into Ancona at 8pm. It felt like two different cities: one old, one new. The modern port was full of enormous ferries that dwarfed the historical city. Our ferry sailed at 9pm, so we went to grab some food from a café. Klara had a salad, and I had spaghetti Bolognese. Klara paid again. I asked for her address and promised her that I'd repay her for everything.

She seemed annoyed. Either that or she didn't understand.

"I just feel bad. You shouldn't feel like you need to look after me."

"It is time, I think." Klara finished her drink and got up from her seat.

We got onto the ferry and went to sit up on the deck. We watched Italy disappear behind us and I drank whiskey sours until my fingers tingled. They were Klara's favourite, and she insisted.

We went to sit in the lounge at around midnight. I watched her chest rise and fall with each sleeping breath. She looked like an ordinary woman. There were faint wrinkles around her eyes where her laugh had been sketched into her face over time. A small mole on her neck, spindles of baby hair curling out from the sides of her head.

I wished there was some mark that distinguished a good person from a bad one.

During my sleep, I had a nightmare.

Eva was drowning in the ocean. She was wearing a wedding dress and her body was tangled up in it. I was watching from a boat – a rowing boat, right out in the middle of the ocean. Mum and Dad were in the boat with me, and GG and Benny. Tommy was there too. They were all watching Eva struggling. Her head was dipping below the waterline, her neck was craned right back, her lips pointing up to the sky, desperate for air. I couldn't move, like in most of my nightmares. I could only watch as she sputtered in the saltwater, flailing in the heavy white dress. She kicked out and screamed and my Mum said it was nothing to be ashamed about. Then I realised that I wasn't wearing any trousers. We were back in the kitchen at home and my Dad's fists were clenched and he was shouting and swearing. But Mum was smiling and reassuring me.

I must have awoken with a start because Klara asked whether I'd had a bad dream. She was sitting opposite me, drinking a glass of orange juice.

"Bad dream?" I repeated. It was morning and I could feel the warmth of the sun flooding through the windows.

"It is the boat. The water. Once, I work on the ferry in Bilbao. The Bay of Biscay. The sea is very…" She made a choppy wave gesture with her arms. "I had many bad dreams. Often I would stay up all night, even when I am not working. I would play cards sometimes, just me."

"I always have nightmares," I said.

She patted my arm. "Do not worry. We are there in twenty minutes."

We went up to the deck as the ferry approached the walled city of Dubrovnik. I'd never seen anywhere like that place. Perched on the horizon, the city looked like one enormous castle topped with a terracotta roof. Klara and I stood out on the deck in the gentle morning sunshine for a while, feeling the cool air on our faces, listening to the chug of the ferry engines and the song of distant seabirds.

After a little while on the deck, we went back to the truck. Within half an hour we had arrived in Dubrovnik. Klara drove me to a cash exchange and I swapped my Swiss Francs for a mixture of Euros and Croatian Kuna. Then we drove out to the train station. Before we said goodbye, I wrote a note for her on a napkin that had come with the hamburgers. I wrote it quickly and in a biro pen, but I hope that she found it. I stuck the note inside the Stevie Wonder CD case in the glovebox.

I'd have liked to stay in Dubrovnik a while, but I had to continue my journey. For the first time since arriving in Zurich, I felt good. I felt confident that Eva would see me and we would make things OK again. I'd travelled a long distance with Klara in not much time at all.

I tried to hitch a ride from the road outside the train station, but I waited for three hours standing in the sunshine without any success. I sat in the shade for half an hour, drank a litre of water and tried again to hitch. Not one person stopped. Looking back, I was waiting in totally the wrong spot. I should have got onto a road that headed north and out of town. But I was tired and I didn't know any better.

I started getting worried that going all the way up to Slovenia would be impossible to do. I had just six days before Eva's birthday. I went inside the train station and checked the next departures. I only recognised one name on the list: Split. And that was only because I'd been checking my map to see how I was going to navigate my way up the Croatian coastline, and then up to Zagreb, the capital city, or, in an ideal world, Ljubljana – the capital of Slovenia. Split is the next major coastal city north of Dubrovnik. The next train was departing in half an hour, so I picked up a new bottle of water, some bread and a chocolate bar, and cleaned up in the toilets. I washed my feet, under my arms, and, after double checking that nobody else was in the bathroom,

I splashed water on my groin. I still didn't feel clean though, and I was looking forward to using my money to stay at a hostel.

My train ticket cost 150 Kuna, which I think is about €18. I didn't want to spend anything, but I felt like I was left with no choice. I walked over to platform three and waited for the train to pull in.

When it eventually did, I was surprised it could still be used as a train. The tracks screeched as though under an immense pressure from the carriages as it squealed to a halt in front of me. The carriages were made up of sheet metal panels that had dozens of dents and scrapes. The train had been spray painted by graffiti artists, but the paint was flaking away from the metal.

Inside, the walls were smoke-stained, and the cushions on the plastic seats had been worn down by decades of fidgeting bums. I was the only person in my carriage, though. The train moved through Dubrovnik, and out through the suburbs. I managed to yank the window open to let some cool air float through the otherwise empty carriage.

The train started to make noises that suggested we were about to be derailed at any moment – as though the tracks were loose or designed for a completely different vehicle. A couple of hours into the journey, it became unbearable. The grinding of metal on metal deafened me. I had to cover my ears. The train screeched to a halt, taking thirty seconds of braking to completely stop. At first, I thought we were at a stop which accounted for changes from another line, but the engine had been turned off and everything was still. We didn't move for twenty minutes. I looked to see if anyone had left the train, but there was nobody, so I checked the other carriages. I was the only passenger.

The station was made up of one small sandstone bungalow. The place was called Obzir, as far as I could make out. The sign on the building had faded with dust. I checked the breakdown of all the stops on my route, and Obzir was only four stops out of Dubrovnik. The train should have been three or four stations further along its route. I grabbed my bag and walked off the train, across the tracks onto the platform – a four metre terrace at the front of the deserted building. There was nobody around. No car park. Not even a distinguishable road coming into the station. I walked to the front of the train to see the driver, but there was nobody on the train at all.

I kicked the metal carriage. I was stranded in the middle of nowhere, with nobody around to help. I kicked the train again and again, and threw rocks that I found between the train tracks at its metal body. Then I heard a man shouting. I turned towards the bungalow and a fat man was running towards me wearing a red and gold conductor's hat and carrying a signalling paddle. I stopped kicking the train, but the man was still running towards me, shouting in Croatian and blowing hard on the whistle hanging around his neck.

"I'm sorry," I said, holding my hands in the air.

He shouted and made elaborate gestures with his arms and hands. It must have rained before I arrived, because his white shirt was soaked. I could see the outline of his nipples.

"Do you speak English?" I asked.

He turned and pointed along the tracks towards Dubrovnik and then pointed in the direction the train was meant to be going – to Split.

I pointed at the train and said, "To Split?"

The man looked at me, his stomach swelling with each panting breath. The shirt buttons around his belly button strained as his lungs filled with air, and it looked like they might pop open. He pulled a handkerchief out from his black trouser pocket and dabbed his forehead. "No train today," he said.

"When is the next train?"

"Tomorrow."

"What time?" I asked.

He rolled his eyes and said, "Come."

I followed him into the bungalow. It consisted of two rooms. A small office with a desk, two chairs and a bathroom. The man led me into his office and instructed me to sit. I wondered if he was going to call the police because I had been throwing rocks at the train. But he didn't pick up the phone. That's how I knew I was stuck there for the night, at least. He wasn't calling anybody.

We didn't speak for ten minutes. Probably because I couldn't speak Croatian and he didn't speak much English or wasn't prepared to. Then the man got up and unbuttoned his white shirt, peeling it away from his arms and back. He had a very thin white vest on underneath. I got up and went to walk out to let him change in private, but he quickly jumped up from his seat and blocked the door with his sweaty arm.

"Sit," he said.

I did as he said. He slipped his vest up and off over his head. He took both the shirt and vest over to an electric heater in the corner of the room and hooked them on the grate, before switching it on to its highest setting. Then he took off his shoes and trousers and put his feet up on the desk.

"I'm Radimir," he said, handing me an open packet of cigarettes. I took one but realised I didn't want it when he offered me the lighter so tucked it behind my ear instead. "You wait here tonight. Tomorrow you go."

"I need to get to Split tonight," I said.

Radimir shook his head. "No trains." His hands rested on the top of his belly while he spoke.

"But I have to go." The warmth from the heater helped to distract from the fact that I was the hostage of a topless Croatian train conductor.

Radimir said, "No trains."

After a minute, he pulled a clear glass bottle and two glasses out from his desk. The bottle was unmarked – no label, nothing. He poured out the liquor and handed me a glass. I waited for him to drink some before I dared to touch it.

"Schnapps," Radimir said.

I finished the glass and Radimir started laughing. It burned all the way down my throat and settled in a fireball in my stomach. I chased it with a beer from my rucksack and Radimir poured me another glass. I took my time with the second drink, and after I'd finished the third glass I was hammered. We didn't talk much. There was no way we could. Instead we played draughts across Radimir's desk and carried on drinking. There were hundreds of ants crawling across the floor and up onto the table. Every few seconds Radimir would crush one with his thumb and then he would wipe the gunk on his y-fronts.

After a couple of hours I went for a walk outside. The train was still waiting on the tracks. I got on-board and ran through the carriages. The schnapps had given me a feeling I'd never experienced before. I'd been drunk a few times – at the Frog and the Two Pigs, and when me and Tommy used to drink cider in his garden shed. But this feeling was something else completely. I wanted to run and run and smash into things with my whole body. I charged up and down the train, swinging from the rails attached to the ceiling, kicking the plastic seating and windows and jumping on the tables.

Then I got off the train and ran along the tracks, towards Split. The whole landscape was empty except for a bunch of spindly plants. It felt as though I could run and run until I reached Split, the docks and the harbour and the ocean. I didn't need any money or clothes or a place to sleep. I wanted to run until the stones wore away the soles of my shoes, until my lungs popped and deflated like old balloons. My feet were beating the hard ground, sometimes crunching in the spots of gravel along the tracks. There were some large rocks and boulders I had to hurdle along the way, but that only made me run faster.

It felt like I'd been running for hours when I eventually stopped, but it can't have been much longer than fifteen minutes. It's tough to say. I collapsed and lay out flat. I stayed there, waiting for darkness to come and swallow me up and then spit me out into the new day. I ripped up handfuls of the long grass that surrounded me. The dark set in and I watched the stars appear through the black sheet of sky. They moved as I watched them. They pinballed around in the blackness. I watched the stars until my eyes watered from keeping them open for too long. I didn't move for a long time.

It took a few hours to start to sober, and when I finally felt sure the feeling was passing I walked back along the tracks in the darkness. In the bungalow, Radimir was sitting in the same place, smoking a cigarette and sipping his glass of schnapps. When he saw me, he started laughing. He laughed and slammed on the desk with his fists. One of the glasses fell off and smashed across the floor. I picked up my bag and ran with it outside and onto the empty train. His howls travelled out to where I was – so loud still that I felt as though he was only a step behind me. The wind on my back became his smoky breath lingering on my cheek, and the thought of him being nearby kept me awake for a long time. Sitting on the train, I stared at the station building – only allowing myself to blink when I couldn't stare any longer. Hours must have passed. In the middle of the night I walked to the end carriage – the one furthest away from the station building – but Radimir's laughing was just as loud.

I climbed into the overhead storage rack where I hid until morning.

I woke up when a man threw his rucksack on my face. I was still up in the overhead storage rack, and I guess he hadn't realised I was there. At first, I thought it was Radimir, and I curled up into a ball and prayed it wasn't. After a few moments, I opened my eyes and saw that the carriage was full.

I jumped down from the overhead storage rack and took a seat by the windows. An elderly lady with weathered, crinkly skin said something in Croatian and wagged her finger at me with disapproval. My head was thumping – it felt like my temples were swollen and my eyes were hyper-sensitive to the light. I drank as much water as I could and tried to get some bread down, but that only made me feel sick. Once the train started moving, I had to run to the toilet and throw up. My puke was a weird grey colour, but I felt a lot better afterwards.

The train only went as far as the city of Mostar, where everyone had to get off. We were shepherded onto three coaches without an explanation, but I guessed it would form the last leg of our journey. I'd already decided the previous night that I wouldn't take another train. I didn't want to end up with another Radimir.

After two hours on the coach, I arrived in Split. I stank, and I needed to wash a few of my clothes, so I decided to stay at a hostel. I still had five days to get to Bled, so I wasn't too worried about stopping for a night. I checked into the Adriatic Star, a hostel on the waterfront, by the Diocletian's Palace – an ancient building filled with market traders selling jewels and art and crockery and replica football shirts.

The hostel manager, Valentina, showed me the room, and I realised why the place was so cheap. The bed sheets were marked with bright orange stains, and the floor was covered in black dirt. I was glad I had a room to myself, though. I was daunted by sharing a room with total strangers.

Valentina was paranoid about me trashing the place, despite its already filthy condition, so she insisted on photocopying my passport five or six times, as well as outlining the long list of costs for damages. I was tempted to leave before I'd finished checking in. I wanted somewhere I could relax and feel comfortable. But it worked out at £8 per night – the cheapest in the city – so I decided it would be best to stay. I took a shower as soon as I got into the room and washed my t-shirts and boxers in the sink before hanging them up to dry out the window. The shower was covered in rust and only spat out cold, murky water, but it felt amazing. Once I'd dried myself off and dressed, I went to explore the hostel.

There was a large communal room and two guys were sitting in there on beanbags drinking beer. It was only lunchtime, but at the time I wasn't bothered by it. I was still hungover from Radimir's homemade schnapps, but I remembered the Russian dolls always used to swear by the hair of the dog, which I had to Google to learn meant continuing drinking. I thought I might as well join them for a drink if it'd make me feel a little better.

I went back into the town and bought a six-pack of Pivo, which I figured meant beer of some description. I carried it back to the hostel without a bag and went up to the communal room. The two guys were still in there. One of them had bought a 24-pack of beers and a bottle of whiskey, but the other didn't seem to have any. I put my drinks down on the table and introduced myself.

"I'm Billy," I said, shaking both of their hands. "Can I join you?"

"Of course, of course!" The guy with no beers said. "Any man with beer is welcome in this circle." He was French and spoke with his hands more than his mouth, in large, arcing motions.

"Careful of Louis," the other guy said. "He'll drink all your beers and make you feel like he's your best friend in the world. Beer is his only friend."

"And whiskey." Louis picked up the whiskey and poured himself a half glass.

I couldn't place the accent of the other guy, so I asked him where he was from and he told me he was local, and that he had lived in Split all his life. His name was Marko.

I had two beers and listened to Louis talk about his great European voyage.

Philip Bowne

"But this is only the beginning," he said. "Soon I will be in Africa. The Congo! I will hitchhike to the heart of darkness. Right along the river Congo."

"Impossible," Marko said.

"How will you hitchhike through a jungle?" I asked.

"Boats. I'll hitch to the centre of the Earth. You watch!"

"You're a fake," Marko said, shaking his head.

"I'm only staying in hostels because I can afford a luxury. There will be no luxury on the Congo, not even a bed to rest my head!"

"He claims to come from Paris without paying a cent," Marko said.

"It's true!"

"All with that bullshit letter," Marko said.

"What letter?" I asked.

"A letter from my late father." Louis pulled a letter from his inside jacket pocket and flicked it with his index finger. "He told me if I am ever to open it, what is inside will ruin my life."

"Bullshit." Marko laughed and gulped down half a can of beer.

"How could it?" I said.

"Don't get him started," Marko said. "He's full of shit. I'm only giving him beer for his company. What are you doing in Split?"

I told them about Eva, and how I needed to get to Bled in a few days to save our relationship.

"Now what?" Louis asked. "You give up?"

"I'm stopping here for a night, then I'll hitchhike up to Zagreb or Ljubljana. I'll get there somehow."

"You're crazy," Marko said.

"Bravo!" Louis said. "Maybe I can help. I could drive you to Zagreb."

"Really?" I said.

"Sure, I will have a car tomorrow."

"Don't listen to him," Marko said. "He's full of shit."

"You will see," Louis said.

"How do you have a car?" I asked.

"It doesn't matter how. It only matters that you get to Slovenia. No?" Louis shuffled his narrow hips back into the bean bag.

"I guess so," I said.

"You don't need to pay me. Just a few beers and we can call it even. I'll drive you up to Zagreb tomorrow afternoon. By 4pm tomorrow I will have the car."

I didn't know what to make of them, especially Louis. We carried on drinking and listening to Louis talk for a couple more hours, before he led us to his room. Inside, he chopped up three onions and crushed a clove of garlic, and then placed a frying pan on an electronic hotplate and started frying them in olive oil.

"I picked these from a field just north of Salzburg," Louis said. "I have a whole bag of onions and garlic. We just need some meat and voila."

"You want us to buy you meat?" Marko said.

"Don't be crazy! I know somewhere you can have all the meat you want for absolutely nothing." Louis lifted the pan off the hotplate and started eating the onions and garlic with a fork. "I can show you tonight. It's beyond all of your dreams. As much meat as you can fit in your belly. You won't believe me!"

"Let's go," I said.

"No, no," said Louis. "Tonight I show you. Until then, we drink!"

We carried on drinking right through the day. At first I struggled to get the beer down, but after three or four cans, my hangover started to ease and I started to feel drunk again. After a few hours we had finished all of mine and Marko's beers, and the whiskey only had a drop left at the bottom. Louis lay on the floor with his eyes closed, arms and legs spread as far from his body as he could stretch them, garbling on about his great Congolese adventure.

"It will be magnifique!" Louis said. The drunker he got, the more his English slipped into French. "The deepest river in the world!"

"More space for you to drown like an idiot," Marko said.

"When you travel the real way, Marko, you will know the importance of such things. When you learn to live with nothing, just the shirt on your back, and when you depend on the fruits of your own hands and feet—"

"And an electronic hotplate."

"That comes with the room!"

"I don't have one," I said.

"It's not my hotplate!" Louis said, sitting up and slapping himself across the face. His cheek was marked with the red outline of his fingers.

"Forget it. Can we go to this food place?" I said.

"Yeah," said Marko, unscrewing the whisky and pouring the last drops onto his pink tongue.

"Not tonight," Louis said, lowering his back down onto the floor. "You bastards can be hungry tonight. Tomorrow, maybe."

Marko and I left Louis sleeping on the floor and went out to find some food. It was nearing 11pm, and the seafront was lined with lit-up rows of bars and restaurants. I looked out to the water, trying to see as far as I could. I used to do that as a kid, when my parents would take me down to Bournemouth. I'd always try to see beyond the horizon. I'd stare at it for ages, willing my eyes to see further. I stared out at the sea that night in Split, but everything was black.

Marko said he knew where we could get a boat. We picked up a six-pack of beers each, a loaf of bread, a pot of raspberry jam and a knife, and I followed Marko to a shop along one of the side streets leading away from the water.

"You must be quiet," Marko said as we approached a white building. He told me to wait at the front. I could hear men shouting at a bar nearby, and a couple of minutes later a crowd of men came out and started fighting. I hid myself down a side street and waited for them to leave. I was waiting for fifteen minutes before Marko came back, dragging an inflatable raft behind him. The gravel was scratching on the underside of the raft and making enough noise to wake up the entire city, so I ran around to lift the trailing end off the floor before he got us arrested for stealing.

"Are you crazy?" I said. "We can't steal this thing."

Marko carried on moving, so I chucked the bag full of beers, bread and jam into the raft and we jogged on our tiptoes back down to the shore. Marko was out in front, carrying the raft with his hands behind him, and I was holding it from the back.

"Relax. It's not stealing. I own this shop."

"You own the raft?"

"Of course."

"So why did you tell me to be quiet?"

"If my wife she wakes up, she will come here and make me go back in there."

"And what's the problem with that?"

"I will tell you later."

We got to the shore and placed the raft in the water, then jumped in. I was sitting near the front on the inflatable rib. Marko threw me an oar and I started paddling. Marko sat at the back, steering us with his paddle.

We zig-zagged between the lines of floating buoys that stretched out towards the milky moonlight. Occasionally, the paddle smacked one of the buoys and I was convinced I'd hit a person, or a fish. Marko laughed at me. He was supposed to be steering, but was nearly asleep at the back of the raft.

It only took us fifteen minutes of gentle paddling before we stopped. Then Marko took off his shoes and socks and dropped his feet in the water despite the chilly air. He was onto his third beer when I opened one. We let the raft float out onto the open water.

"Why are you living at the hostel?" I asked him. "Have you divorced your wife?"

"No, it's much worse than that."

"She divorced you?"

"No," he said, and gulped down the last of his can. "I'm a rafting instructor. As you probably guessed by now."

"So what?"

"Let me explain. I go out on the same route every day with groups of tourists. Every day is exactly the same. I know the river like I know my own ball sack." He opened a fresh beer and pulled out a packet of cigarettes from his jacket pocket, lit one, and offered me the packet. I didn't take one.

"Doesn't sound so bad to me."

"You haven't heard it yet. I took a group out three weeks ago, doing the same things as I've done for fifteen years. It was fine. It's not a demanding river. Even at this time of year. The rainfall is higher in October, but still the water is only white in a few small places. But at the end of the rafting, there is a rock that I always let my groups jump from. Every rafting and canoeing instructor uses this rock to let their groups jump into the water. It's fun. The rock is probably twenty feet above the water." Marko sucked on his cigarette and flicked his ash into one of the empty beer cans.

He continued, "So the rock can be very busy. And three days ago there were probably 40 people waiting to jump from this rock. So we waited and watched everyone jump, and clapped when they came back up to the surface. Everything was fine. All the other groups jumped in and there were no problems. My group was last to go. I had ten Dutch people, and in they went. Plop, plop, plop. One by one they all dropped in absolutely fine." Marko started biting his thumbnail.

"But the last girl. This sweet girl, barely 19 years old. She is last to jump. There are still 40 people waiting to see the last person drop down into the water. But she is terrified of height, and I am standing behind her as she is looking down and telling her to do it. I'm laughing. I've seen a million people do this jump. Every day of my life for years and years I have seen it. So I said, 'Do it! Don't make me push you!', but I didn't expect her to really do it. Not if she didn't want to. But she must have been so embarrassed not to do it, that she turned around and jumped right off."

"And then what?"

Marko leaned out of the raft and slapped the water. It made a harsh clapping sound. The raft floated into the channel of light that radiated from the city and illuminated the black water. Marko's eyes glowed white. The dark and heavy bags beneath his eyes looked swollen, and for the first time I noticed the receding patches in his blond hair above his temples.

"At first, we all cheered. It was funny. I walked up to the edge of the rock and saw the water moving away in circles from the tiny splash she made in it. I didn't think anything of it. But then her head burst up through the surface, and she was screaming. I can hear her screaming now. It stays with me. I made her do it."

The raft had drifted towards the shore, so I grabbed the paddle and started paddling back into the open water.

"What happened to her?"

"She broke her back. I got her to hospital but she couldn't move. She can't feel her legs. She can't walk."

We drank the last of our beers and ripped up chunks of bread, some to eat, some to throw out of the raft and into the water for the birds. The boat floated out away from the lights, and Marko's face disappeared beneath the starless sky.

I woke up to the sound of Valentina yelling at Louis for pissing in the hostel reception. His room was six or seven down from mine, but the walls in the place were so thin I could hear every word. I'd left the curtains and the window open the night before and passed out on top of the duvet, and as I lay there listening to the argument, the cold early morning breeze pushed the white netted curtains into the room and up towards the ceiling.

Valentina was screaming at Louis, demanding that he pay for the cleaning cost.

"I no speak Anglais!" Louis yelled back at her. She would have known he was lying to her. He must have spoken in English when he checked in.

"You filthy French bastard," she said. "You piss over my hostel, you pay for it!"

"Madame, I no understand!"

The argument went on like that for a while. I rolled out of bed and stuck my head out of the window. The sun was high up, gently warming my face.

"You pay, or you leave!" she continued.

"I no speak Anglais, Madame!"

After that a door slammed and a few minutes later Louis was tapping at my door. I let him in and he dived into my bed. He was wearing only a pair of white Y-front underpants.

"What did you do?" I asked him.

"Sleepwalking," he said. "I pissed all over the reception. I don't remember it. She caught me trying to do a shit on the doormat. She woke me up as I was about to go."

"You gonna pay her?"

"I cannot."

"How much does she want?"

"800 kuna. For a piss! Can you believe it?"

"So you have to leave?"

"I will not."

"She's gonna kick you out."

"I don't think so."

"But we're leaving this afternoon anyway, right?"

Louis pulled a cigarette out of his underpants and lit it.

"Stop!" I said. "You can't smoke in here." I jumped up and went over to him to put it out, but he sprang out of bed before I could reach him.

"If I get fined, you get fined with me." Louis giggled and held the cigarette up above his head and waved it close to the smoke alarm on the ceiling.

"You're a wanker," I said, and went for him. I took a swing for his nose with my right hand but missed. Thinking about it, I didn't even want to hit him. I'd never hit anyone in the face before, and the idea of it freaked me out. If Tommy was there, he would have broken all the bones in Louis's face. The smoke alarm started going off.

Within twenty seconds, Valentina was pounding her fist on the door.

"Get out!" she screamed. "Open the door!"

I was standing on the bed, trying to turn off the smoke alarm by pressing the button on the plastic box. It wasn't working. I started hitting it then, trying to smash it clean away from the ceiling like my Dad had done. But I caught my knuckle on it and it ripped the skin away, so I didn't want to hit it again. I also realised that I would probably need a strimmer in order to finally put an end to it. Louis was sitting on the floor smoking, laughing at the whole situation. I climbed down from the bed and opened the door to Valentina.

"Pay now or get out!" she yelled. "Now!"

"I'm sorry. It wasn't me. How much will it cost?"

"1000 Kuna."

"For smoking?" I said.

"Now!" Valentina said. Louis was still sitting propped up against the wall, smoking his cigarette. A fleck of hot ash dropped from the cherry onto his bare chest, and he slapped it away.

"Don't worry, Valentina. I will pay you shortly." Louis took a long drag on his cigarette, and she walked away, cursing us loudly in Croatian as she went.

That morning I went out to have a look around the city. I walked around the market and looked at various wines and oils and other souvenirs they sold. I didn't buy anything, though. My budget wasn't looking great after staying at the hostel and buying food and drink. I barely had any Croatian Kuna left, and only €60.

I went back to the hostel after walking around the city. I wanted to see Marko. He let me into his room after I banged on the door for a minute. I must have woken him up, because as soon as he opened the door he turned around and fell back into bed. Dark black and blue circles marked outlines around his eyes, and the whites were bloodshot. His legs and back were covered in purple blotches where the skin was bruised. The room smelled of whisky and sweat. First thing I did was open the window.

I said, "Let's go into town," and left Marko to get dressed. Louis was sitting in the communal room, expressionless, plotting a route along the River Congo. He didn't have any eyebrows. I didn't bother to ask what had happened, mainly because I didn't want him to come with us. I was already dreading the journey to Zagreb with him, but it was too good an opportunity to turn down. Instead, I waited a few minutes for Marko and we went to sit on a bench by the harbour, eating bread and jam bought from a supermarket in town.

"Tonight is my last night here," Marko said. "I can't afford to stay any longer. I have to go home to my wife."

"You never told me why that's a problem."

"I haven't told her about the girl." Marko placed his knife and fork on the table and started crying softly into his hands. "She will hate me."

"She won't," I said. "She'll be happy to have you home."

"I went to the rock last night," he said. "To the same rock she jumped from. I jumped in, hoping I could break my own back, but I couldn't. I must have jumped in thirty times and climbed out again. I couldn't do it."

"It was an accident."

Marko pushed his knife and fork onto his plate. He hadn't eaten anything.

"When I was a climbing instructor, I had a big fall. I thought I was going to die. I fell through a crevice that was over fifty metres deep. The rope saved my life, but it got caught in my mouth and ripped all my teeth out." Marko smiled and I realised that all of the teeth at the front of his mouth were perfectly square. "I didn't deserve to live that day."

"Don't be stupid. That's crazy talk."

Marko didn't say anything for a few minutes. He sipped his coffee and then said, "What about you and the girl? Crazy talk."

I laughed. Marko gave me a hug before he left and said I would see him again someday. I spent the next couple of hours drifting in and out of sleep by the water, waiting for 4pm to come around and to get travelling north. I tried to get myself up and moving, but I didn't have the energy. My eyes wanted to close and stay shut.

Despite the fact it was only fifteen degrees, my face caught the sun while I was asleep. I splashed sea water over my forehead and had lots of water to drink, but the skin was still sore and felt like it was stretched tight across my bones, like the skin on a bongo drum.

Louis was drinking when I got back at around 3pm. He was sitting in the communal room with his unopened letter on his lap. Apparently he'd grabbed a load of beers from the back of a delivery truck while the driver was smoking a cigarette.

"Why are you drinking?" I asked. "You said we're leaving at 4pm."

"Yes, yes, I know. The car won't be ready until 6pm. It's not a problem. We can have a couple of beers, and then go. It won't be long."

By 4pm, Louis was drunk. By 6, he was hammered, and the car had been delayed until 10pm.

"It'll be here later!" he insisted. "We can eat and become sober, and then take the trip up through the night. I could go up to Ljubljana, for your trouble."

I kept waiting and waiting, and by the time 10pm came around, Louis told me that the car wouldn't be ready until the following morning. I knew I had been stupid to trust him. I wanted to kill him, for making me wait on the empty promise of a free ride north. But I kept quiet. I decided to forget it all and leave first thing in the morning – it was pointless to argue about it and I didn't want to get on the wrong side of a madman.

Louis decided it was time to show me where he could get meat for free. I'd spent too much money, so figured I'd may as well join in whatever his scheme was to get some free food.

We left the hostel around midnight and Louis led the way. We walked twenty minutes uphill, outside of town through hayfields. There were no streetlights. Louis had a pocket-sized torch, but everything was black. We weren't talking, either. Louis said we had to be silent once we got on the path out of town. I still had no idea where he was taking me.

Ten minutes along the dusty track, Louis jumped a fence into a farmer's field. I followed. The distant lights of a farmhouse glowed in the night, and the chirping of a thousand crickets filled the empty landscape like a song of the stars. Louis and I were still silent.

We walked into the field some way, the stars growing brighter with each step.

Louis said, "Here it is," and before I had the chance to ask him what, he had grabbed an animal in a headlock and pulled a kitchen knife out from his trouser pocket. The blade flashed in the starlight and was followed by a screech. I covered my eyes and turned my back. The animal collapsed to the ground and Louis giggled. "Get here," he said. "You gotta help me carry it."

"What?"

"Back to town. We have to carry it back and I'll gut it. Then the steaks are on me!"

"We can't do that, Louis."

"You want goat burger instead?"

"It's a goat? What did you kill a goat for?"

"A man's got to eat."

"I'm not doing that."

"You have no choice."

"I told you, Louis. I'm not carrying that thing anywhere."

"Listen, Billy. If you don't help me take the animal back, then I'll run to the farmhouse and tell the farmer what you did. Then BANG. You're dead. So what do you say?"

I helped him pick up the goat and we took turns carrying it over our shoulders along the dirt track, back to the lake. The blood trickled down my neck and the animal was starting to stink. Its hair brushed against the hairs on my neck and made me feel sick. It weighed about the same as a young boy. As I carried it, I thought of Christoph and how he cared for his animals. I'd only come along because I thought his scheme would have been funny. I hated myself that night. Louis whistled all the way back to the waterfront and spoke about how we would eat like kings for the next few days.

I still don't know if he was broke like he made out. Marko never seemed to think so. I never considered that he might be penniless until I saw how delighted he was that night. I don't think any man could be happy with killing something unless he absolutely needed to.

It took us nearly an hour to walk back to the seafront with the goat. Once we got down to a secluded spot, I jumped straight into the freezing cold water. I was that desperate to wash the blood and sweat off my skin.

Louis pulled out the kitchen knife and slit the goat along the underside of its body, right down to its arsehole, and a pile of blood and guts spilled out. The stink of it followed, and I thought I might be sick in the water.

"Do you do this kind of thing a lot?" I asked him.

"My father was a butcher."

"I mean, do you kill other people's animals? Is that how you're getting by?"

"I've done many things to stay alive."

"How do I know you're not just some rich pretender?"

"Do rich kids do this kind of thing?"

"Probably."

"Pah!" Louis scooped up the internal organs that he had removed and dropped them into the sea. "I never liked the insides."

Then he made me hold the back legs and we dipped the carcass into the water in order to clean it out. It took Louis another half an hour of butchering before he had all the meat off the animal that he could cook in a frying pan on his hotplate. It wasn't much, especially for the size of the animal. He rolled it up in the lower half of his shirt, and we walked back to the hostel.

Back at the hostel Louis washed the meat again in his bathroom sink while I chopped his onion and garlic. He fried it all up in lots of olive oil. As he cooked, the hotplate was resting on the window ledge with the window open as wide as it would go. There was no way he would take the risk of giving Valentina the chance to smell something cooking. He claimed that he had successfully avoided her to the point where she had given up on chasing him up for the money. I didn't believe him.

I grabbed a bottle of whisky Louis had in his room and stayed with him while he ate. I didn't go near any of the food. It made me gag watching him eat, so I turned my back on him and drank while he finished it.

"I'm transcending," he said, clasping his hands behind his head and stretching back in his chair once he was done.

"That good?"

"You should have tried it."

"I'm OK with a drink."

"Give me some of that," he said.

I passed him the bottle and we took turns to drink from it. Louis had red cheeks and a pinkish smile stretched across his flat face – he had something other than beer and whisky in his stomach for a change. It was good to see him contented. I didn't like him, though. In fact, if it weren't for the circumstances, I wouldn't have spent any time with him at all. I'm sure he felt the same about me.

Still, we kept drinking until the bottle was gone and Louis was naked and lying on the floor talking about life in Paris and his trip to the Congo. I chucked a towel over his middle so I didn't have to look at his dick and then lay down on the bed so I didn't have to look at him at all.

After telling me all about when he used to joyride cars in Lille with his uncle, he started talking about the letter he'd never opened.

"My mother, she gave it to me on her deathbed. She said if I open it, it will ruin my life."

"You said your father wrote you the letter," I said. "You're full of shit."

"No, no, no. My mother. It was my mother. She wrote it to my father on her deathbed, and my father gave it to me on his deathbed. See? And I have never touched it. But I carry it everywhere with me." He got to his feet and grabbed the letter from his wardrobe. "What do you think it could be?"

"I don't know. Maybe it's a cheque for a million euros."

"They didn't have a euro between them."

"Will you ever open it?" I asked.

Louis was sitting on the edge of the bed and running his finger over the flap of the envelope, flicking the end up slowly, so as not to peel it away from the paper. I could tell he wanted to open it. It was killing him. That's when I knew he wasn't lying about it – when I saw the tears trickle down the high bones on his hairless cheeks, and he threw the envelope at the wall and slid off the bed and into a ball on the floor, sobbing into his knees. I didn't move to comfort him – partly because I was so drunk myself, and also because he was naked and it would have felt weird for me to touch him.

He cried for a few minutes and then stopped, got up and started hitting the walls with his fists and head, running around the room like he'd been trapped inside it for fifty years and was dying to break out. His dick was swinging from side to side like a miniature pendulum on a grandfather clock. I didn't want to look at it but there was nowhere else to look. His balls were curled up into a tight sack like a frozen brain. He hit things until his knuckles bled, and finally walked up to the open door of the wardrobe and kicked it clean off its hinges. It all happened in less than a minute.

After the wardrobe door hit the ground, Louis ran into the toilet and started throwing up. I was still crashed out on the bed, watching and listening to everything that was going on, but not doing anything. Louis remained in the toilet, throwing up every few minutes, for an hour at least. I was still awake once he fell asleep on the bathroom floor, so I got up to have a look at him. Chunks of sick blotted his cheek, and a large patch of yellow vomit had missed the toilet and marked a patch on the floor by the shower. It was peppered with flecks of onion and balls of chewed-up goat. I don't know whether he'd just got drunk or whether he'd given himself food poisoning. I threw a towel over him and returned to the bedroom. The envelope was on the floor, so I grabbed it and took it back to my room, leaving the door propped open so I could return it when I was done.

I didn't open it right away. It didn't feel right, and at first I wasn't totally sure what I was going to do with it. I thought about burning it. It was ruining Louis's life – torturing him every day. I was sitting in my room for a long while, staring at the white envelope, trying to get a feel for what was inside and trying to decide what was the right thing to do.

I wanted to get Louis back, for messing me around. I'd accepted that Louis was full of shit and wasn't going to get me a free ride anywhere. I knew I'd been naïve. I walked down into the hostel kitchen and crept in. It was empty, and I found the stash of cutlery and borrowed a butter knife. I slid the butter knife beneath the flap of the envelope and slowly prised it open.

It took me several minutes. I still didn't know what I was going to do with the letter once I'd read it, so I wanted to open the envelope carefully in case I needed to put the letter back inside. My hands were shaking. The adhesive crackled as I worked the knife across the flap, and when I moved the blade too fast it made small rips in the paper. When it was finally done, I pulled the piece of paper from the envelope.

I look back now and think what I did was wrong. It was Louis's letter and its message was none of my business. But at the time I was too angry and curious to stop. I'd assumed it would be written in French, but I'd planned to try to understand it using Google Translate. But when I opened the envelope and pulled the letter out, slowly unfolding it with my fingertips, I saw that the paper was completely blank.

I never saw Louis again. I checked out of the hostel at 8am the next morning.

Since I didn't trust the trains to get me to Zagreb, and I didn't want to spend another night stranded with a character like Radimir, I went to the outskirts of the city and waited at a petrol station to see if I could catch a ride. At the hostel I found a piece of cardboard and a felt tip pen and wrote 'ZAGREB' on it in big letters. I figured it would help me to get a ride from the right people.

A trucker offered me a ride but I couldn't understand him properly and he wasn't going to Zagreb, so I decided to hold out. After my luck with Klara, I figured it was only a matter of time before somebody going the right way would pick me up.

This was not the case. After waiting for two hours on the highway I started to lose hope. I was standing at a junction that left the city. Barely any cars passed there, and when they did, it didn't seem like anyone was even considering stopping. Many drivers made the circular signal with their index finger. One guy stuck his middle finger up at me as he sped off with his sunglasses on.

After another hour, I walked back into the outskirts of the city and found a café. There were men eating sandwiches stuffed with meat and chips sitting up at the bar, drinking beers and chatting beneath the ceiling fans. I spotted an empty table with two plates of half-eaten food that had been left behind. I didn't want to buy anything, but I was hungry, so I grabbed the leftover hamburger from one plate and a handful of chips from the other and dipped back out. I ran a couple hundred metres away from the café, just to make sure nobody followed me for stealing their lunch while they were having a piss or something. Then I found a bench and went to sit down and eat the food. It was greasy and salty and the tomato ketchup tasted a lot like vinegar, but it was satisfying – my stomach felt full and I was ready to go and try to get another ride.

Time wasn't on my side. On that morning, I only had three days before I was due to meet Eva – and still 285 miles to cover. The journey to Zagreb would make up most of those miles – 220 in total.

I threw rocks at the road sign while I waited. I was about to start hiking north, along the main highway, when a beat-up Subaru skidded off the road and the driver put his window down. I was nervous. Whoever was driving the Subaru was driving very fast, which, I figured, probably meant they were dangerous. I worried that they might kidnap me and keep me as a hostage. Dad would be reluctant to pay the ransom, especially after the news that Benny was getting his inheritance.

But I knew that the Subaru was probably going to be my best shot at getting to Zagreb, so I walked up to the car slowly. Without thinking, I quickly kissed the cross on the necklace Christoph had given me. I guess I hoped it might bring me good luck.

I told the driver I was trying to get to Zagreb.

"We can't take you all the way to Zagreb," the driver said. He had a deep voice. "But we are going to Karlovac. We can take you there. It's one hour from Zagreb." He had dark eyebrows and a shaved head. A young woman was in the passenger seat, and there was a baby boy strapped into a car seat in the back. I briefly wondered if he was a hostage, but by then I knew I was overthinking it.

"Great," I said, picking up my bag. "Thanks."

The man had his hand out of the window and tapped on the car door.

"Let's go!" he said.

I climbed in the back. The man introduced himself as Jakov. He spoke to the woman in Croatian for a couple of minutes and then she asked me a bunch of questions about my journey, and where I'd come from.

"My wife wants to practice her English, so she will not stop talking," Jakov said.

Her English wasn't great, but I was happy to talk to her. They'd saved me from a long trek, and my chances of getting to Eva in time were vastly improved. We moved out of Split and through the barren Croatian landscape. It was the closest thing to a desert I'd ever seen, even though winter was approaching. The Subaru roared along the arrow-straight roads. I imagined the road carved into the rock by the Romans – ancient men digging out the sandstone and stacking it along the roadside, moving forward, deadly straight, into the hills. The landscape was marked with patches of green – hedges and brush zipped past my window before I could see what it was.

The woman – I never learned her name – started telling me stories. Jakov listened and I caught him smiling in the rear view. They seemed like an OK couple. The baby kept quiet most of the way – he had a dummy in his mouth and was sleeping or playing with his rattling toys.

"Do you live in Karlovac?" I asked them.

"Not exactly," the woman said. "We don't live in anywhere."

"We live in the car," Jakov said, and laughed. "We travel around Croatia from city to city."

"Doing what?"

"Playing cards."

"How?" I asked.

"I go to the bars where the students drink, start a game of blackjack or poker, let them win some money, gain some confidence. Then they start to bet bigger and bigger, and then I win all of their money. Then we go to the next place."

"Why students?"

"They are stupid enough to play cards with me."

The woman wasn't talking. She couldn't keep up with the conversation.

"Do you enjoy it?"

"It's the only way I can earn enough money to get us out of this country. We want to move to Germany."

"Do you think you'll leave soon?" I asked.

"I hope, yes. There is no work for me here."

"Don't play him for cards," the woman said. We all laughed.

Jakov floored it all the way up the highway towards Zadar, then followed the road inland. I peeped over his shoulder to see how fast we were going. The speedometer was tickling the

165kmph mark, and Jakov was steering with one hand, smoking a cigarette out of the window. I clenched my fists and thought about how much ground I was covering, thinking how lucky I was to be going this fast – trying not to have a panic attack. I kept telling myself it was a good thing.

Somehow, the baby slept through the speed. I tried to close my eyes and drift off, too, focusing on the kaleidoscopic dance of light behind my closed eyelids.

When we got to Karlovac in the late afternoon, I thanked Jakov. We shook hands, and his girlfriend hugged me. I went to get food and water at a supermarket in the centre of town. I bought a sandwich and a bag of paprika-flavoured crisps. I was lucky that Croatia is a comparatively cheap country to eat and drink. I only had enough Croatian money to buy a little more food and water in Zagreb, as I didn't want to change any of my Euros into Croatian Kuna.

I went to sit on a bench in town and ate my food quickly. It was only 5pm, and I felt like I could get a ride to Zagreb in the early evening. Jakov said it was only an hour's ride in the car.

An old lady started walking towards me as I was sitting on that bench. She must have been eighty years old, possibly older. Her back was crooked, and she had a pink scarf wrapped over and around her head. Her walking stick clicked on the ground as she made baby steps towards me. She was smiling, but her front teeth were missing. When she got to me she held out her hand. Her fist was closed, and as she reached me, she nodded for me to take whatever she was presenting. Naturally, I put my hand out. She dropped a single plum into my hand. It was shrivelled and soft.

"200 Kuna," she said, outstretching an empty palm. "200 Kuna."

"No, I don't want it," I said. "I don't have any money." I laughed at the fact she expected me to pay almost £20 for a single plum. I wasn't worried at first, I simply tried to hand the plum back to her, but she wouldn't take it.

"200 Kuna," she insisted, looking around at people passing by, and raising her arms in the air. People were looking.

"Listen, I don't want this," I kept saying. "I don't want this." That's when I felt a hand on my shoulder. I turned around to see an enormous man – he was 6 foot 7 or 8, and wide. Wider than a doorframe.

"You pay the lady," he said.

For a second I couldn't say anything. I felt my stomach twist and the thump of my pulse beating in my ears.

"Or I call the boss." The huge man pulled a 90s Nokia from his pocket and wiggled it in my face.

Before thinking better of it, I jumped up and ran. The man quickly got after me, I could feel his heavy footprints pounding inside my chest. I ran down a side street filled with workmen smoking in their overalls and old women chatting in small huddles. Water droplets drizzled down from the grey skies. My bag slowed me down, and I thought about ditching it in the panic. But it was too late. As I went to turn the corner, the man caught up with me, yanked me by the arm, grabbed me by the throat and pushed me up against a wall. I couldn't breathe. His hand felt cold on my neck, and flecks of his spit landed on my face as he laughed. His breath smelled of garlic mayonnaise.

He didn't say anything else. I had my eyes closed as tight as I could, screaming that he could take everything I had and praying that I wouldn't die. I heard my nose crack and felt my top lip turn warm as blood spilled out.

After laying there for a while crying and Googling "how to tell if your nose is broken", I heard a voice from above me.

"Hey man," he said. "You OK?"

I locked my phone and stuffed it into my pocket and rolled over to see a blond-haired boy around my age looming down over me. He was fiddling with a fidget spinner, but when he saw the blood smeared across my face, leaking out of my nose and mouth, he tucked it away in his pocket.

"Oh, shit," he said. "What happened?"

I groaned and said something about a plum. I felt dizzy, and I felt like I wasn't ready to have a conversation without crying.

"I'm Cooper," he said. "I'm from Aspen, Colorado. But now I live in Texas."

"I'm Billy," I said, but I could hardly get the words out.

"Wanna get a beer, Billy?"

"I need to get out of here."

"Yeah. We should clean you up." He handed me a napkin for my nose. "I don't think it's broken. Looks like a stinger, though."

"What are you doing in this place?" I asked him, head tilted back, pinching my nose to stem the nosebleed.

"On my way through, thought I'd check it out. I've been out in Europe since September. Driving around."

"Have you got a car?" I asked.

"A rental. She's my baby – a little Mazda."

"Where are you going next?"

"The Museum of Broken Relationships," he said. "Broke up with a girl. That's why I'm here."

"Me too."

"I was just kidding. Sorry, man. I came here to get away from my family. My Dad has gone cuckoo. He's campaigning for Trump down in Texas. It's crazy, man."

I'd seen Trump all over the news. He looked like an angry pug wearing a toupee. He wanted to build a wall to keep the Mexican people out of the US. GG always told me that good fences made bad neighbours, and that Trump was doing it all wrong.

"I guess you guys have it too, right?"

"What do you mean?" I asked.

"You got Brexit. I saw that. I thought that sounded like a breakfast cereal."

When I thought about it, Brexit did sound a bit like a breakfast cereal. I thought back to the night of the referendum and Eva's EU cake and when we finally had sex. I regretted not being able to vote. I convinced myself that if I'd been able to vote, it would've been different, and Britain would've stayed in the EU and Eva would've stayed with me. But I guess it doesn't work like that.

"So, I guess you guys will probably have a wall, too."

"It's not like that," I said. "It's more about being independent and stuff. We're not racists."

"I guess I don't know enough about it."

"I'm not sure anyone really does."

Cooper cupped his hands together and blew onto them to warm up. I thought about my next steps. There wasn't much time.

"Cooper, it's six-thirty. Isn't it a bit late for a museum?"

"Yeah, I'm going there tomorrow. I gotta drive through to Zagreb yet. That's where it is. It sounds so funny, it's full of items that people have sent in from all over the world, items that were significant to their relationship at some point, all with the little stories attached."

"You're going to Zagreb?"

"Sure am."

"Can I come?"

"Don't see why not. You got any money for a beer?"

"Not really."

"Did you get robbed?"

"No, I'm just skint."

"What the hell is 'skint'?"

"I've got no money."

"Come anyway. You could use a beer."

We found a Burger King and I cleaned up in the toilets. Cooper bought some tampons and I shoved one in each of my nostrils. He said it's what you're supposed to do. He bought two cheeseburgers and gave one to me, but I could barely open my mouth because my face was so tender, and when I tried to chew it felt like my teeth were going to fall out.

Neither of us had a clue where we were, so it took over an hour to find Cooper's Mazda. When we eventually did, he picked up sixteen beers from a shop and we got back on the road, headed for Zagreb.

"Where are you gonna sleep tonight?" he asked. "I got a bed booked at a hostel, but I can't sneak you in."

"I'll find somewhere." As I climbed into the low sports car, Cooper grabbed his dog-eared copy of *On the Road* from the dashboard and shoved it in the glovebox.

"You really got no money?" he said, slamming the glovebox shut.

"Not much. I have to save it to get me to this place in Slovenia."

"Oh yeah? What's it called?"

"Bled."

"Never heard of it."

"Me either."

"Why you going there, then?" he asked.

"I have to meet my girlfriend there. Well, she broke up with me, so she was my girlfriend. But I think we can fix it if I get there in time."

"Heavy. Hope she appreciates you getting your face broken for her."

"I think I'll make it."

"You'll crush it!"

We didn't speak for a while. Cooper took his window down and stuck his head out. His long blond hair flapped around in the wind. After a minute or so he pulled his head back in.

"You want a beer?" Cooper cracked open a can and took a long swig.

I thanked him and took one.

"You can always sleep in the Mazda, if you want. As long as you promise not to drive off with it."

"I wouldn't know how."

"You can't drive? You're what, eighteen?"

"Yeah. Haven't got round to it yet."

"You Brits are so funny like that. Me and my buddies been driving since we were fifteen. You can't even touch the wheel at that age."

"It's not so bad. I wouldn't be able to afford it anyway."

"That's another thing about you Brits. In fact, all Europeans. I was thinking about this the other day, driving through Budapest. You all live on top of each other, in those crazy blocks. It's weird, man."

Cooper liked to talk. He told me all about anything and everything. He told me about his brother who was born with a rare kidney disease, his parents who both worked in oil and gas, and about his life in Aspen before his family had to move to Texas because of his Dad's new job.

"It sucked. I love Colorado. Texas is the gooch of the whole country. I just haven't made any real friends yet. And I got a shitty job at a gas station. That's why I came out here."

"That's a better reason than I've got," I said.

Cooper was an even more reckless driver than Jakov had been. I wasn't sure if he was trying to impress me, but he ragged that car for everything it had. We were only half an hour into the drive and he'd already drunk three beers. That's when he decided to come off the highway. He said we could go the scenic route. I wasn't that bothered – he didn't seem drunk and I was glad not to have been mugged for all my money. In many ways, finding Cooper was the best thing that could have happened to me.

He hammered the Mazda around the winding B-roads, braking hard and as late as possible at corners. I held on to the door and braced my stomach. It's always awkward when you're the passenger and you want someone to stop driving like they have a death wish.

We were within twenty miles of Zagreb when the Mazda started to smell funny. At fifteen miles, smoke started billowing out from the bonnet, so Cooper slammed on the brakes and skidded off the road. The car came to a halt and Cooper kicked open the car door and sprinted down the road, shouting, "It's gonna blow!"

I was still sitting in the passenger seat. I didn't know a lot about cars, but I was convinced that they didn't blow up out of nothing. Even so, I wasn't willing to take any risks, so I got out as quick as I could and went to find Cooper.

I shouted his name several times but he'd disappeared. It was like he'd never existed. There was nobody around.

I was alone with the rocks, stretching out their arms and legs in long shadows in the dust. The Mazda had grazed a boulder on the side of the road when Cooper braked and panicked, and there was a long scuff down the left-hand side.

"Cooper!" I yelled, hoping he wouldn't run too far from me.

Cooper's head popped up from behind a large rock, fifty yards away from the car. "Hey, man."

"What are you doing?"

"I've never seen a car do that before. I thought it was gonna blow up."

"I gathered."

"What are we gonna do?"

"We could push it," I said.

"It's too far. Let's wait for someone to come by. We can get a tow."

We had only seen two other cars since coming off the highway, and none for twenty minutes at least. But I was in no position to argue. Night was coming near.

"OK," I said. "We might have to spend the night out here."

"You think?"

"If nobody comes by."

"I got enough beers to see us through."

At this point, I seriously considered leaving Cooper to walk into Zagreb by myself. I figured I could probably make it within five hours, and then I could try to hitchhike on to Ljubljana first thing the next morning. I looked at him as he guzzled a beer. He had a blond goatee beard that made him look like a cat that had dipped its face in a bowl of milk. I was pissed off he'd driven so recklessly – his showing off had broken the car. If I didn't make it to Zagreb in time, I wouldn't have enough money to get all the way to Ljubljana, and I wouldn't get to Bled in time for Eva. She would think I hadn't bothered coming. I weighed everything up and decided I couldn't leave Cooper. He'd helped me out. He was a friend already.

Night came and we waited in the car, drinking beer. Cooper smoked cigarettes but I didn't want any. Cooper didn't mind the fact I didn't smoke. A few cars drove by but nobody stopped. We resigned ourselves to sleeping in the car for the night. We would wait it out until morning and then push the car down the road until someone helped us.

"We should set up a roadblock, like in the movies," Cooper said. "Then they'd have to stop. Then we could jack their car." He laughed a goofy American laugh, a whooping smoker's laugh.

When it started to get cold we closed the windows and doors and Cooper smoked five cigarettes, one after another. He didn't have a limit. Apparently he'd been smoking with his older brothers back in Aspen since he was twelve. The only air inside the car was replaced by the smoke.

Cooper talked about lots of things. I remember a long speech about baseball, and some story of his family friend that found a musket when they were digging out their garden.

"Back home I have a ragtop," he said. "I always used to leave it open, unlocked. Never any stuff in there. I just didn't want anybody to take a knife to that ragtop. It feels like silk, man."

I couldn't concentrate on what he was saying, but every few minutes he would say something like, 'bang for your buck', or another American phrase that would result in me suffering a fit of laughter. My whole stomach and ribs hurt by the time I'd controlled myself.

Everything was dark when I had to open the door to throw up. Cooper patted me on the back as I vomited and handed me a fresh beer to wash the taste away with.

"Don't worry," he said. "That always happens."

After hours of sitting up listening to *Limp Bizkit*, the feeling started to fade. Cooper switched the music off and fell asleep. Soon the feeling was all gone. The dream of floating off above the towns and cities, the people and cars and the continent, and even above the skyscrapers and into the vast and empty sky, it was all over. The goose bumps on my arms prickled up in the cold night, and I was empty.

I slept a few hours, and when I woke up I pulled the tampons out of my nostrils and chucked them in the ditch. Cooper was complaining after waking up at 8am because the sun was glaring through the windscreen, and he was too tall to comfortably sleep in such a small sports car. I ate some leftover bread from my rucksack and shared it with Cooper. That was all the food we had, and we were all out of water.

We started pushing the Mazda. It was a small car, but neither of us was feeling too great after the drinking and smoking the night before, and as a result we had to stop to catch our breath every couple of minutes. We weren't getting anywhere.

Cooper kicked a rock off the road and into the brush.

"I gotta try and get her going," he said. "You push, and I'll see if I can start the engine once we're moving."

I pushed, but I couldn't get it moving. I wasn't strong enough. We were both sweating and we decided to rest for twenty minutes while we figured out what was best to do. Cooper went to sit in the driver's seat and I leaned against the car, next to him.

"We'll try it again. I'll help push. I can do it if I run with the door open and jump in once we're rolling."

"OK," I said. I knew this might be our only shot to get into Zagreb without walking. I couldn't afford to delay anymore. I got around to the back of the car, placed my hands on the dusty bumper and pushed through my heels, willing it to get going. It started to budge. Cooper was a strong guy. Soon we were jogging along, rolling it towards Zagreb.

"Keep her going," Cooper yelled. "I'm gonna jump in now." He jumped in and I started pumping my legs even harder. I heard the engine coughing up a big ball of oily mucus. The Mazda was working again.

"Get in! She's alive!"

I ran around to the front and jumped in.

"Whoooooooeeeee!" Cooper whooped and yelled. We were going to Zagreb.

"I can't believe it worked," I said, once we were a few miles into the journey. Cooper was driving carefully this time.

"I knew she'd come through. I'm gonna need to take her in to get fixed up, though. Could be tricky."

"Maybe the engine just overheated."

"Maybe. We can give her a try once we've been to the museum."

"I don't think I can go. I need to get to Ljubljana."

"Course you can! It's gonna be hilarious."

"But I have to meet her tomorrow night. I'm still in the wrong country."

"It's not far, dipshit. Every place in Europe is just around the corner."

"Not when you've got no money."

"How 'bout this. We go to the museum. Stock up on food and beers and tobacco, and then head onto Ljubljana. I'll drive. I could do with heading up that way, anyways. There's a military prison there that's been converted into a hostel. It's still got all the prison bars and everything. It sounds awesome."

"How do you find out about all this stuff?"

"The internet, my friend."

"What if the car doesn't work?"

"She's working OK now, isn't she?"

"It might not start again."

"Then we push! You're gonna get your girl. You wait and see."

I didn't say any more. Cooper had decided for me.

We parked at the top of a hill outside town, so Cooper could get the car going again. Then we went to a supermarket and I got the usual things – bread, water, and a chocolate bar. Cooper bought two sandwiches and a big bottle of Coke, crisps, crackers, cheese slices, and a slice of pizza. It was amazing that he wasn't fat. I'd lost a lot of weight since leaving England – I could see my ribs pressing their outline against the skin on my flanks. My face looked gaunt and pale, and my arms felt like matchsticks.

We ate and Cooper led us to the museum using a sat-nav on his phone. It was only a ten-minute walk from the centre of town. When we got there, Cooper insisted we have a beer at the café outside, simply because they were advertised as 'colder than your ex's heart'. It was only 10am so I wasn't too keen, but he bought mine for me so we drank, and then went inside.

The museum was filled with items that belonged to lovers at some point or another. Each had a story attached to it – as Cooper had promised. He ran around as quickly as possible, laughing loudly to himself and then running over to grab me and show me the story he found so funny. This happened five or six times. "Billy, look! Billy!"

"What?"

"It's a toaster."

"And?"

Cooper couldn't control his laughter. I couldn't tell if he was high on something. I didn't know anything about drugs. I think that was just how he was all the time.

"What does it say?" I asked.

"It's called 'The Toaster of Vindication'."

"Go on."

"It says: 'When I moved out, and you left me, I took the toaster. That'll show you. How are you going to toast anything now?'" He started cracking up again. I laughed too. "Funny, huh?"

"Check out the axe," I said.

Across the room, an axe blade was buried deep into a block of wood. Cooper read the story aloud. "It says his wife fell in love with another man, and he axed the shit out of all her furniture. She came back for her stuff and it was all chopped up like firewood."

I walked around reading all the stories. There were red high heels from Paris, a cuddly toy from Lithuania, a garden gnome from Ljubljana. Each with their own story. I thought about what I would send to the museum, if I needed to. I thought about it for several minutes. I'd only known Eva for a few months, but it struck me that I owned nothing that could be a symbol of us. Of a love – or a lost love. There were hundreds of e-mails, and text messages, but there was nothing tangible. There was nothing I could pick up and hold and prove that this thing was when we went to that bridge in Brighton, or a shell from the pebble beach. Everything we shared was up in space – in telephone lines and Wi-Fi passwords. Everything was trapped in wires and screens. There were memories, but you can't trust those.

A girl across the room was crying and everyone was looking at her. It made me feel awkward. She was walking around on her own and reading the stories, sobbing to herself. I walked to the far end of the room to try to block out the sound. I turned my back on Cooper and went into the toilets. Listening to the girl made me think of Eva and then I started to cry. I felt like a kid again. The crying came through my whole body and I couldn't control it and I was shaking. I locked myself in a cubicle, buried my face in my hands, and cried for several minutes. When I went to leave the cubicle, a man with a moustache was washing his hands. He stared at me in the mirror. My eyes were all red from crying. We didn't speak.

I went back out onto the museum floor and thankfully the girl was gone. Cooper was back at the toaster, inspecting it closely. He wasn't laughing at all this time. He licked his finger and ran it along the top. A few burnt breadcrumbs stuck to his fingertip, and he peered at them.

"You OK there?" I asked.

He looked surprised to see me.

"Yeah, man. Let's get out of here. I'm kinda done with this."

"OK," I said, having wanted to skip the unnecessary stop from the get-go.

I went and grabbed my rucksack. Cooper had already walked out. As I was leaving, I stopped and looked at the toaster and read its story again. It was sent to the museum from Aspen, Colorado.

We walked back to the Mazda and I pushed it down the hill while Cooper got it up and running. Thinking back now, we probably didn't need to push it to get it started, but it didn't matter. The car was running. Cooper drove back up the hill to pick me up.

It took us half an hour to work out which way we needed to leave Zagreb. When we had finally worked it out, we got stuck in the inner-city traffic for a further twenty minutes. It was still only midday.

Just outside of Zagreb, we got stuck again in another line of cars, heading out of the city. Several police cars overtook us and carved straight through the traffic, their blue lights flashing and sirens wailing. We sat and waited. An hour passed, and then two. We barely moved. I was getting anxious there was a big problem.

"What the hell can hold up the road for two hours?" I said.

"A crash, or something. I dunno. Chill out, Billy. We'll get through."

A third hour passed, and we were still crawling along the road. Many of the cars in front of us had turned around and gone back towards Zagreb. I suggested to Cooper that we do that, but he was adamant it was only a matter of moments before the traffic would clear.

After another hour, Cooper told me to go and take a look.

"Walk up there and see what's holding us up," he said. "I'm not going anywhere." He was eating crackers and cheese.

Philip Bowne

I got out and jogged past the rows of cars. The line of traffic in front of us stretched out forever. It was at least a mile long, probably longer. A group of people gathered around a campervan said something to me in Croatian and pointed up at the road ahead, but I ignored them and carried on. I expected to see a horrific crash – a twenty car pileup with blood and bodies and bits of bodies scattered all over the road. But there was no sign of any crash. The holdup was a result of hundreds of people walking along the road. Lots of different people – mothers and fathers, friends, children and babies. At first I thought it was a protest, but on the outskirts of Zagreb it made no sense. They weren't shouting anything or holding signs or throwing petrol bombs or anything. They were just walking.

I ran back to tell Cooper what was going on.

"There's hundreds of people walking on the road, about a mile up from here."

"Why?"

"I don't know. They just are."

"What did they look like?"

"The women are wearing headscarves. The police are watching them."

"Shit. It's refugees," Cooper said, stuffing a cracker into his mouth and crunching it between his back teeth. "I didn't think they'd come this way."

"Where are they from?" I asked.

"Probably Syria," Cooper said. "Don't you watch the news?"

211

"I try to avoid it."

"Well there's thousands of guys like these with no place to stay. But nobody seems to wanna take them in."

I'd seen flashes of the crisis on the news, but it caused Mum and Dad to argue about what should be done. Dad said the refugees needed help, but Britain couldn't help everyone. Mum said that other countries were doing loads to help and that Britain could do more. Dad got angry about taxes and resources, so I left the room and went out. I never stuck around when they talked politics.

The police were trying to organise the refugees into single file at the side of the road, but the verge was too narrow, and there were too many of them. The road was blocked.

"Think it's best to go back to Zagreb," Cooper said.

"I can't. I have to be in Bled tomorrow."

"Sorry, chief. There's no way I'm waiting out in this all night."

"It's OK."

"Come with me. I'll get you to Ljubljana tomorrow."

I couldn't go back to Zagreb and spend the night there. A crippling anxiety would have come over me if I knew I still had 100 miles to travel on the day I was supposed to meet Eva. I was already starting to feel short of breath, and my heart was twitching beneath my t-shirt.

"I'll have to keep going on foot."

"You can't do that," Cooper said. "They'll rob you!"

"No they won't. I have nothing to be stolen, anyway."

"They could be terrorists." Cooper put down the cracker he was about to cram in his mouth. "They could be anyone."

I tried to defend my decision, but I was terrified. The British press had been warning about the migrants for weeks.

They believed that there would be thousands of terrorists integrated among them. I imagined that if they found out I was British they would take me hostage and kill me if they didn't get what they wanted. I tried not to think of that and reminded myself that I had only one more day to get to Bled. I had no choice but to keep going.

"It's better than waiting for them to clear," I said. "There's too many people up there. We're never gonna get through."

"It'll take you two days to walk there."

"I can run past them and try to hitch a ride further along."

"Nobody's gonna pick you up today, man. Not with all this going on."

"I don't have a choice."

"You really going?" he asked.

I nodded and stuck out my hand for Cooper to shake, but he didn't shake it – he leaned over the gear stick and grabbed me, squeezing me tight.

"Good luck with the girl," he said. "You gotta let me know how it goes. Come out to Texas sometime and I'll show you around."

"Deal."

I got out of the car and tapped it on the bonnet. I started walking up the road and Cooper made a U-turn out of the line of traffic. He beeped his horn several times and stuck his thumb up out the window as he accelerated back towards Zagreb. I didn't think that would be the last time I'd ever see him, but as soon as he was out of sight I realised we had no way of contacting each other. I could tell he didn't want me to go.

I ran back up to where the refugees were walking. It took me a little longer, which was promising, as they had managed to move some way forward. I tried to run around them but there was no way around – there were people everywhere. The police were escorting them at the front and sides, so I couldn't get past. I had no choice but to try to worm my way through the crowds.

It was slow going. The people were crammed together and there were no gaps to pass through. The sound of marching feet resonated along the road and the police officers shouted things in Croatian every so often. I gave up trying to pass through them and started walking with the crowd. People were looking at me and pointing and talking about me in Arabic. They didn't like me being there. I tried to move away and get out, thinking I had made a mistake and they were going to beat me up and steal my things like Cooper had warned. I regretted not staying with him in the comfort of the Mazda with the prospect of an easy drive through to Ljubljana tomorrow. But I couldn't sit still. I had to get there.

As I was trying to move out of the walking procession, a girl around my age started laughing at me. She wore a head scarf, like the other women. The scarf was bright blue with teal stripes running across it. The thick green jacket she was wearing was worn and dirty. I waved at her and she laughed even more. I got that feeling in my stomach again, like when I'd met Klara, and I thought it best not to look at the girl for a couple of minutes. It was obvious I wasn't supposed to be there. I felt awkward at first, and I thought about turning back and finding another route to Ljubljana. But people started talking to me and I learned that they had walked all the way from Syria. I didn't know where Syria was at the time, but I knew it was a long way away.

They asked me why I had two black eyes, and I told them about the plum incident. The swelling was still pretty bad, and

I didn't want it to get better because I thought it might impress Eva. I listened to their stories about home. A group of four Syrian brothers told me about the civil war they were fleeing from. One of the brothers, Abbas, was walking with crutches. He had one of his legs blown off by a mortar in Aleppo. The men took turns to carry him on their backs for a few minutes at a time. Abbas laughed and shouted, "Taxi!" as his friends carried him. They all laughed. I felt OK with them.

"Do you wish we go somewhere else?" Abbas asked me.

"I don't think so," I said. They all laughed.

The girl who had started laughing at me was called Lana. She was nineteen years old and studied pharmacology in Damascus. Her family had to flee the country when the bombs started dropping on the city. Lana's mother had died in an attack. Her father and younger brother were with her, walking ten metres ahead of us. The Hungarian border had closed so they were forced to take a different route and were walking from Zagreb to Slovenia, hoping that they could take a train to Austria.

We walked for hours. The adults were talking and some sang, trying to keep their spirits high. But the children were not children at all. They walked without laughing or talking. They didn't play with one another. One boy of six or seven walked for hours in total silence. No complaining, no crying. He didn't talk at all.

Many of the people had worn their shoes so thin that the soles of their feet would scratch on the tarmac, and so many had given up on shoes altogether and were walking barefoot. One man's heels were cracked open on the road and blood was leaking out, leaving a trail behind him.

After a long time, the group stopped. A BMW was parked up on the side of the road, and a man wearing a black suit was handing out bread and water. His car was full of supplies. When we arrived, he was passing out water from the boot – there must have been sixty bottles crammed in there. When that was all handed out, he opened the door to the back seats and passed out bread and jam.

An hour further on the road and around eighty of the group stopped to rest. Another eighty or so continued along the road, towards the Slovenian border. My toes were numb from the cold. I took my shoes off and pressed my thumbs into my heels to relieve some of the swelling. I had a huge yellow blister on my heel that had opened and when I lifted the dead flap of skin away it revealed a tender pink patch of flesh underneath. Sweat had trickled into the wound and the saltiness made it sting. An older man handed me a plaster and smiled.

"Please," he said.

I took it and thanked him. He walked away and handed out plasters to other people. A cluster of dark grey clouds had formed overhead, and spots of rain began falling onto the tarmac.

Everyone had taken their shoes and socks off. I looked around and saw everyone else's feet. Most were cracked, blistered and bleeding. Parents rubbed the feet of their children. A young girl was lying on the roadside, crying while her mother massaged her foot and kissed it. She was only eight or nine years old. She was pointing along the inside of her foot and screaming with pain.

One of Abbas's brothers, Yusuf, came to sit with me. He told me we were close to Harmica, which is a small village at the Slovenian-Croatian border. We were only five miles away. Hearing that made me smile. I had only come about twenty-five miles, but the fact I was almost in Slovenia made a huge difference. My feet felt lighter at the news. It made me feel like I wanted to walk all night, all the way to Ljubljana.

After twenty minutes or so the group held a big meeting to discuss what they were going to do. They spoke in Arabic, so I didn't know what they were saying, but soon they started shouting at each other and the children looked scared and tired and fed up. The group argued for a while, before Abbas came over to me and told me what was going on.

"Half of the group wants to rest here, and the other half wants to keep going," he said.

"And what do you want to do?" I asked him.

"I go where my brothers go."

"Will they stay here?"

"Tonight we walk, I think."

"Can I come?"

"Of course you come!" Abbas put his arm around me and gripped me in a headlock.

I got some bread out from my bag and ripped off half for Abbas.

"It's OK," he said. "For you." He refused to take it, so I grabbed his hand and put the chunk of bread in the palm of his hand. He thanked me and started to eat it in tiny bites, savouring each crumb.

Everyone else was starting to get ready to leave, so I drank the last of my water and changed my socks, then I put my shoes back on and laced them up. Only a handful of people wanted to stay. They were too tired to walk any further, so they unravelled blankets and placed them on the grass verge. They didn't have a tent to sleep in and a light drizzle had started. As we walked off I watched a mother and father holding on to each other, their child wrapped up in between them. The father was crying silently as his child drifted into sleep.

We walked on towards Harmica. At every road sign the group cheered. Everyone wanted to go north. We may have had different reasons, but we were all in it together.

We were going faster than we had before the split. We followed the road, and near Harmica we cut through a field of horses. Some of the men petted the horses as we walked by. It reminded me of my walks with Eva in Eastbourne. One evening we went through the town and walked past restaurants and coffee shops and bars, until we came to Hampden Park. There, I cut across the grass where it had been worn down to a brown dirt track by people taking the shortcut. The improvised track led twenty metres across the grass, and ended when it met the gravel pathway. Eva didn't follow me. Instead, she walked up the rest of the path, before turning left and onto the same gravel track. She avoided walking on the grass completely.

"Why didn't you follow me?" I asked her when she caught up with me.

"I don't follow desire lines," she said, arms tucked across her breasts. The sun had scattered a new formation of brown freckles across her nose and cheeks.

"Desire lines?"

"Cow path, goat track, pig trail. They have many names. My favourite is desire lines."

"What does that mean?"

"It means you follow the shortest possible route to getting where you want. The path you walked was the line of your desire."

"What's wrong with that?"

Eva stopped and turned around, looking over at the desire line I'd followed.

"It ruins other people's grass," she said, and laughed.

"But it was already like that."

"I know, Billy. What I'm saying is, you can follow desire lines, but look at us. We are in the same place. You always end up in the same place. So what does it matter?"

"I guess."

"People don't know how to wait."

"I'm sorry," I said.

"You don't need to be sorry, Billy."

"I'll stop doing that. I'd never thought of it in that way."

"It's not a bad thing to follow your desires," Eva said, rubbing my shoulder. "But you should know that just because you follow something, it doesn't mean you won't end up on the same path, to the same place. Most often you will end up in exactly the same place, you know?"

I looked down at the freshly trampled grass in those Croatian fields and thought how wrong Eva was. I looked at that new path we were treading and I saw it as the beginning of the route to the desires of every heart in that group.

I patted a horse on the head as the other men had done. She was big and her hair was brown and her mane was even darker than the rest of her. Her brown eyes looked through me as she chewed on the stems of long grass. I imagined the horse was

Baba Ganoush. She looked at me and grunted, blowing air out of her nose and nickering.

"I'm sorry for shooting you," I said, patting her heavy flank. I was sorry, too. Not only had the scheme cost me all my money and my girlfriend, it made me feel disgusted with myself, for causing pain to such a beautiful animal. I waited with her until the rest of the group passed me. I patted her thigh and flank and thought about Sam. I wondered whether he was OK and what had happened once he'd got to the hospital. A big part of me worried that he wouldn't be around when, or if, I ever got back home. I should've gone to the hospital to see him that day he fell ill. I'll never forgive myself for not seeing him.

I left the horse and carried on walking at the back of the group once everybody passed. The group soon found its way back onto the roads and we could reach out and kiss Harmica. The final couple of miles were spent singing and whistling and Abbas hopped on his crutches. The sound of his sticks on the road were like a clock counting the final seconds of a day's work.

At Harmica, the mood dropped. At the end of the long road into the village, the men at the front of the group spotted barriers. When we got closer, we realised that it was a police barrier. Armed riot police were guarding the border. Nobody would be let through. The border was closed.

The news quickly spread throughout the entire group. There were whispers about the authorities taking fingerprints and many were fearful of being sent back to Macedonia or Turkey or even Syria.

Abbas, Yusuf and the other brothers reached the metal barriers and produced their documents, asking to pass through into Slovenia. But the policemen shook their heads from behind their huge riot shields.

They were standing in a line, about fifteen of them, shoulder to shoulder, blocking the road. When the rest of the group caught up, a crush developed. People were pushing from the back, forcing everyone forward.

The pushing became more forceful, and the police used their riot shields to bash the group back a few metres, but that made things worse. The group thinned out so only a few men were left protesting with the border police.

Yusuf was shouting at them. "Are you human being, or not?" Other men were waving their arms and shouting in Arabic. Blood was streaming from one man's nose. The police said nothing.

"Are you human being, or not?" Yusuf yelled again, his voice cracking at the top of his throat. When they still wouldn't answer him, he kicked out at the riot shields. Then he shoulder barged into the line of police. That was it. At that point, one of the cops pulled a can from his belt and sprayed gas into Yusuf's eyes. Yusuf fell to the ground and rolled away from the barriers. He clutched his face, rubbing his eyes and shrieking in Arabic. The crowd backed off and Abbas moved over to his brother on his crutches. He dropped down onto the floor beside him.

It seems pathetic now, but all I could think about was that I had to meet Eva in twenty-four hours. With my British passport, I could have got past the police. But I would have been too embarrassed to have strolled across the border leaving my friends in the cold.

By this time, most of the group had gone to lie down on the grass at the side of the road. They set out their blankets and lay down to rest. I didn't have the strength to go on, even with my passport. It was only the group that had kept me going. A young mother wrapped her baby up in her own jumper, to save the child from the cold night. The baby was sleeping on the side of the road, and the police watched on. I went to join Yusuf, Abbas and the two other brothers. They let me share their blankets.

It wasn't for a long while after that night that I thought about what I'd seen. I wished Britain could be a country that was able to provide refuge for everybody that needed it. But there was always talk that there aren't enough nurses or doctors or teachers or policemen, and more people would only make that worse. I still don't know what the answers are.

The houses in the small village of Harmica were in darkness. There was only light in one window, where two children, a boy and a girl, watched what was happening. They sat on the windowsill and watched for several minutes, faces pressed against the windowpanes.

Even though I felt safe with the group, I was too cold to get comfortable. I opened my eyes in the middle of the night and walked around to try to get warmer. Jumping on the spot, I noticed lights in the bushes across the way from where the group was sleeping. I walked up to see what it was – part of me thought I was dreaming or hallucinating, because as I moved closer, I saw dozens of flying lights moving in and out of the forest clearing. I'd never seen a firefly before. They formed ribbons of light in the cool, dark air. I liked to think of them as the fire of dead souls floating through the night. I dreamed about them as many things. For a while they were lighthouses. Then they were green stars flickering in the brush. I wanted to catch one between my hands, and watch my fingers light up with that hopeful green light – but I couldn't.

Yusuf and the brothers woke up in the dark at 4:30am, and the whole group was awake half an hour later. A spokesperson came over to the group at 6am and announced that there would be coaches coming to take them to Ljubljana – from there they would be taken by train to Vienna. The group was filled with hope and joy at this news. They started singing and dancing and cheering "Vi-enn-a, Vi-enn-a!"

Yusuf told me I should go with them. He said I was their friend, and they would like to share the journey with me. I was more than happy to agree – I was exhausted. My eyes felt crusty, like I'd slept with my eyelids superglued together and now I'd woken up I had to try and force them open again.

We waited. The woman who announced that the buses were coming said that the first bus would arrive at 4pm. They didn't explain why it wouldn't arrive until the afternoon. Nobody cared. They were moving forward. It was agreed that the women and children would go first.

Harmica is only an hour and a half from Ljubljana, so I worked out that if I got the second bus, with Yusuf and Abbas, I should make it to the capital by 10pm. Bled was only forty-five minutes' drive from the capital, so I decided to stay and wait for the bus to come, and from Ljubljana I would take a taxi on to Bled.

At 9am I went for a walk and found a small supermarket. I bought ten bottles of water, six loaves of bread, six bags of crisps, ten chocolate bars and a big bag of sweets. I only had euros to offer as I'd run out of Croatian Kuna, but as we were so close to the border with Slovenia it didn't seem to matter and the shop assistant didn't mention anything. The food and drink cost me €22, leaving me €18.

I stole one of the supermarket baskets with wheels and a handle and walked back to the group. When I got there, I shared out everything I had. People smiled and gratefully ate and drank. Nobody took more than their fair share, and they made sure I had enough of everything to fill my stomach.

The rest of the day was agonising. We sat waiting for that first bus to come. I didn't want to sit still but my feet needed a break. I lay down and watched the clouds pass over the top of us. Yusuf joined me and started to pick out shapes in the clouds – there were elephants, spaceships, butterflies and lions. His eyes were still bloodshot from the pepper spray. He couldn't look into the sky for long.

An old man from Harmica came up to the barriers at about 2pm. The border police stopped him passing through and warned him to stay away. He was carrying brown paper bags filled with fruit. All he wanted to do was help, but he wasn't allowed to give us any fruit. The police spoke to him for ten minutes before he turned around and walked back into the village. Twenty minutes later he reappeared again, this time with two huge bottles of water. He struggled with the weight of the bottles, and I thought he might collapse under the strain. When he made it to the borderline, the same thing happened. The police didn't allow him to pass. The man turned around and scurried off. I like to think that he was swearing at the police in Slovenian.

We passed time by playing thumb wars and slaps – games I was surprised the Syrian guys knew as well. After another hour, the old man appeared again, this time carrying a football. A few kids in the group noticed him and got up onto their feet, waving their arms in the air, begging him to pass it to them. This time the old man kept his distance from the police, knowing they would stop him. Instead, he placed his hat on the floor, bounced the ball in front of him, and volleyed it straight over the police and into the area where we were sitting. One of the men jumped up and started doing keepie-uppies. We cheered and waved at him, and some of the kids yelled their thanks. The old man laughed, picked up his hat, and walked back into the town.

We kicked the ball to each other for a while, playing in the road like children. The feeling of despair had vanished, and the group was full of life and joy and hope.

At 4pm the first bus arrived. The wives and children kissed the men goodbye as they piled onto the coach. Before the vehicle had even pulled away into Slovenian territory, many of the women sitting at the window seats were asleep.

I slept until 6pm and we waited until 8:45pm before our bus finally arrived. It was over an hour late. We piled on and stuffed most of the luggage in the hold beneath. I kept my bag on me and got on the bus, taking a seat next to Abbas. The driver didn't smile. When the border police moved the barriers, the whole bus whooped and yelled and cheered, waving goodbye to Harmica and the border as we moved into Slovenia.

The bus was stuffed full of people. The gangway was crowded with people standing, and every seat was taken. Nobody cared. We chatted the whole way there. Abbas told me about his old job as a market trader, selling hand-crafted wooden crockery. He said he had to stop working when the war started. He said that he hoped to get a job making things again, one day.

The coach pulled into Ljubljana train station at 10:27pm. Everybody thanked the bus driver and left the bus to meet their families and move on to Vienna. I said my goodbyes to Yusuf, Abbas and the rest, and then they moved away into the station doors, onto the next part of their journey.

I wish I could tell you that my journey with the refugees granted me maturity and perspective. I wish I could tell you that I returned home and felt like a new person – a man, grateful for what I had and thankful to my family for keeping me safe. But that's not the truth. The truth is, I didn't care. My mind was still fixed on Eva. All I wanted was to reach her and to hear her say she loved me.

When I found a taxi, I chucked my rucksack onto the back seat and climbed into the passenger seat. The driver was talking into a Bluetooth headset. He smelled of coffee and cigarettes.

"To Bled," I said. "I need to go to the church."

He carried on talking into the earpiece.

"I need to go now," I said.

He flicked the engine on and pulled out into the road. I drummed my palms on my thighs, willing him to drive faster. The voice in his ear stopped and he pressed a button on his phone to end the call.

"You want to go to the church?" he said.

"I need to be there for midnight."

"Well I can take you as close as we can get." He eased his foot down on the accelerator, overtook a car in front, and slipped into the stream of moving traffic. We soon got out of Ljubljana, and onto a dark road that crept through the countryside. The driver spoke on his Bluetooth headset for the whole journey. I didn't know if I would have enough money to pay the full fare. I grabbed my rucksack from the back seat and put it by my feet, so I'd be ready to make a quick exit. I pulled out a chocolate bar from the front pocket of the bag and had three squares. I offered the driver the bar and he had a square while talking on his headset. That made me feel less guilty about planning to jump the taxi. At least he'd have seen that I can be a good person.

We arrived at the outskirts of Bled at 11.15pm. I only had forty-five minutes to get to the church and see Eva. I remembered the last conversation we had, when I went into her workplace and spoke to her on the phone. The phone had cut out before I had a chance to tell her I would come.

Soon we were into the town. It looked similar to Lucerne; built around a lake, surrounded by mountains. Bled was just a miniature version of her hometown. I wondered why Eva chose to come here. She may as well have stayed at home.

The taxi came down the hill into the town. We passed through one-way streets on the way down to the lakeside. When we were at the lakeshore, he stopped. I couldn't see a church.

"€30," he said.

"Where's the church?" I asked. My heart was trembling. I had to run away. I couldn't afford to pay him €30. I only had €18. His hand appeared under my nose. I thought he was going to hit me or choke me until I paid. I flinched, and then realised he was pointing out to the lake. I turned my head and saw the white church tower illuminated against the black mountains. It cast a long reflection on the black water, reaching out towards me on the shore. The church had been built on a tiny forested island, out in the middle of the lake.

"Are there boats running?" I said.

"No," he said. "But I don't mind you praying in here." He laughed.

I gave him all my money, and before he could count it, I grabbed my bag and kicked open the door, sprinting in the opposite direction from where the car was facing. I ran into a dark street and waited until I figured he must have gone.

After hiding for ten minutes I walked around to the edge of the lake. Couples were eating and drinking beneath patio heaters at restaurants along the waterside, laughing, clinking glasses, celebrating being together. I looked for a boat, but they were all tied up around the far side of the lake. I checked my watch: 11:32pm. She probably would have been waiting out there, on the island. I thought it might all be a big joke on me – she knew I would go all the way out there and she would have enjoyed the thought of me making a fool of myself. She didn't even know if I was coming.

I threw down my bag and peeled off my shoes and socks, my jacket, jeans and shirt. I tried to hide all my stuff behind a locked bicycle, but it was all on show. I didn't have time to worry about it being stolen, about losing my passport and the consequences of being stranded in Europe, hundreds of miles from home.

I didn't bother dipping my toes in the water. I paced back a few steps and for a moment I stood shivering in my pants. Then I kissed the cross on the necklace Christoph had given to me. I thought out a prayer in my head, asking for everything to go well and for Eva to be there and to want me.

I sprinted to the edge of the water, throwing myself out into the blackness. Knees tucked into my chest, I bombed in, sending a huge cascade up into the air. I sunk a few feet down, stunned by the cold. Maybe there was another church, somewhere else in the town. Maybe she was watching me with some new boyfriend that had a compost heap the size of Kilimanjaro. They were laughing at me in my baggy chequered underwear.

But it seemed like something she would do. The sort of test she would think up. It would be too easy if it didn't involve a midnight swim in the open water during autumn. I kicked my legs and moved forwards, out into the lake.

I had no idea how far the island was from the shore – it was hard to tell in the dark – but at a guess I thought it might take me twenty minutes, maybe more. I imagined Eva getting up and leaving the church if I was late, jumping into a boat and rowing straight past me. She always hated it when I was late. Her nose would crinkle up and lines would appear around her eyes. The thought pushed me to swim faster, smoother. I was a skimming stone, zipping across the water towards the island.

After twenty minutes, I stopped. I turned to face the shore and see how far I had come. I still had my watch on because it was splash proof. 11:55pm. I didn't have time to waste. Maybe she was waiting there, thinking of me, hoping for everything to be OK again. I kicked my legs. Numb from the cold, they didn't feel like they were moving.

I was close to the island, but my swimming had become laboured; my arms and hands slapped the water, my legs kicked without rhythm. I panicked – I realised I had never been in open water before. I stopped to tread water, looking down hoping to see my feet. There was nothing but blackness. My arms and legs felt full of sand and my feet cast in a block of cement.

I sank down several feet. There was nothing below me, or above. It was hard to know whether my eyes were open at all. But I didn't want to give up. My feet started kicking by themselves, lashing out at the cold water. The air in my lungs bubbled out of my mouth. I was light in the head, sleepy, ready to drop to the bottom.

I burst up to the top and broke through the surface water. I had to get to the island. I paddled like a puppy. I hardly moved for a couple of minutes, still coughing and short of breath. I couldn't miss her.

At 12:07am, I pulled myself out of the water and onto the concrete staircase that ran from the shore right up to the church. It was enormous. I imagined it ran right down to the depths of the lake, and way up. Lying on my stomach on the cold concrete, I couldn't even see an end to the stairs from the bottom; it looked like they rose into the sky and went on forever.

I was exhausted, shivering and numb. Climbing the stone stairs, I couldn't breathe properly. My legs didn't want to haul me up to the top. They felt frozen, without blood flow. I fell on my knees and crawled. Stones cut open my kneecaps, and a trail of blood trickled down to my toes. When I reached the last few steps, I saw the church. The bell tower stretched high into the sky. I pushed open the heavy wooden door and stepped in.

It was warm inside. The black marble floor caught the light of candles that split through the darkness. The bell rope hung down from the tower, at the front. All the seats were empty. I couldn't see anyone.

I ripped the white tablecloth away from a table to wrap around my body. A Virgin Mary statue fell onto the floor and rolled down the aisle. The thought of being close to Eva warmed me up. It was 12:15am. The candles didn't look like they had been lit for long. I thought that it must have been her. I took a seat in one of the pews and waited. The gold altar shone in the candlelight. I looked up into the high ceilings and examined the frescoes. The Virgin Mary was there, judging me from above.

Twenty minutes passed. Eva must have been close. She could have rowed her boat right past me. My thoughts wandered to memories of home, of Tommy and the day we lost all our money, of what would happen when my parents found out. I thought about the wedding that would be happening in a matter of weeks, wondering whether it was happening at all. All I did know was that a lot of things were coming to an end, and I didn't know how I could be happy again. I didn't know what was going to happen to me, and that scared me. That's what it means to be an adult. Being an adult doesn't make you confident and happy and content and grown up. Nobody can be any of those things. Being an adult is being terrified and cowardly and frightened of everything all the time.

My knees had stopped bleeding – they were clotted with grit and gooey blood. I scrubbed the dried blood on my shins. All I needed was a crown of thorns and a crucifix and I would have looked like the man Himself.

I got up and walked around the church, reading some of the signs up on the walls. They explained how the church had been renovated several times after earthquakes, lightning strikes, fires.

I moved along the wall and read them all. The last explained the legend of the sunken bell.

A young widow, Poliksena, once lived at Bled Castle. Her husband was killed by robbers and his body was thrown into the lake. After his death, she gathered all her gold and silver and had a bell cast for the chapel on the island, in memory of her husband. But the bell never arrived.

During the transport of the bell, a terrible storm struck the boat and sank it together with the crew and the bell. To this day, the bell is said to ring from the depths of the lake. Poliksena lived out the rest of her days as a nun in Rome. After she died, the Pope had a new bell created, and sent it to Bled Island. It is said that whoever rings this bell three times and believes in God, will have their wish come true.

I walked up to the rope. I didn't believe in God. I had no reason to, and I still don't. I just wanted her to know I was there, that I had tried. I wrapped my hands around the rope and pulled down on it, hard. It didn't ring. I could barely find the strength to pull at all.

Defeated, I walked away from the rope. I grabbed a couple of pillows from the pews. I had decided to sleep in the church and go back in the morning. The swim back would've killed me.

I placed a few cushions down on the marble floor and dropped my tablecloth on top of them. The rope dangled down by the altar. Without thinking better of it, I sprinted down the length of the aisle and jumped at it. Stretching out my arms and legs, I reached out with everything I had left and clung on. My bodyweight forced the rope down, and with it, the bell jerked and bellowed – ringing out loud across the lake, the town, the continent.

I prayed she would hear it from somewhere.

That night I stayed in the church, but Eva never appeared. When I woke up in the morning, I'd rolled onto the black marble floor. I got to my feet and left, still only wearing my underwear. The sun was crawling over the mountaintops. It seemed there wasn't anybody on the island. What I hadn't noticed the previous night was a small restaurant and outdoor seating area next to the church. I needed some clothes, so I went and tried the restaurant door but it was locked. I walked around the island, still wearing the tablecloth. It was tiny – about ninety metres across. I didn't know what to do, or how I would get home, or feed myself, or anything. Everything was done. It was all over. After half an hour sitting in the dirt, I walked around the back of the restaurant building. The back door was unlocked.

Inside, the chairs were up on the tables and a brush was resting against the wall in the far corner. In the kitchen I fired up the gas hob and cooked six eggs in a frying pan with olive oil. I ate them with some bread and then looked around for something to wear. An apron would have done it. That was the best I hoped for. But when I went into the room off the kitchen I found the laundry room, and in there I managed to find a pair of blue and white checked chef trousers and a sweater. I got dressed and washed up my plate, and the frying pan, then left the restaurant.

In the daylight, I saw how far I'd swum. The taxi driver had dropped me off at the furthest point from the island, at least twice the distance from the shore than it was to the closest side. Waiting at the top of the stone staircase, I looked out across the lake, watching teams of rowers climb into their long metal boats and a fisherman casting out with a cigarette in his mouth on the lakeshore. At the bottom of the staircase, the wooden decking was still wet from where I'd climbed out of the water.

Around it, a few hardy dragonflies hovered around the water lilies, drifting up and zipping away, before flying back to the same spot, looking for something they might never find.

I'd planned on waiting for somebody to come to the island with a rowing boat, so I could get a lift back to the shore, but the swim to the closest point on the lakeshore was only around a quarter of the distance I'd swum the previous night. I took off the trousers and sweater and dived off the wooden decking, swam back to shore, and then walked around the lake to the spot where I'd left my bag and all my clothes. It took me around half an hour in total.

I was surprised to find none of my things had been stolen since I left them there. Especially as there were already people walking to work, and families cycling around the lake. Lots of people would have seen my bag, coat and trousers that held my phone and wallet. But nobody had touched my stuff. I got dressed and gathered my things and walked around to the town centre.

The first thing I did was go to a café to charge my phone. I managed to get it to 20% before the café owner told me if I wasn't going to buy anything then I had to leave. So I unplugged my charger, thanked him, and walked out. I needed to call home. I had no choice – I didn't have the strength to hitch rides and walk miles along empty roads and eat nothing but bread. I couldn't face it. I felt weak, especially after meeting Abbas and the other refugees. But I was alone. I didn't want to be alone any longer. I just wanted to go home.

Mum picked up the phone. She started crying when I told her what had happened. I told her everything. About the bet, the horses, the journey to find Eva. I told her I had nothing, and that I had no money to get home or even to buy food. She cried without saying anything. She cried until the battery ran out on my phone again and I cried in the street. I went to sit by the lake and watched the rowing boats slide along the glassy water. The men in the boats were lean and strong. Their shoulders bunched up in their sweatshirts as they pulled the oars through heavy water. After watching them for half an hour, I heard sloppy footprints coming from behind me. A man was walking around the waterside in full scuba diving equipment – wetsuit, fins, oxygen tank, goggles, weight belt, mask and snorkel. A camera was dangling around his neck, encased in a waterproof plastic case.

"How you doing there?" the man said. He was Irish. "Wanna come diving?"

"Not really," I said. "I'm leaving soon."

"Oh yeah?"

"Yeah."

"I just got in today. What are you here for?"

"I was meant to meet my girlfriend, but I was too late."

"Ah, shur. That's a shame. I'm on the adventure of a lifetime."

"Yeah?"

"You bet, kiddo."

I looked out at the lake. The rowers were still shooting across the still water. It was a small lake. I wouldn't have expected people to scuba dive to the bottom of it, especially this late in the year. I wondered if the man was diving for Poliksena's bell.

"What's the adventure?"

"I'm on a World War One themed diving holiday." The Irishman lifted his mask and snorkel and grinned at me.

"What do you mean?"

"I'm diving to the bottom of this lake here. Find me some World War One shit."

"Like what?"

"Sticky bombs, mainly. Bullet shells, landmines. Could be anything down there." The Irishman was still grinning at me as a group of three other wetsuited men walked around the edge of the lake.

"Wish me luck," he said, as the group waded out into the water. I watched him pull his mask down over his eyes. The heads disappeared below the surface. The Irishman's head went last, and I watched the trail of his air bubbles. I followed his path for a minute or so, until the bubbles vanished completely.

Later, I walked to the ATM and checked my bank balance. Mum had transferred £500 into my account. I was going home.

5

On the flight back to London, I couldn't stop sobbing. The act of leaving in failure was too much. Shortly after take-off I tried to hide behind another passenger's discarded copy of *The Independent*. I must have been too loud, because the woman next to me offered her tissues. She looked at the headline of the paper and nodded as though she understood: Donald Trump had won the US election. She patted my shoulder in consolation and spent a long time talking to me about the checks and balances in the US governmental system. She spoke about the House of Representatives and the Senate and the Supreme Court. It didn't make much sense to me, but I wasn't really listening. I couldn't tell her that I didn't care about anyone else's problems. Instead I pretended to read through the rest of the newspaper, ignoring the woman's attempts to solve the crossword puzzles together. That was when I learned that Leonard Cohen had died the day before. I spent the rest of the journey with the melody of 'Hallelujah' in my head. I'd never heard of Leonard Cohen before, but 'Hallelujah' was one of Eva's favourite songs. Everything reminded me of her, and the empty church.

When I landed, Mum and Dad were waiting in the arrivals lounge. They spotted me as soon as I stepped through customs.

Mum hugged me and said she was so relieved that I was OK. I tried a smile, but it probably came across as a grimace. My eyes were still a little bruised and there was a little gash across the bridge of my nose. I kept my head down and they didn't notice.

"You're so skinny," Mum said. "Have you been eating?"

"Not much."

"Well, we've got gammon for dinner. You like gammon."

Dad's first words to me were, "You need to pay back every penny."

We walked out to the white Skoda and we drove back to Cheltenham. Dad didn't say much. I imagine he was sick of me and everything else. Mum tried to keep the conversation light and positive, but I didn't want to talk at all. I watched the tyres of the other cars spinning and spinning. I started looking at the people in their cars when we were alongside them on the motorway. It made them uncomfortable. One man put two fingers up at me, but I carried on staring at him. I realised that this was the closest I would ever come to these people, before they turned off at a junction and disappeared into another life.

It was only when we got home that Mum started crying. Dad had gone straight to the garage and she was sitting at the kitchen table, pouring herself glasses of wine.

"Why did you do it?" she said. She asked the same question again and again, until eventually I decided to counterattack.

"It was a crime of passion," I said.

"What's that supposed to mean, Billy?"

"You know. You know what it's like to cheat for a lover."

"Oh, Billy. If GG's been talking about how me and your Dad met, then he had no right. That was a long time—"

"No!" I said. "I'm talking about now. I'm talking about you and that guy."

"What guy?"

"The Mercedes guy."

Mum either had no idea what I was talking about, or she was a better actor than I'd realised.

"Before I went away. The black Mercedes. The Mercedes Man."

"What are you talking about?" she said, picking a ball of fluff from her cardigan, trying to act casual. And then she started to laugh, which pissed me off even more. "How do you know about that?"

"I've seen you."

"It wasn't what you thought, Billy."

"No?" I was getting angrier by the second. "What was it then?"

"It was nothing."

"An affair isn't nothing."

"Oh, Billy. I know your Dad and I aren't— We're not— But Jesus, Billy, I'm not having an affair!"

"How am I supposed to believe that?"

"The man in the black Mercedes – his name is Mike."

"I don't care what his name is."

"He's a private detective."

"So you're having an affair with James Bond."

"I'm not having an affair. I swear to you. I hired him. To investigate Benny. He only came here to pass on his findings."

"Why were you investigating Benny?"

"We didn't trust her. It just didn't seem right, Billy. You must realise how it looks."

Things were starting to make sense. Sort of. "So, he was the guy who told you Benny is already married?"

"Yes, except now it turns out she isn't. She was, but now she's not."

"I'm confused, Mum."

"We're all a little confused, Billy."

I poured myself a glass of Mum's wine.

"Basically, it was a mistake," Mum said. "The detective got it wrong."

"Was he even a private detective?"

"Yes."

"I struggle to see how."

"Well, it happened that way, OK? There was a woman with a similar name, a mix up with the dates, that sort of thing."

"I don't believe you."

"Honestly, Billy." Mum grabbed my hands in hers. "It was a mistake. Benny isn't married. She's actually a very lovely lady." Mum looked me in the eyes, long enough for me to know she wasn't lying. At least, long enough that I chose to believe her. She may well have been lying, but we aren't born distrusting our mothers, and it was easier for me to accept that Benny wasn't a bigamist and Mum wasn't having an affair. I was two problems down already.

I spent the first fortnight in the house watching TV and avoiding my parents. Every night I tried watching porn on the internet, hoping it would help me get over Eva. I'd turn out my lights and close the curtains and go onto one of those websites, but I couldn't even get a boner. It was all so fake. I couldn't bear to watch it.

I worried that I might never be able to get a boner again. I tried thinking about Eva when I touched myself, but that only made me upset and nothing else happened.

Tommy still wouldn't answer my texts. I walked over to his house one afternoon and his mum answered the door in an orange dressing gown with her hair wrapped up in a towel. Her big toenail was yellow and disfigured. It looked like a fungal infection. The nail had ridges running along it like corrugated iron sheets.

"Tom's not here," she said. "He ran away." She brushed her knees together and crossed her stubbly legs.

"Have you heard from him?"

I could hear footsteps at the top of the staircase behind her.

"Hurry up and get back to bed," Simon said. "Who is it anyway?"

"Nobody," Tommy's Mum called back. She looked down at her feet as she slammed the door closed.

Besides the revelations that Benny wasn't married and Mum wasn't shagging in a Mercedes, not much had changed at home. Mum was still at Slimming World, trying to lose weight she didn't have, and Dad was always in the garage, boxing and working out. He'd converted it into a proper home gym with a treadmill, a rack of weights and a spinning bike. He'd painted the walls white and tacked up posters of Muhammad Ali and Ricky Hatton.

Tuna had convinced him to buy rubber flooring off the internet. Mum told me that Dad was due to have his first fight in a few weeks. She didn't seem angry or disappointed when she said it, thumbing back the cuticle moons on her fingernails. She didn't seem glad or proud or smug, either. She simply accepted it.

My parents lived separate lives that only converged over passing the mustard at the dinner table. I felt even more detached. Dad would tell me every day that I needed to get a job and that for every day I didn't have a job he was charging me interest on the money they had lent me to get home from Slovenia. Letters addressed to me dropped on the doormat every other day. Missed payments, final warnings. They threatened to take me to court and warned that bailiffs would come to take the equivalent value of my debt in goods. I thought about ringing them up and telling them to come and take whatever they wanted. I didn't have anything worth any money. I imagined two big men carrying the TV out the front door as Dad came home from work. It probably wasn't the best idea.

GG and Benny had been visiting regularly. Mum was trying to keep everyone on good terms, but I doubt it had worked. Dad could barely bring himself to speak to anybody but Tuna. His days were spent working and boxing, eating and sleeping. He'd also bought a huge tractor tyre which was left sitting on our front lawn. I wondered what it was doing there when I first got home, but I didn't want to ask either of my parents. It was a big black rubbery mass that swallowed nearly the entire green space. I thought that maybe my parents had finally lost their minds and had installed it as a central feature. A few days later, I heard grunting and yelling from outside the front of the house, and I saw Dad squatting down and flipping the tyre end over end, with Tuna egging him on from the side. It was like watching World's Strongest Man. Dad flipped the tyre back and forth, end over end, for a good twenty minutes, before letting out one final grunt to give cadence to his work and high-fiving Tuna after the tyre dropped onto the grass.

I didn't hear anything from Eva. I didn't try to contact her, either. I couldn't. In the first days after swimming out to the island, my brain turned itself inside out, trying to find the reason for why she wasn't there. But it didn't matter anymore. She wasn't there. I was.

I mourned our relationship at the foot of the Eagle Tower. I would often spend the afternoon sitting down on the brick wall opposite that monstrous building, staring up into the office windows, imagining showing it to Eva as an example of brutalist architecture. I stared at the building from all angles. When I first met Eva, I was glass. Now I felt like concrete. Sometimes, looking up at Eagle Tower, I'd see Dad appear at the photocopier by a third-floor window. He would stare out across the town, his mouth stretched flat across his vacant face. He never noticed me.

After a while, I started to do things. I started running around the racecourse like I had before everything. It was getting dark earlier, and the Christmas lights buzzed from the lamp posts along the High Street.

When I built up the courage, I decided to phone Sam. I hadn't talked to him since he was taken to hospital during race week, but I still had his landline number written down on the scrap paper he gave to me. I worried that he might not have made it through whatever was causing him the pain in his sides.

I convinced myself that he had probably died. Before I pressed the call button, I prayed that he'd answer and be alive and well. I prayed a few times after going to that church in Bled. I still wore Christoph's necklace every day, too. It wasn't a religious kind of praying. I didn't direct my thoughts and wishes to any God. I knew that was all a load of crap. Diana proved that to me. Eva proved that to me, also. I prayed to make my own hopes and wishes clear to myself, by turning them over in my thoughts. I know it sounds stupid, but I needed something. I prayed for Sam for several minutes. I thought about his white moustache and his chequered farmer's cap that smelled of straw and manure.

The phone rang for ages, but eventually Sam answered. "Long time no hear," he said as soon as I told him it was me.

"How have you been?" I asked.

"Oh, you know. Much of the same. I'm not fit enough for the work now, though. So I've been busy with the garden." His voice was a little weaker than I remembered.

"What happened when they took you to hospital?" I asked.

We had to wait while Sam coughed away from the phone. "They did all their scans and checks and what not. Thought I was gonna die, if I'm honest. The pain was so bloody awful."

"What was it?"

"Only kidney stones. But I was in agony. After the scans they had to go straight in and get 'em."

"Are you OK now?"

"Went straight up my penis with a laser. Thank god they put me under anaesthetic, so I couldn't feel anything. Nurse comes in before and rubs cream on my old man and says it's gonna be OK.

I says, 'It's not your dickie they're zapping with a laser gun'. She went away after that."

"They put a laser up there?"

"Would you believe it? I thought they'd cut me open round the back, but they zapped me, right up there. Had a camera in there, too."

"Down the piss pipe?"

"They call it the ur-e-thra."

I fidgeted, unable to sit still. It was like my urethra could hear what Sam was saying and was trying to block it out.

"I'm just glad I don't have a great big long one, you know? That's all I could think as they did it, I was just so glad not to have nine or ten inches to zap down. It worked, mind you. They zapped 'em down into little bits of gravel and then I pissed it all out. That's the worst bit, actually. I pissed a lot of blood after they got 'em out. Nurse came in again and says it's gonna be OK. I'm there pissing pints of blood and kidney stones out my dickie. I says again, 'It's not you pissing blood and rock'. She went away again after that."

"Sounds awful, Sam."

"That's not it, my boy. They went back up there again the same day."

"More laser business?"

"No, they put a stent in my kidney."

"What's that?"

"It's a bloody long bit of wire they feed up there and they wedge it in your kidney to keep it from getting blocked up again."

Listening to Sam made me feel better about everything. I'd lost all my money and Eva, but at least I hadn't had my knob lasered. And at least Sam was still around.

"I'm glad you're OK. I was worried about you."

"I'm on the mend. You get used to it when you're as old as me."

Then I told him everything. About hiding from Radimir in the train, about Christoph and Diana and the cows, about Klara and her big truck. He listened and laughed. We were on the phone for so long that I noticed the phone had warmed the skin on my ear when we said goodbye.

That afternoon, Sam picked me up and we drove out of Leckhampton. He parked by Gloucestershire Airport, at a vantage point that overlooked the airstrip. The planes came in over our heads to land. Their engines rattled the old car and the scented Christmas tree air freshener bounced from the rear-view mirror.

"I often come here to watch the gliders," he said. "I'm not so fussed about the planes. Bloody noisy things."

"Why gliders?"

"They don't have an engine, see. They get winched up into the sky and they float. They're silent. Like being in a cloud."

We stopped there a while, watching the gliders shoot in and out of the clouds. When we weren't talking, I could hear the faint sound of whistling wings above our heads.

"I think that's what it'll feel like when I die," Sam said. "Like gliding."

"I always thought it would be like the TV turning off."

"You're a pessimist," Sam said. "You should be more hopeful at your age."

"It's like being born, I think. You don't know anything about it."

"What would Him upstairs have to say about that?"

"Bowie or Wogan?" I said.

"Don't be stupid," Sam said. "Have some respect."

"I don't know. I've never believed in that stuff." The glare from the low winter sun was burning through the windscreen and into my face. I pulled the visor down and looked outside at the cars rushing past us and the gliders floating above everything.

"You could be right, course. But I don't think so," Sam continued. "We die but we carry our lives with us all along the way. So that moment when we die, it's the most perfect moment of your life. Everything comes to you at once and you understand it all."

A glider whizzed over our heads and landed with a loud thud in a grassy section of the airfield. I thought it had crash-landed, but Sam said that's how it's supposed to happen.

Mum's secret sharing club had expanded in the time I'd been away. It now had an official title: East Gloucestershire's Secret Sharing Club. Capital letters and everything. Mum had made business cards, too. On Mondays, Wednesdays and Fridays, our living room would be packed full of women who devoured gossip and Battenberg. Mum even managed to introduce a membership fee. People paid £40 for a year of membership to her weekly sessions. I didn't understand why people would pay to anonymously share their secrets. None of it made any sense to me, but they seemed to get on with it fine. The people of Cheltenham couldn't get enough of it. I wouldn't have thought secrets would be such a valuable commodity. I mean, there's only so many secrets, or burdens, that one person can have. At least that's what I used to think. Mum's club attracted the same faces, week after week. They seemed to have an inexhaustible collection of secrets. Either that, or they made things up just to be able to hear what everyone else had to say.

Even from upstairs I could hear the women giggling and gasping as each secret was revealed to the group. Whenever they met I would put on some music to try to drown it all out. One afternoon I played my Arctic Monkeys album as loud as I could without Mum getting pissed off and telling me to shut up. I could still hear the laughing and gasping. One woman seemed to laugh in a way that tried to be loud. It rattled through the walls and into your ears. I got as far as track four before I gave up and went out into the back garden.

It had changed a lot that year. The grass was up to my knees and drooping with rainwater. The shed was rotten, and the window was still smashed from when I played cricket with Tommy as a kid. I walked through the long grass, treading on old plastic toys. I found burst footballs and plastic bags buried in the overgrowth. I stopped to think about everything that had happened in our garden. I remembered the blue-and-white paddling pool that had popped when Dad jumped in for a laugh. I remembered hiding beneath the wooden garden table and how cobwebs had collected between its slats.

It was a big garden, but it didn't look like much when it was so overgrown. I thought back to when I played on the lawn as a kid, and the back garden had felt like another world. As I trampled through the weeds, I wondered if my nostalgia had caused it to swell in my memory. Maybe it had never been that big. I got as far as the brambles, which dominated the final third of the garden, right up to the back fence.

Then I went to the garage and got the strimmer. I started by taking the grass down at the front part of the garden. It took a long time, and I didn't make much progress. The strimmer was small, only designed for neatening up already tidy borders and grasses, and I figured the blade was probably blunt after Dad's attack on the smoke detector. I needed an industrial-sized thing to get through all that grass. But the strimmer was all I had, so I cut down as much as I could before I got cold and bored and went back inside.

But I started doing a bit of gardening each day, and after a few sessions, I'd cleared most of it. The brambles at the back were my final task. Whenever I turned the strimmer off to take a break or move into a different part of the garden, I often heard the faint sound of boxing gloves beating into leather. Dad escaped to the garage just as often as he used to, if not more so now that Mum's club had taken over the household. He had worked himself into a good shape. His shoulders looked thick and heavy. I thought about getting into boxing myself when I looked at how much his physique had improved, but then I realised that would mean working out with my Dad in the garage, and I soon changed my mind.

One week before the wedding, GG came round. I hadn't seen GG since before I went away, chasing Eva. I wanted to go to his house and play pool or watch *Match of the Day*, like we used to, but it was awkward. I hadn't seen him since I went and asked to borrow money after I lost the bet.

"How are you, mucker?" he said when he walked in, grabbing my earlobe and yanking it down a little. I hugged him.

"I've missed you. I'm sorry for what I said before."

"Don't be silly. We've all missed you, my boy," he said. "Where did you get to?"

"I went away for a while."

"I know that much, Bill. Your mother was having kittens when you disappeared like that." He grinned. "You'll have to tell me all about it. Where's your father?"

"He's in the garage, doing his boxing stuff. He's been playing Iron Maiden tracks all day and grunting. I don't know what he's doing."

"Let's go and see." GG smiled and we walked out to the garage. Mum was busy with the Secret Sharing Club in the living room, so I slipped out without her even knowing. She wouldn't have been happy that I was going in there. She would have seen it as taking Dad's side, but it wasn't anything like that. I just wanted to see what happened behind the closed door.

When GG pulled open the garage door, Dad didn't hear us enter because "Run to the Hills" was playing at maximum volume, and he was busy doing star jumps at the back of the garage. Tuna was slapping Dad on the back and head and yelling at him. GG shouted a few times, but Dad couldn't hear over the music and he had his back to us. I flicked off the stereo.

"What are you doing in here?" Dad turned around as soon as the music stopped. He was topless, as usual. He spent most of

Philip Bowne

his waking hours topless. His eyes were loaded with rage – Tuna
had clearly been working him into a state. Dad looked ready to
kill someone.

"We thought we would come and watch you train," GG said.

"I'm Tuna," Tuna said. "You must be the old man."

"Tuna?" GG said.

"Long story," Tuna said. "Good to meet ya."

"And you," GG said, shaking Tuna's hand.

"Well, we can't all stand around," Tuna said, picking up a
spare pair of gloves and handing them to me. "Put those on, Bill.
You can do a bit of sparring with your Dad."

"What?" I said.

GG laughed.

"You heard me, Bill. Now's your chance to have a go at
him. You've always wanted to, haven't ya?" Tuna glared at me.
When I thought about it, I'd often imagined what would happen
if me and my Dad had a fight. Growing up, there were many
occasions that I'd wanted to hit him. But I'd never thought
those dreams would play out in reality. It's the sort of thing
that isn't supposed to happen. We're not supposed to fight
our dads.

"I'm not sure that's a good idea," Dad said. "He's never
boxed before."

"He's gotta start somewhere," Tuna said. He tossed me a
gum shield that was wet with someone else's saliva – probably
Tuna's.

I looked at Dad and then GG. They were waiting for me to
decide. I wanted them to decide for me, to stop it from happening
and get me out of that garage. I didn't know how to hit people.

251

I didn't want to know. I couldn't hit Louis when he set the smoke alarm off because I couldn't stand the idea of actually hitting someone in the face. If Tommy had been there I would have let him fight my Dad. Tommy probably would've knocked him out.

"Go for it, Billy. It's only a bit of fun." GG put his hand on my shoulder. I turned around and looked up at him.

"I'm not sure," I said.

"It's fine," GG said. "Go for it."

Dad grinned. He still looked like he was ready to murder someone. I wondered what he was thinking – whether he wanted to hit me or if he found it as weird as I did. After the money I'd cost him, and the extent to which I'd been one of his life's disappointments, I figured he would probably want to smash my head into a pulp, like an avocado into guacamole.

"Excellent. You've got five minutes to get warm, then we'll begin." Tuna moved over to the back of the garage with Dad, and they started doing burpees and star jumps and shadow boxing. I waited at the front of the garage with GG and started stretching out my arms and legs.

"Don't worry, Bill. He won't do anything stupid," GG said. He flicked the stereo back on and "Run to the Hills" came blaring out again. "Quick question, Billy. Why's he called Tuna?"

"I don't know. He wouldn't tell me."

"Perhaps he's big on fishing."

"Mum thought he was part of a prison gang."

"With a name like Tuna?"

"She said she thought each gang member might be named after a different type of fish."

"What?"

"I dunno. She just hates the idea of Dad getting involved in this stuff." I took off my t-shirt, mainly because Dad was shirtless and I thought that was how you had to box, but partly because I was hoping it would inspire some primal instinct in me to fight. Tuna looked over at me and laughed.

"I've seen more meat on a gippo's whippet, Bill," Tuna yelled across the garage.

"Ignore him," GG said. "He doesn't know what he's talking about."

I slipped my hands into the leather gloves and GG helped me lace them up. The fabric inside them was coarse and scratched the skin on the backs of my hands. I pushed the gumshield into my mouth but it was moulded to fit someone else's teeth, so it cut into my gums. After a couple more stretches, Tuna called us into the middle of the garage and made Dad and I touch gloves. I caught my reflection in the mirror up on the back wall. The outline of each rib was marked clearly on my skinny torso, as though trying to break the skin. There were red patches of shaving rash on my neck, and my mouth was surrounded by white pimples. Dad danced around the garage on his tiptoes, throwing jabs, ducking imaginary punches.

"Right, you know what you've gotta do," Tuna said. "I'm not gonna carp on about rules and regulations. Get stuck in. Three rounds, three minutes a piece." Tuna's refereeing stance didn't reassure me. I felt like I'd wandered into some shady bare-knuckle boxing club. The cobwebs quivered in the garage rafters.

I looked at Dad as Tuna stepped away. He was poised on his toes, waiting for me to move. I put my gloves up in front of my face, so close that I could barely see Dad for the sticky red leather.

They reeked of sweat. I mimicked Dad's movements, bobbing up and down on my toes, ducking and weaving. Dad threw a couple of range-finding jabs, but none of them connected. I didn't throw a punch. Iron Maiden were still blaring out from the speakers. Guitars wailing and drums crashing.

I looked up at the Muhammad Ali poster. When Dad had bought it, I'd made some dig about being surprised he'd let a Muslim into his house. Dad had laughed at me and said, "Don't worry – he's got to stay in the garage." When I didn't find that funny, he called me a snowflake, which was a phrase he used a lot, even though neither of us knew what it meant. Now, since Ali's death, he'd written "Rest in peace, Cassius" at the bottom of the poster. Slightly above Ali, there was a picture of Ricky Hatton. His nose was like a cheese twist: wrapped around itself several times. I didn't want my nose to look like a cheese twist. I liked my nose.

Dad hot-stepped around the ring with his guard up, measuring me, calculating what my weaknesses were. He looked the part. His stance was purposeful and calm. The first round flashed by with a couple of blocked punches. Dad worked my guard with a flurry of one-two's, each blow accompanied by a sharp exhale. A pneumatic sound. But none of his shots had landed. The fight was a total mismatch. I might have been quicker than Dad, but my limbs were puny compared to Dad's thick, hairy arms.

Tuna squirted water into Dad's mouth at the end of the round and offered him some advice through gritted teeth. I'd expected Dad to kill me, but I'd managed to survive the first round.

"You know you can hit him," GG said, as I caught my breath back. "That's what boxing is."

Tuna called us back into the middle after a minute and we started up again. Dad was more aggressive from the start. The first time Dad hit me it didn't hurt. His glove smacked me in the stomach, hard, but the shock of it meant that the pain didn't come. A shot of adrenaline kicked out of my heart. Dad's face lifted to reveal a black smile – his gum shield jutted out over his bottom lip, making his jaw look larger. It wasn't my Dad I was fighting, but some sweaty caricature of the man.

I moved in closer to him, my guard still high. Dad's hands were down by his sides. He didn't think I would hit him. He didn't think I could hit him. I wanted to show him he was wrong about me. He was wrong about everything. All he cared about was money and having something to show to people. All he cared about was hitting his bag and polishing his golf clubs. That's all that mattered to him. He'd lost the ability to love.

I felt the adrenaline turn to anger. The purest anger I've ever known. I bit hard into my gumshield, tasting blood from the cuts on my gums. Dad's eyes widened. He watched my movements closely. I decided I was going to hit Dad with all the force I had. I envisaged myself breaking his nose and the blood and spit shooting out of his mouth. I imagined his knees buckling as he collapsed to the ground.

Dad was thinking the same thing. He must have been. When I play it back in my mind, that's how I see it. I see it as the moment we both connected – we both shared the same thought at the same time. He wasn't my Dad in that moment, and I wasn't his son.

We both stepped forwards – making the same move to throw the same punch that would knock the other's head off. And as we pulled our fists back behind our shoulders to unleash that decisive blow, the garage door swung open, and a blinding sunbeam filled the dingy garage. I stepped on Dad's foot and he lost his balance. He fell into me and crashed to the ground, cracking his head on the iron dumbbells. At that moment, Mum appeared in the doorway. Blood trickled down the back of Dad's bald head. He looked up at Mum – her body was silhouetted against the bright white sunshine. Dad raised his glove to the wound.

GG said that I won the fight, although I'm not sure it's possible to win a boxing match without punching your opponent. Either way, it was nice to walk away with my nose intact. I'd never meet another girl with a nose like Ricky Hatton's.

After the fight, Tuna helped Dad inside, and Mum cleaned the wound on his head with a piece of wet kitchen towel. I put my shirt back on and waited in the living room with Tuna and GG.

"You got lucky there, Bill. You were about to taste leather."

"I think Billy won, even if he didn't throw a punch," GG said.

"There's no winners in sparring, Grandad," Tuna said. "If we got these two in the ring that would be a different story. Martin would mess you up, Billy. I can't lie to you. That'd put some cream in your coffee, eh Grandad?"

"Maybe," GG said.

"Maybe? You know what I mean. Martin would have stewed him up in a pot with rice and beans if Billy hadn't tripped him up. It would've been chili con carnage."

Dad was crying out as Mum dabbed the cut in his head. They were in the kitchen, and we could hear his groaning from the living room.

"So why do they call you Tuna?" GG asked.

Tuna looked at us both, assessing us, meeting our curious eyes with his. I struggled not to stare at the pinkish skin on his cheeks where the scar tissue had not fully healed. The fact that I couldn't figure out why Tuna was given his name had bothered me ever since I'd met him in our garage, several months before. Part of me wondered if it was his real name, after all. I'd thought about whether he was once a deep-sea fisherman, or a fishmonger, or maybe he was part of a prison gang. It was impossible to know.

"Hang on," Tuna said. He was reading a text message. "I'm gonna meet Seaside and get a ploughman's." Just as I thought he might finally tell us, he jumped up and left to buy a sandwich.

"Who's Seaside?" I asked.

"His name's Paul," Tuna said. "And he's black."

"What's that got to do with anything?" I said. GG shrugged his shoulders.

"Black Paul," Tuna said. "Black Paul becomes Blackpool. Blackpool becomes Seaside."

"Must be a gangster with a name like Seaside," GG said, glugging down the last of his coffee and resting the mug on the table. Tuna ran out the front door. Once he'd left, GG asked me about the money I lost.

"I can lend you some money to get you back on your feet," he said, fingers locked together in his lap.

"It's OK," I said. "I'll figure something out."

"You know, Billy, you don't always have to do the stupidest thing you can. Betting money you don't have is stupid. Shooting a horse is really stupid. And chasing some girl across Europe is stupider still. But refusing help? That's the stupidest thing of all."

"I couldn't take your money, GG."

"You haven't asked what I want in return yet."

"What do you mean?"

"It's Benny," said GG. "She really wants this wedding to be special. But, you know, some things are difficult at my age."

For a moment, I thought GG was going to ask me to consecrate the marriage on his behalf.

"Benny wants a big reception with dozens of guests. I haven't had the heart to tell her that nobody's coming. The thing is, we don't know many people. Benny only has her brother, and I haven't got out much since your Gran passed. As for my old friends, most of them are dead, and those that are still alive have lost their marbles or else they couldn't sit through the ceremony without pissing themselves. But a young lad like you, you must have lots of friends."

It was a reasonable assumption, even though it was totally wrong. I only had one friend, and he was on the run. "I don't know, GG. I'm not sure who I'd get to come."

"I know how it is. Who wants to go to some geriatric's wedding, right? But there is a free bar. If you could ask a few people, I'd be very grateful."

"Sure, GG. I'll do what I can."

Once GG had left, Mum went mental.

"You can get rid of that fucking speedball now!" she screamed at Dad. The whole street must have heard. She said that he was an embarrassment to the family and that it would be "the ultimate humiliation" to take him to the wedding in the state he was in. I walked out when she started throwing things against the wall.

I couldn't stand the noise and I felt the least I could do was to try to honour GG's request about the wedding. I went to see whether Tommy was back in town. He'd been staying offline, but I thought that might just be his way of keeping a low profile.

Simon answered the door. His dressing gown was loosely tied at the front, and I could see the top of his pubes and his furry brown belly hair.

"What do you want?" he said.

"Is Tommy around?"

"No." Simon slammed the door.

I booted the front door three times and ran away. Simon opened the door again and started shouting at me. As I ran, I heard him yell something about spreading my nose across my face, like butter on toast. I didn't want to go home. I walked around the town centre looking at watches in windows, searching for jobs, thinking about the women that walked past me and wondering whether they were thinking about me. As I wandered around town, I got thinking about the difference between problems as an adult and a kid. An adult's problems don't just go away with a kiss from your mother. Adult problems take time, and pain, and they hurt. I was lucky to have escaped these adult problems for so long. Tommy had been dealing with them since he was a kid. His Dad ran out on him, and his Mum had violent boyfriends and Tommy had to grow up through all of it. It felt like I'd figured out why all adults are miserable.

When I got home, I'd expected the argument to still be raging, but instead Dad was tucked up on the sofa and Mum was tenderly nursing his wound. It was disgusting to watch them play this game of doctors and patients. Dad had a thermometer in his mouth and Mum had brought him a bowl of grapes. I watched for a minute as she tested him for concussion. I had to leave when she started calling him "my little soldier." Maybe adult problems are just as stupid as teenage problems.

I went up to my room and thought about what I could do for GG's wedding. In the end, I composed a short invite. "Dear _____, you are cordially invited to the wedding of George and Benny on Saturday 17th December at Burbridge House. I know you don't know either of them, but they would really like you to come. Please note that there will be a FREE BAR. Also, please note that Benny is a woman (not that there would be anything wrong with it if she was a guy). I look forward to seeing you there, Billy." When I was satisfied, I sent it to everyone I knew on Facebook. I sent it to Tommy, to a guy called Buck I used to play football with, and even to Katie Marshall. I sent it to the Russian Dolls. I even sent it to a girl called Violet who often liked my

Facebook photos, even though she lived in Birmingham and I'm convinced we'd never met. There was a small chance Violet was actually a bot account, but I had nothing to lose. When I was finished on Facebook, I phoned Sam and explained the situation, and he said he'd be honoured to attend. I invited everyone.

Everyone except Eva.

The next day, Mum was hosting the secret sharing club, so I went out into the back garden. I started working on the dead trees towards the rear fence.

I took an axe out from the shed and hacked away at the branches. They broke away easily, like they were made of polystyrene. It didn't take long to hack the first tree down to a lonely stump in the ground. There were four in total. After half an hour, Dad came out to see what I was doing. I thought he was going to give me a bollocking, so I stopped and put the axe down. Dad moved slowly towards me. It was obvious that every movement hurt him. His face was sewn into a tight grimace.

"Don't stop on my account."

I picked up the axe again, feeling the weight of it in my hand, and moved onto the second tree, swiping the blade through the branches with ease. Dad watched me for a few minutes. I didn't look at him but I felt like he was smiling. I don't know why.

"You can take the axe to that shed," Dad said. "That's been rotten for years."

I chopped down the remaining three dead trees and wiped the sweat away from my forehead onto my t-shirt. Dad had started piling the dead wood up by the house. It strained him to squat down and pick it up, but he wanted to help. There was a big bandage on the back of his head that was spotted with blood. It was a deep cut. Mum was worried that he'd have to get it stitched up.

Dad wanted to clear out the dead wood with me. He was probably just sick of listening to the secret sharing group, like I was. I didn't mind. It was more awkward than ever after the boxing incident, and I wanted things to be back to normal again – as normal as they could be. I started to see Dad differently after everything that had happened. I stopped resenting him, and I started to feel like he was someone I wanted to know – someone I wanted to have in my life. I felt that Dad respected me for putting the gloves on and choosing to fight him, rather than running away. As children we fear our dads. As adolescents we hate them. My hatred for Dad was passing, slowly. I figured that must have meant I was growing up. But I didn't feel like I imagined an adult should feel. I still felt confused and lost and lonely. And I still disagreed with my Dad about everything. I don't think that will ever change.

When we'd moved all the dead wood out of the way, I emptied the shed of all the tools and junk that we'd been keeping in there for years. The wooden panels were rotten, warped and ready to fall away at any minute.

"Are you sure you want me to destroy it?" I said.

"It's what needs to be done."

Once I had Dad's permission, I didn't hesitate. I smashed the axe through the window and cracked it through the wooden panels. In my mind it was Julia, the rotten boat I found when I arrived in Lucerne. The front of the shed came away instantly, firing out rotten splinters. Dad was laughing and holding his neck to try to support his injury. I kicked out at the wet wood and cracked the axe into the side panels, and then the back. It all fell away as though it were made of cardboard. The shed was now just a frame with a roof on, and it swayed like a drunk about to topple.

"Finish him!" Dad said.

I took the axe and used the butt to dislodge the roof sheets and send them sliding off the frame and onto the ground. Dad cheered. He was waiting for the finale. I needed to make it special. I took the axe by the throat of the handle and swung it around my head three or four times, before stepping around in a circle like a shot-putter and whipping the axe through the first leg of the frame. It buckled, as though falling onto one knee. I moved onto the second, and then the third. For the final leg, I stepped back and threw the axe at the wooden strut. It didn't connect as cleanly as I'd envisaged. The blade missed the target, but the weight of the axe was enough to break through the rotten wood, and it came down anyway. I broke down the remainder of the roof and, as before, Dad and I moved the wood into a neat pile by the house.

By the time we were finished, it was dark, and the secret sharers were long gone. Mum was alone in the living room, putting up the Christmas tree. I went upstairs to wash up and while I was in the bathroom I got a Facebook message. I thought it would be another wedding acceptance. It seemed that the free bar was enough to lure even the most obscure invitees. But in fact it was from Christoph. "Hello my friend," it said. "Diana and I are in London. You must come to the city and we can go for Guinness! Sending Christmas greetings and wishing good health for you and your family. Your friend, Christoph."

I replied immediately. "Hi. Would you like to come to a wedding?"

Saturday came, and Benny and GG were married.

In the morning, I woke up and got showered, shaved the little hair from my face and put my suit on. Mum and Dad got ready and we had smoked salmon and poached eggs for breakfast – something Mum only ever does on special occasions. I was surprised at how relaxed they were. Dad didn't seem angry, like he had been when he'd first found out about the wedding. He was busy reading over his speech and dabbing aftershave onto his wrists and neck. Mum was on her computer, setting up the website for East Gloucestershire's Secret Sharing Club. She thought it could be a big business opportunity and had booked the community centre for her next twelve sessions. She'd invited all her new members to the wedding, as part of a sign-up offer.

At midday, we climbed into Dad's car and Mum put on her Christmas CD. Mum had to drive because of Dad's injury. She didn't seem to mind. She hummed to Boney M and tapped her palms on the steering wheel. After forty minutes in the car, we arrived at Burbridge House, which is way out in the country, with a mile-long gravel drive leading across the estate. Over the lawns I saw a deer walking into the woodland shadows.

The wedding had attracted a strange assortment of guests. There was me, my Mum and Dad, Tuna, Mandy, and a few of GG's old friends. Benny's brother did make it in the end, but he didn't speak to anybody and left straight after the ceremony. I wondered whether he was even her brother at all. Tommy made it too. He was still on the run but had only got as far as Gloucester. He was convinced that the authorities were looking for him, so he refused to be in any of the photos. He wore a baseball cap and sunglasses throughout the ceremony.

Old Sam was true to his word. His Micra was already in the car park when we arrived. He was wearing a fine three-piece suit and he struck up a friendship with the Russian Dolls, who hoped his insights might improve their betting fortunes. Yes, the Russian Dolls were there too. They were wearing old suits and it looked like they'd all got dressed together in a completely dark room. It was like they were wearing each other's clothes, because the biggest one's cuffs came halfway to his elbows and the smallest one's hands were lost inside his sleeves. They fidgeted throughout the ceremony, clearly worried that the free bar thing had been a hoax. They still called me Virgin Boy. Some things never change.

There was one girl that nobody seemed to know. She might have been Violet from Birmingham, but it was hard to tell from her profile photo. There were four women from East Gloucestershire's Secret Sharing club. They remained huddled on the periphery for most of the evening, people-watching. Christoph and Diana had come up from London for the night, and Mum and Dad had said they could stay with us. I was glad to have a chance to repay their hospitality, in some small way at least. Mum had drunk a couple of gin and tonics when we arrived, and she kissed both Christoph and Diana on their cheeks. She said that anybody who helped her boy in his hour of need was always welcome in her home. Even Dad was in a good mood. I think he'd probably had a few shots, but he was smiling again. It was like having his head smashed in by his own son was exactly what he'd needed. I could have done that months before, if he'd only asked.

At 2pm, Benny walked down the aisle with Mum and Mandy. Benny wore an elegant all-white silk trouser suit with delicate white heels. Mum and Mandy were wearing their white tuxedoes with black shirts and white leather dress shoes. They looked like a jazz trio from the 70s. GG wore a black suit with white shoes. He waited patiently at the altar with his hands behind his back, smiling as he watched his wife-to-be approach. I sat next to Dad. With his neck brace on, he had to move his entire torso to watch the procession walk down the aisle.

Mum and Mandy shuffled behind Benny who swept down the aisle with all the confidence of a high-fashion model in Paris or Milan. Benny didn't want flowers at the wedding: she said that flowers were environmentally irresponsible, but she had allowed Mum and Mandy to each carry a small bouquet of silk flowers down the aisle. They were both holding the flowers rigidly, with hands like puppets.

I thought back to the time Mum and Mandy were drunk in the kitchen at home and Mum called Benny a slut. It felt like things had changed since then. Even if nobody had said it out loud, it felt like Mum and Dad had learnt to accept GG and Benny's relationship. They may not have approved of it, but they didn't have much choice. It seemed to me that life worked that way. That's one thing I'd learnt from losing Eva. Either we accept the things that are out of our control, or we're suffocated by them.

Thankfully, the ceremony was brief. The thing I hate about weddings and christenings is that they take so long. It's a bit different with a funeral, of course, although I'd only ever been to Gran's. It's good to take your time with death, but so long as everyone's living, there's no need to drag things out. Time goes too fast to be wasted. GG and Sam could tell you that, but I was starting to realise it even at eighteen.

Soon the celebrant got to the bit that creates tension at every wedding: "Should anyone here present know of any reason that this couple should not be joined in holy matrimony, speak now or forever hold your peace."

There was an eerie silence. That question should be banned from weddings. It only serves to set the imagination running. If I was getting married, then at that point I would look at my wife-to-be and think of Mum's secret sharing club. I'd see that my wife was full of unknowable thoughts and secrets. It'd put me off. Besides, surely there's a better moment to raise an issue. If the bride's been shagging the milkman, then it might be something to address before the couple are about to sign their hearts away.

Mum was rocking her left foot up and down, squeezing her hands together in her lap until her knuckles glowed white. Silence. Benny smiled. Mum didn't say anything.

I also liked that they didn't get married in a church. I'd had enough of churches. Despite that, it was a weird atmosphere, with the women dressed the way they were, with Tommy in his baseball cap and the Russian Dolls wearing suits and work boots.

And it was strange watching my own Grandad get married, having grown up with my Gran for so many years. That said, I liked Benny. She hadn't given me any reason to dislike her. She hadn't given Mum or Dad a reason to dislike her, either. Whatever Mum was led to believe about her can't have been true. It can't have been. The detective, if he even was a detective, must have been wrong.

The couple repeated their vows and GG slipped a gold ring onto Benny's manicured finger. They kissed, and Benny was smiling and crying – the tears fell from the sides of her face because her cheeks were lifted by smiling so much. Then they played the wedding march and we all stood up to clap and throw confetti. GG winked at me as they walked out towards the reception room. And that was it – they were married.

We had a drinks reception in the dining hall and the old men chatted with my Mum and Dad and Mandy. It was all about how lovely it was and how great GG and Benny looked and how bad the weather's been and someone had a problem with asbestos and somebody else's daughter has a terrible commute to the hospital each day where she's made to pay for her own parking but she's a nurse and that's the state of the country now so we'd better get used to it and Brexit won't change anything because it's all been going down the pan for decades. I couldn't take any of it in. I went outside with Tommy because he wanted to smoke a joint, and when we returned Christoph and Diana were in animated conversation with my Mum. I knew they'd be telling her about their miracle. I looked at Diana, pretending to smile. A smile can hide a lot of things.

When I thought about it, it didn't bother me that the miracle wasn't true or that their god wasn't real. Sometimes it's the believing that matters.

I was unsure about inviting Davey, Wayne and Frank – the Russian dolls – but because GG needed the numbers, I thought I had to.

I knew Tommy and Tuna would hit it off with the Russian dolls. They chugged beer after beer, playing boat races against each other with cans of Stella that had been smuggled in, despite the fact it was a free bar. I got involved in the antics for a while, but it was weird to be drinking like that in front of Mum and Dad and I hated downing drinks anyway because it made my throat so cold and it felt like the beer frothed up around my tonsils.

After six or seven beers, the Russian dolls decided to start a conga train. They shuffled around the room picking up the other guests, singing out "doo-do-do, come on and do the conga! doo-do-do, train across the floor." Christoph was straight on-board. He jumped in at the front and honked an imaginary horn. I went to stand with Diana while we waited for the conga to end, but Wayne, the medium-sized man of the three chubby gravediggers, came and grabbed our hands and made us join on the end. Soon everybody was a part of the conga train, all hands on the hips in front of them, kicking their legs out like it was a can-can.

After the conga train finally ended, Sam came up and asked me who the Russian dolls were.

"They're a funny bunch, aren't they?" he said.

"I used to work with them at the church," I said. "In the graveyard."

"They told me they're estate agents."

I looked over at the Russian dolls. They were dominating the dancefloor. Frank was lying on his back, and the other two were spinning him around by his legs. They all had their ties tied around their foreheads.

"They're not estate agents," I said. "They're gravediggers."

"Which church did you work at?" Sam asked.

"St. Edwards," I said. "Why?"

"OK," Sam said, sipping a neat brandy. "There's not a hope in hell they'll be burying me."

"They buried me a few times," I said.

Mum came to talk to us after that and I introduced her to Sam and she thanked him for coming to the wedding and for giving me the opportunity to gain experience working at the racecourse.

"Billy, introduce me to your friends on the dance floor," she said. "I've never met them, but everyone at the church says they're lovely."

I looked over to see if the dolls were still break-dancing. Luckily, they weren't, but Davey was casting out an imaginary fishing rod from one side of the room, and Tuna was the catch of the day, his index finger hooked into his cheek as though he'd been caught. He flailed around on the floor as Davey reeled him in.

"I'd rather not, Mum," I said. "They're drunk."

"So what?" Mum said. She was drunk too. Her eye make-up had smeared down her cheeks. "Come on." Mum grabbed my hand and led me over to talk to the Russian dolls.

Philip Bowne

"Davey, Frank, Wayne," I said. "This is my Mum, Suzi."

The dolls stopped dancing and came to shake my Mum's hand.

"What was he like then, lads? On the job, I mean," Mum said, grinning.

I shivered when my Mum said 'lads'.

"He was a nightmare, Suzi," Wayne said, with a dumb smile across his chubby face.

Before she could respond, Frank reached out and grabbed my Mum's hand, stooped down and kissed it with his beery lips.

Wayne and Davey watched Frank's hand-kissing gesture and must've decided it would be weird if they didn't kiss my Mum's hand as well. They both bent down and kissed her knuckles – it was like they were meeting the Pope. Mum's lips spread into a delighted grin that I hadn't seen since she bought a vegetable spiraliser and made courgette spaghetti.

"Oh, you're too sweet," Mum said.

Tuna was watching us from across the dancefloor, and, with nobody else to dance with, he came over and kissed Mum's hand.

"Hallo!" Christoph said, Guinness in hand, waving at my Mum and staggering over to have his turn kissing her hand, Diana trailing slightly behind. They chatted in a big huddle for five minutes or so, Tuna, the Russian dolls, Christoph and Diana. They talked about Dad's boxing and Mum lied about him cracking his head after a slip in the shower. Christoph told stories about working as a doorman in Hackney for a short spell in his thirties. Sam joined the group and told Tuna about working with horses, and they argued for ten minutes about whether eating

271

horsemeat is acceptable. Sam didn't think it was, but of course Tuna was convinced everybody should eat it and that Sam should stop being such a 'namby-pamby vegan wanker'.

"Horse is the new chicken," he said. "You wait and see."

I was on my fourth beer when Tuna came up to me with his mouth stuffed full of food. It was surprising that he wasn't fat, because I'd only ever seen him eating, drinking or smoking.

"Tell you what, Bill," he said. "These balsamic-glazed pecans are the best fucking pecans you'll ever try. I'm telling you."

The waiting staff walked around carrying the canapés on slabs of stone. Tuna stopped one of the girls serving them and cleared half her canapés onto his napkin.

"You tried the citrus-cured sea bass with crème fraîche?"

"Are you a big fan of fish, then?"

"I like all food."

"Is that why they call you Tuna?"

"What, because I like all food?"

"No, because you like fish."

"Do you like fish?" Tuna asked.

"It's OK."

"Well, I'm not gonna start calling you The California Halibut, just cause you like fish, am I?"

To be honest, The California Halibut sounded like a brilliant nickname. Even if it was a bit long-winded, it was a country mile better than Virgin Boy. "Why do you know so much about fish, then?" I asked.

"It's not just fish. I'm a chef. Have you tried the serrano-wrapped pear with goat's cheese?"

"No."

"You haven't lived."

"So why are you called Tuna? What's the big secret?"

Tuna rolled his eyes into his head as he took a bite out of a goat's cheese tartlet. He actually looked like a dead fish for a second.

"Does it matter to you that much?"

"Yeah. Where does the name come from?"

"From my name."

"Tuna is your name?"

"No."

"So, what is your name?"

Tuna looked around to check that nobody else would hear him. "John West."

"John West?"

"You know. John West. The tuna company."

"That's your name?"

"Yeah. That's my name, alright?"

It took me a couple of seconds to click what John West was, but then I remembered seeing the name on tins of tuna in the cupboard at home. "Is that it?"

"What do you mean, 'Is that it'?"

"I thought you might have been part of a gang or something. Why didn't you just say that your name's John West?"

"It's not something I'm proud of, pal. Would you shout about it if you were named after a fish stuffed in a can? Would you celebrate being named after a brined product?"

"They don't always come stuffed in cans."

"Well, that's the stigma."

"I don't think it matters."

"It does matter. Besides, I'm Tuna. Have been since I was a kid. I don't even know who John West is – it isn't me. Keep that between us though, yeah?"

"OK," I said, knowing I would tell GG as soon as I got the chance. "Between us."

I left Tuna as he was stuffing his face with more complex-looking appetisers and I went to speak to Sam. I must have been drunk, because I confessed to him about shooting Baba Ganoush and losing all my money. I didn't want to tell him any of it. I hadn't planned to. I thought he would hate me. Sam listened to me tell the whole story without saying a word. I told him about losing my jobs, having no money and needing to go and see Eva, the girl I loved. I told him that I was desperate, and I didn't think I had a choice. I said I was sorry for asking him for a racing tip. He nodded along, patiently listening.

When I was finished telling him everything, my eyes were watery. Sam passed me his lapel handkerchief. "Now that is a surprise," he said. "But you're only young. You're only a young lad."

"What does that mean?"

Sam stopped and thought about what it meant. I think I know now what he meant, but at the time his words didn't bring me much solace. "You'll have thousands of evenings to drift off to sleep and think about all this. To work it out and realise why you did what you did. It might not take you thousands of nights. It might only take a few hundred. But my guess is that it'll be a few thousand.

And when one evening it all clicks together, and you realise why you did what you did – well. Then you'll know. You don't know how young you are until you're older, see."

It occurred to me that maybe Sam was a bit drunk too. He wasn't making much sense. I finished my pint and stood swaying on the spot. "So, you're saying that it won't be better until I'm older?"

"Maybe," he said. "But then, some things never get better."

"I don't think I'll ever get over Eva."

"Maybe not. But that's OK, too."

"Why?"

"Billy, there's some sadness I wouldn't give up for all the gold in the world. You'll feel the same when you get to be as old as me and your Grandad. In the end, your sadness is the most precious thing you have."

Before I could get my head round that, it was time to sit down for the meal. I was at a table with Mum, Dad, GG, Benny, Mandy and Tuna. I wasn't sure how Tuna had even been invited to the wedding, let alone ended up on the top table.

When the food was done, Dad got up from his chair and tapped his champagne glass with his dessert spoon. It didn't make the ringing noise like it was supposed to, and I thought the glass was going to break, but there were so few people in the room that everyone stopped talking to listen to him soon enough. I hadn't expected Dad to make a speech. I'd doubted whether he'd even attend the wedding. But since the fight he'd seemed different – it may have been something to do with the fact he couldn't move his head, but he seemed calmer. He'd come out to help me in the garden and we had talked – something that was rare for us.

"It's come to that time," Dad began.

Mum laughed loudly, and everyone looked at her as she glugged down a glass of Prosecco.

"I never thought I'd be in this position, if I'm totally honest. Best man at my own Dad's wedding. It's a strange one." Dad swivelled his shoulders around and grinned to indicate that he was in good spirits. A few in the crowd chuckled a little. "But I am glad that I'm able to talk now. It's not the sort of thing you expect in life, like I said, but it's a blessing." He paused and looked for the right place on his script. "Like I say, I'm honoured to welcome Benny to our family and to celebrate the union of these two people, and with it the union of our respective communities." Dad lifted his eyes from the page and looked at us earnestly. "We are all the same inside. We all bleed the same blood." Things were getting a bit awkward. Dad was making a real effort, but racial politics wasn't the safest territory for him. I think everyone was relieved when he cleared his throat and moved on.

"It wasn't easy for any of us when Mum passed away, and I know it's been especially hard for my Dad. But he has the keys to unlock a new life now, and I think we can all learn something from that." Dad pulled his set of keys out from his trouser pocket and began jangling them at arm's length. "We all have the keys to unlock our own happiness." Dad's keys rattled through the room and everyone gazed at him like it was leading to some sort of punchline. But Dad didn't say any more than that – he shook his keys up and down and looked around the room. Slowly, people started to join in. The old men got up out of their chairs and rattled their keys back at Dad. Then the others joined in – Sam and Christoph and even the Russian Dolls. GG was smiling and laughing as Benny danced to the tinkling percussion of house keys and garage keys and keyrings, chinking together in some strange orchestra. Tuna climbed onto his chair and saluted Dad as he shook his keys. The secret sharers looked horrified – they probably thought that the Secret Sharing Club and the wedding were an elaborate façade to a swanky swingers' party. Mum laughed like she had when GG twanged his cutlery on our dining room table – pretending to embrace the moment, but quietly hating it and willing it to end as soon as possible. I pulled my key out from my pocket. I only had one key, and a Big Ben keyring attached, but it was the gesture that counted, so I joined in. I looked at all the various sets of keys around the room – Sam had dozens of keys collected over years of life, and locks, and opportunities. Dad had a heavy set of ten or twelve keys – some of them I didn't recognise, and he had probably forgotten what they even unlocked.

After Dad's speech, a jazz band took the stage and started playing songs from the 50's or 60's that I didn't know. The singer was a chunky man who could belt out big, raspy notes. GG and Benny had their first dance to "Isn't she lovely," by Stevie Wonder. After that, all of GG's old friends joined in on the dance floor. One of the eldest, an ex-army man named Terry, came over and took Mandy's hand, leading her up for a dance. The curvature of

Terry's spine made him look as if he'd spent his entire life rolled up in a ball inside a washing machine. But he could still dance, and Mandy laughed as he twirled her around the floor.

Of course, Tuna was dancing too. He moved like he actually had been stuffed in a can for ten years, bouncing around the dance floor like it was the last thing he'd ever do. I expected him to throw up a bellyful of hors d'oeuvres. Sam was dancing with Diana. The Russian Dolls were dancing with each other. They clicked their fingers like they were in a barbershop quartet, and then Frank tried to twerk. I couldn't find Tommy. The last time I saw him he'd been trying it on with the girl who may or may not have been Violet from Birmingham. Either he'd seduced her, or the authorities had snatched him discreetly.

Mum guzzled three glasses of champagne and dragged my Dad onto the dance floor. He held my Mum stiffly, one hand on her hip, the other in her hand. It looked like a robot had taken my Mum out dancing. But they smiled, all of them, even my Dad.

I got myself a drink from the bar and watched the dancing. I thought about everything that had happened that year. I thought about the graves I'd dug and the bodies that filled them. I thought about Mohammed, Paulo and the summer school. I let my mind wander back to Tommy and shooting the horses. I thought about my Gran, and the ring I sold. I thought about all the money I'd lost. I thought about Klara and Cooper and the refugees, Christoph and his cows, and the lie Diana had told him. Most of all, I thought about Eva. I thought about the day we spent on the bridge, the journey I'd taken to find her, and the empty church.

I sipped my drink. I was the only guest not dancing, but I didn't mind that. I liked to watch. The old men scuffled around the shiny wooden floor in their polished black shoes, some of the men in pairs, pretending to be couples. Many of their wives were dead or too ill to come, but they made the most of their time up there. I watched for several minutes as the glitter ball spun above their heads and shot light around the dark room.

Then, without thinking too much about it, I got up, and left.

Things moved slowly. I didn't do anything for a few weeks. Dad would come home from work and shout at me because I was sitting around in my pants. I spent a lot of time watching YouTube videos of muscular men giving motivational speeches. They had no effect on my mood. Dad said I was a waste of space. I didn't talk much. I wasn't eating a lot, either. Winter had closed in and everything felt dark and cold and pressed down on my soul. I spent a lot of time in my own head.

Dad stopped boxing. He even took the speedball down. But my parents found new things to fight about and argued as much as they did before the wedding. A lot of things went back to how they were. Occasionally, I went to go and see the Russian Dolls in the churchyard. If a lot of people had died and they needed help, I would pick up a shovel and start digging with them again. It made me feel better. Not because I was suicidal or anything like that. It felt good to work. There was something healing in the repetition of digging. I liked how I could watch the work progress in front of my eyes. After digging I would go down into town and stop by at Chicken Valley for some fried wings and a Coke. I didn't like the chicken too much. I went because the same girl was working there each night. I thought maybe I could get to know someone new. I would sit there and eat my wings and imagine myself walking up to the counter and asking her out. I didn't, though. I didn't speak with her much. She sometimes asked me how my day had been. Once she asked me what I did, and when I told her that I was a gravedigger she giggled and let me take the Coke for free.

As the weeks went by, I started going back to help in the graveyard more often. I'd pack sandwiches and take a carton of orange juice and a flask of tea. The Russian dolls were always glad of the help. They always bought me a couple of beers after work to say thanks. But really, they were helping me. I didn't try and talk about Eva with them. They knew not to ask. I'm pretty sure my Mum had told everyone in Cheltenham about how I'd been spectacularly dumped by a Swiss girl.

Weeks passed. Spring broke through the blinds. Eva started writing e-mails. She said she was sorry for what happened, that she was in Bled that night I swam to the church, but she couldn't bring herself to meet me. She even said she thought she saw me jumping into the lake. She said she was worried I might hurt myself. She was embarrassed, and ashamed, and upset. I didn't respond. I carried on gravedigging and trying to save some money to pay my Dad back, and then pay off my gambling debt. GG gave me a little bit of money to help with the extortionate interest repayments, but he said I had to work to pay off the rest myself.

I wanted to forget all about Eva. I was doing well. I wasn't as upset as I had been. But then she wrote to me again. She asked if we could meet in London – she said she had arranged to see a talk about making plastic straws illegal. She said that she missed me.

She said that her job was going well, but that she felt lost and lonely, and that she would often lay awake at night thinking about the way we used to talk while we lay there in the dark holding each other, listening to the song of the crickets and the screeching foxes.

I thought about meeting up with her. I still thought about her every day – I'd often scroll through the pictures of us on my phone. I couldn't bring myself to delete them. That summer we were together, her hair was kissed blond at the tips, and her body was brown and lean. I studied the photographs of her closely. Everything about her was neat. Everything was in the right place. Her collarbone was a straight line sketched across her chest. Her wisps of hair were painted with the most delicate brushstrokes. The images recreated that feeling inside of me that I hadn't felt since she left. It was the weight of excitement from being around her in the first days, combined with the hollowness of being without her that I'd felt on my journey. More than anything, the pictures reminded me of my loneliness.

I didn't respond to the second e-mail. I didn't know what to say. I just got up every morning and went to dig graves and tried not to think about her. The days were getting longer. The sun stretched itself an extra few minutes each day. Colour was slowly returning to the world. Another two weeks passed. Daffodils shot through the soil. The air became lighter and sweeter with the spring. I was still digging. I'd started working full-time. Frank said if I was going to turn up every day then I'd may as well get paid for it.

I didn't hear any more from Eva until I came home from work on a Friday evening and she called my mobile. I was sitting in the hallway unlacing my work boots. There was a cottage pie in the oven that Mum had cooked, and I could smell the meat and gravy and I could feel the hollowness in my stomach. I watched as Eva's name flashed up onto the screen. The phone started vibrating and moving around on the wooden floor.

I watched it for a moment. I thought about what she might say, and how my life might be different if I picked up the call and held the phone to my ear and listened to her voice again. Every part of me wanted that. Just to hear her talk.

The phone kept buzzing. I imagined her on the other end, crying, sitting alone in her dark room and longing for me the way I had been longing for her. Part of me feared that it was an accident, or a pocket-dial or maybe she was drunk and there was no reason for the call at all. I thought about all the possible reasons she might call. Then I got up and pulled off my work boots. Mum always made me beat the mud from the soles into the garden. She would've killed me if I'd got any on her carpets.

Once I'd done that, I sat down again at the bottom of the stairs. My phone had stopped vibrating, Eva's name had disappeared, and the screen was black.

Acknowledgements

I couldn't have written *Cows Can't Jump* without the support, encouragement, and insight of my great friend and mentor Michael Johnstone. Mike's knowledge and generosity over the last few years has helped me to push through the novel writing process. I am particularly thankful for his sensible editorial guidance over late night games of Crokinole.

I would also like to express my appreciation to Tyler Keevil and Martin Randall. I was very fortunate to learn from their teaching during my time at the University of Gloucestershire. They were always kind to me, and supportive of my writing and ideas, even the bad ones. Their friendly and encouraging manner provided me with the confidence to develop my early drafts.

Growing up, I was very lucky to have lots of great teachers and mentors. I'd like to acknowledge them for helping me along the way. In particular: Mrs McBain, Miss Moore, Mr Peake, Mr Chatora, Mr Wootton, Mr Woodham, and many others from Southwold and BCC.

Many thanks, also, to Marion from Adventures in Fiction for choosing the novel as the winner of their Spotlight First Novel Prize. And to Ray Robinson, who helped me to develop my writing after winning the prize. Ray's enthusiastic, detailed approach was invaluable, and I feel very lucky to have learned from him.

I would also like to note my gratitude to Archna and Neem Tree Press for providing me with the opportunity to publish this work. They have been a delight to work with throughout the publishing process.